FINAL CUT

Other Folly Beach Mysteries by Bill Noel

FINAL CUT

A FOLLY BEACH MYSTERY

BILL NOEL

FINAL CUT
A FOLLY BEACH MYSTERY

iUniverse Star
an iUniverse LLC imprint

iUniverse books may be ordered through booksellers or by contacting:

iUniverse
1663 Liberty Drive
Bloomington, IN 47403
www.iuniverse.com
1-800-Authors (1-800-288-4677)

ISBN: 978-1-938908-68-2 (sc)
ISBN: 978-1-938908-69-9 (e)

Library of Congress Control Number: 2013921850

Printed in the United States of America

iUniverse rev. date: 10/22/2014

Cover photo by Bill Noel.
Author photo by Susan Noel.

CHAPTER 1

How was I to know that the thunderous crash and bloodcurdling screams weren't in the script? The red light duct-taped to the side door at Cal's Bar was illuminated to warn a handful of bystanders that cameras were rolling. It was a moviemaking sign telling people to shut up and not disturb the magic being filmed inside. I was one of the bystanders. I didn't know what the scene was, but I was fairly certain it didn't involve a wide-eyed crew member charging out of the bar and screaming, "Medic!"

City council member Marc Salmon had taken time away from saving the city and was standing beside me. He yelled for the panicked crew member to follow him across the street to Folly Beach's combination city hall and fire and police department to grab a firefighter who, on the budget-strapped island, multitasked as a paramedic.

Two of my friends were in the bar, so I ignored the red light and barged in to see if they were okay. When the entourage from *Final Cut* had first invaded my small South Carolina barrier island, I'd been among those who'd gathered to watch the filming. From that initial exposure, I'd learned that the process of filmmaking ranged from absolute boredom to controlled chaos. The scene that met me made chaos seem domesticated.

BILL NOEL

Two twenty-something-year-old actresses were huddled in the far corner, dressed in bikinis so small that even their seven-year-old selves would have had trouble squeezing into them. One flailed her arms like she was fending off an attack by seagulls while the other cried uncontrollably. A tripod-mounted movie camera was on its side on the dance floor, its expensive lens shattered on the floor. Two temporary, steel scaffoldings that held three microwave-sized movie lights and a contraption holding a boom microphone were draped across the bar on the right side of the room. On its way down, the steel scaffolding had slammed into a decorative, wooden ceiling beam, knocking it loose. The fifteen-foot long, wooden beam had landed on top of the steel scaffolding. Crushed glass from a Corona Extra neon sign that the set designers had substituted for Cal's usual neon Budweiser sign covered the dark brown, beer- and dirt-stained carpet, and a Modelo Especial beer ad, another addition the crew had made to give the set a more exotic look, dangled precariously from fishing line above the bar. And a cloud of dust from the carpet hung in the air. The bar looked like photos I'd seen after a 7.3 earthquake had devastated parts of California in the 1950s.

A gaggle of people was gathered around a prone figure on the floor. The group included actors dressed stereotypically like drug smugglers, with gold necklaces dangling down the fronts of black, form-fitting T-shirts, and the crew dressed … well, dressed almost like the drug-smuggler-portraying actors. Blood puddled under the moaning victim. His left arm was twisted in an unnatural angle. The right side of the steel lighting rail was draped across his chest, and the wooden beam pressed on the rail. His arm twitched. The victim wasn't one of my friends, thank God, but my relief was short-lived.

A stuntman had wrapped his well-muscled arms around the end of the wooden truss that had flattened the steel beam across the moaning casualty. He strained to lift the heavy rail. It barely moved. None of the bystanders had lifted a hand to help with the rescue.

I was no farther than six feet from the action, so I rushed over, shoved one of the panic-stricken actors out of the way, and told the stuntman that I would lift on his signal. He looked around as if to see if there was someone to help other than a sixty-something-year-old, slightly overweight, rapidly balding, out-of-shape Folly resident. I wondered the same thing but thought it better to focus on the life-threatening steel rail and wood beam. The stuntman seemed to realize that I was the best he was going to get and began counting. At three, we strained to move the deceptively heavy obstacles. Nothing happened. I moved closer to the end of the beam for better leverage. The victim's right hand balled into a fist, and his moans had become muted. We didn't have much time.

"Again," I said. The smell of stale whiskey, perspiration, and sheer terror assailed my senses.

He repeated the count, and I put all my energy into moving the deadly structure. The beam slowly lifted, and the steel scaffolding rolled toward the trapped man's stomach. He screamed.

The air-conditioning had been jacked up to keep the set comfortable for the actors, but sweat rolled down my forehead. I looked around and asked in a loud voice—more accurately, I shouted—for someone to grab the scaffolding and hold it off the body, after which I shouted for someone to pull the grimacing man from under the beam.

Two stagehands finally opted to help. The beam had begun to slip from my fingers. The muscular stuntman was also losing his grip. My mind told me that the stagehands needed to pull slowly on the fallen man, but my emotions screamed, "Yank him out quickly!" The new rescuers put their arms under the victim's shoulder and pulled. He yelled, and one of the men let go.

A Folly Beach police officer had made the trip across the street and forced his way through the wall of onlookers. He grabbed the man's other arm and carefully slid him out from under the scaffolding. My arms, shoulders, and back felt like they were on fire. With marginal aid from one of the other rescuers, the officer had pulled the victim three feet away from the beam, so I let go. The beam crashed down on the light rail with a low thud. I landed on the carpet about as gracelessly.

I took a deep breath, resting my head on the floor, and stared at the water-stained ceiling tiles. The stuntman lowered himself to the carpet, shook his head, exhaled, and then turned to me and said thanks. I moved to a sitting position and smiled. He introduced himself as Thomas Wright. I said I was Chris Landrum.

I would have shaken his hand, but my right arm didn't have the strength to move.

It had been a half hour since every EMT, firefighter, and police officer on the island had descended on Cal's. The paramedics had loaded the injured man into an ambulance, which then screamed off to a hospital in nearby Charleston. The film's director had cursed, kicked one of the hapless barstools, and bellowed that filming was over for the day. Most of the cast and crew had scampered out of the bar before the director could change his mind. Three crew members had remained to sort through the damaged equipment and then made a halfhearted effort to straighten up the bar.

I had moved from the threadbare carpet as soon as feeling had returned to my arms and legs and was seated at a nearby table. Across from me was the bar's owner, Cal, and Jim Sloan, known to everyone except the IRS as Dude. Both were good friends and the reason I'd rushed into the bar in the first place.

"What happened before I got here?" I asked.

"Actor be squished," said Dude, the master of the under- and often nonsensical statement. "Me nearly."

Dude was four years younger than me, a little shorter at five seven, and a lot lighter. He could have been Arlo Guthrie's twin with his sun- and saltwater-wrinkled face; his hair would have been a hairdresser's nightmare, although I doubted that he'd ever been to one. He had owned the island's largest surf shop for twenty-five years and dressed as if he was stuck in a time warp. Dude looked like the aging hippie that he was with his limitless number of look-alike, tie-dyed shirts. His appearance had gained him the part of one of the bartenders in the film. Fortunately for moviegoers, he did not have a speaking role.

"I reckon that Chris already knew that, seeing that he rescued the *squishee*," said Cal.

Cal and Dude, their elbows on the table, leaned in my direction. Cal Ballew, the six-foot-three, gangly Texan, had awkwardly folded his body to fit under the table.

"True," I said and nodded at Dude but then turned to Cal. "What happened before I got here?"

Dude took the hint, leaned back, and nodded for Cal to respond.

Cal smiled at Dude and then looked at me. "The guy's Laurel." He pointed to the felled beam. "He's one of the actors— small role, not too important. Laurel was blocking a scene with Wynn, el numero uno, the big cheese." Cal then tilted his head in the direction of the director's chair where Wynn James, the lead actor, was talking to a police officer.

"What be blockin'?" interrupted Dude.

And this was from someone who was in the scene.

Cal looked at Dude and rolled his eyes. "Practicing. Standing where they need to be so the camera folks, sound guys, and lighting gurus can do their thing before they roll the cameras."

Cal talked like he'd known movie lingo all his life. He had spent more years than most people had been alive traveling the country and singing his traditional brand of country music to anyone who would listen. He resembled Hank Williams, the original, with his quick smile, distinct singing voice, thin frame, and stooped shoulders. Regardless of what he had done all his life, his first exposure to the film industry could have been measured in weeks. My guess was that he had learned what blocking was in the past few days.

"Yeah," said Dude. "That's what we be doing." He then flicked his wrist at Cal in a "go on" motion.

"Anyway," said Cal, "they were blocking a scene when there was a loud, screeching noise from the ceiling, and those two big-ass steel legs supporting the light bar started falling." He held his right arm out vertically and then quickly lowered it toward the floor. "Crash!"

"Wipe out!" said Dude, who then looked toward the ceiling where the trouble had begun. "Me be almost axed."

Cal tapped Dude's arm. "He sure was, he was." Cal nodded. "After the first crash when the light bar smacked into the wooden beam, the beam started swinging. My bud, Dude, was standing under it. Yes, he was."

"Big crash *dos*!" said Dude, who then coughed and wiped perspiration off his sun-wrinkled brow. "Looked toward stars. Celestial, not actor peeps. Saw swingin' steel. Boogied out from under."

Cal looked at Dude, probably shocked by the length of his monologue, and then turned back to me. "Then the light doohickey and the wooden beam came tumbling down. Barely missed Dude." He hesitated and shook his head again.

"Laurel not missed," said Dude, who then pointed to me, wiped the perspiration off his forehead again, and coughed. "You be knowin' the rest." He pulled his elbow to his face and coughed again.

Perhaps, I thought. "You okay, Dude?" I asked.

"Cold avisitin'," he said and then coughed again. "Maybe flu."

I had never known Dude to have been sick and was surprised that he had acknowledged the arrival of a cold. Perhaps nearly being decapitated had stirred up germs. He was lucky to still be with us.

March had come in like a lion and continued to roar. The six-mile-long, half-mile-wide island, known as "The Edge of America" to many, "Folly Beach" to cartographers, and "home" to me, had experienced record rainfalls the two weeks leading up to St. Patrick's Day.

Another kind of storm had blustered into town the first of the month. As early as January, rumors had begun making the rounds about a "blockbuster" film that was going to be shot there. It wouldn't have been the first time that film crews had found the quirky island to be a perfect setting. A handful of small-budget movies and a couple of television shows had been shot on or near Folly. What made the newest cinematic effort so talked about was that it reportedly was to be a monumental production with a hundred-million-dollar budget and would star some of the biggest matinee idols this century has known. It didn't take long for that sensational news to spread to the island's twenty-four hundred full-time residents.

Somewhere along the route to reality from the early mega-budget and mega-star rumors, the production had morphed into one with a minibudget and has-been stars who would be more at home on the current crop of television reality shows. Regardless, Folly Beach was once again hosting the production of a movie, and with few exceptions, its citizens were ecstatic. Still, conversations about casting decisions that had begun months before with exclamations of "Wow!" were then continued with confused looks and "Who?"

An advance team searching for settings with local color had arrived and quickly provided even more excitement for some of my friends. Cal had agreed to rent them his country music bar and allowed it to be remodeled to appear on the "big screen" as The Bar, a grunge-rock establishment. Hardly any remodeling was needed to grunge up Cal's. Bert's Market, Folly's iconic grocery, agreed to serve as the set of a quirk-infested grocery store; only a name change to Eve's would be needed. And my favorite breakfast spot, the Lost Dog Café, was commissioned to serve as the set for a restaurant, dubbed the Blue Dog Café. The restaurant had approximately three trillion photos of dogs covering its walls, so it was easier to rechristen it with the name of a dog rather than to employ the moniker "Julie," which had been the restaurant's name in the original script.

The near disaster in Cal's wasn't the first bolt of lightning from the storm *Final Cut*. The original director, Cesar Ramon, had drowned before the first pixel of the movie was captured. The ill-fated director, along with eight members of the film's entourage, had gone deep-sea fishing off the coast near Isle of Palms, just north of Folly, when they were trapped in a horrific storm. The boat's captain was an alcoholic and someone locals wouldn't venture into a swimming pool with, much less the unforgiving Atlantic. Rumors had circulated that a reduced rental rate combined with the sales pitch of the captain—who, at the time, had been experiencing a rare moment of sobriety— convinced the newcomers to ignore the ominous weather forecast. Despite the desperate pleas of even the most seasoned sailor on the small boat, the captain ignored the black storm clouds, gale-strength winds, and waves that would challenge much larger vessels. Rumors around town were that he needed the money and wasn't going to let anything deter the charter.

Passengers on the doomed fishing excursion included two actors, the girlfriend of one of them, the director, two assistant directors, and two of the project's financiers. Mother Nature unleashed the storm approximately an hour into the outing. A massive wave caught the boat broadside, and before anyone could put together a string of profanities, the craft had capsized. Everyone was hurled into the tempestuous waters. All but the director had survived.

The storm moved on as quickly as it had arrived. When the captain had slurred the order to don life jackets, five of the passengers had wisely paid attention before leaving the dock. The director had taken his first and last fishing trip. No one on the boat was certain how he or she had survived, and no one was certain why Ramon hadn't. However, everyone agreed that it was a terrible accident and that they were lucky to be alive.

I doubted that anyone who survived the storm suspected that it was an omen of things to come.

***

Cal and I were now alone in the bar. Dude had returned to the surf shop to spare unsuspecting customers from having to suffer abuse from his two tattoo-covered employees who were, as Dude had so succinctly put it, "customer-unfriendly." I'm simply old-fashioned enough to call them rude and insensitive.

"That's about as much excitement as this old cowboy's heart can take," said Cal.

The film crew had returned the large items to their "pre-earthquake" locations, but Cal's was still a mess, and its owner was sweeping up broken glass from the neon signs and camera lens. I had moved the tables out of his way so he could clean without having to move anything heavy.

I was no spring chicken, but I was still five years younger than the lanky Texan. And fortunately, I had not spent the best years of my life traveling the back roads of the South in a 1971 Cadillac Eldorado while sleeping most nights on its backseat, a lifestyle that had taken a toll on my friend's body.

I pointed to the heavy structures that were still wedged against the bar. "Any idea what caused it?"

He stopped sweeping, took a deep breath, and looked at the ceiling where the heavy wooden beam had once been anchored. "Nary a one."

The side door opened before I could say that it didn't seem reasonable that gravity alone would have caused the chain reaction that brought down the light bar and the ceiling beam. Charles Fowler sprung in as if he'd been fired from a cannon.

"What the hey happened? Why didn't you call me?" said my best friend—albeit an unlikely best friend.

"Yo, howdy, Michigan," said Cal. He stopped cleaning and leaned against the broom. "The sky just came a tumblin' down. If I'd known that you'd rush over to help clean up, I would've called."

Charles was originally from Detroit but had been on Folly for nearly thirty years since he'd retired at the ripe, young age of thirty-four. He'd worked an off-the-books job for Cal a couple of years ago when Cal hired him as a "bartender"; Cal actually wanted him to catch the culprit who was stealing from the bar. With his vivid imagination, Charles fancied himself a private detective. He was a better detective than he was bartender, but that was like saying that a parakeet had a better chance of flying to the moon than hitchhiking a ride there on the back of a toad.

My unlikely friend was shorter than me by a couple of inches, a little lighter, and had been described by a couple of my friends as "handsome in a weathered sort of way." Even though it was hot outside, he wore a long-sleeve T-shirt with the face of a snarling tiger on the front and the word Auburn in orange block letters above it. In the eight years that I'd known Charles, I'd never seen him in a short-sleeve shirt. Yes, I'd asked him several times why the long-sleeve fetish, and someday I'll get a straight answer. It wasn't going to be today.

Charles carried, swung, and pointed with a handmade, wooden cane. He also tapped on the pavement with it as he walked. I didn't know any more about why he carried it than I did about his shirts. I'd resigned to telling myself that we're all different and let it go at that.

"Well, umm, sure, I would've helped," said Charles as he looked around at the mess. "But that's not what's important." He turned toward me. "There you are, just standing there, smack dab in the middle of a whopping disaster, and never once thought to call me, an official of the film company."

I'd heard what he said but couldn't wrap my arms around it, even though they had finally regained their strength. "Official of the film company?" I said.

Charles's smile traveled from ear to ear. "Yes, sir." He nodded. "I'm now officially what they call in the motion-picture industry a gofer."

I was newer to the film industry than Cal and apparently Charles, but I was certain that gofer wasn't on the same level as director, producer, or star. I looked toward Cal for insight. He shrugged—no help there. I turned back to Charles. "Does that mean you'll get one of the motor homes they have?"

"How about a folding chair with *Charles, Gofer* on the canvas backrest?" chimed in Cal.

"Not certain," said Charles. "Don't suspect I'll be getting all that right away. This is a cinematic production destined to be a cult classic, you know."

"Does that mean a cheap movie with few viewers?" I asked as I stifled a smile.

He wrinkled his nose and stroked his two-day-old beard. "Suppose a novice to the industry might call it that."

"Okay, my friend," said Cal as he stared at the tiger on Charles's shirt, "how did you acquire such a lofty title?"

Cal had a serious expression on his face, but his tongue was clearly pushing against his cheek. It really wasn't fair; Charles was way too easy to make fun of.

"Excellent question," said Charles with a nod. "It was an act of fate. It's like that old-time actress who was discovered in a department store and became famous."

Cal looked toward the ceiling and then back at Charles. "Lana Turner? It wasn't a department store; it was a drugstore."

Charles huffed. "Whatever. The point is she became famous by standing around." He reached down, picked up his cane from the floor, and pointed it at Cal. "That's how it happened to me."

Might as well join in. "Who discovered you?"

Charles raised his chin and turned my way. "Officer LaMond."

"Cindy discovered you?" I said. This was getting to be fun.

Cindy LaMond's day job was an officer in the Folly Beach Department of Public Safety where she'd worked for six years. She was a good friend and was married to Larry LaMond, who owned Folly's only hardware store. And, as known to only a handful of residents, her hubby was a retired cat burglar. Charles had been friends with Cindy for as long as I had. Officer

LaMond had taken an unpaid leave and had been hired by Cassie Productions, the movie production company, to handle security.

Cal smiled and turned to Charles. "And how exactly did Officer LaMond make such a discovery?"

"Glad you asked," said Charles. "I was standing outside your fine establishment." He pointed his cane toward the front door. "Officer LaMond was standing beside me. I think she was working crowd control and—"

"Crowd?" interrupted Cal.

"Yep," said Charles. "Must have been three, maybe four women loitering around, itching to catch a glimpse of the movie stars."

"Back to Cindy's discovery," I said. If I hadn't spoken, Charles would have told us who each loiterer was, where she lived, and if she had pets.

"I was standing beside Cindy." He pointed his cane to a spot beside his right foot. I assumed that was where Cindy was standing. "She turned to me and said, 'Want to be a gofer?'"

"Wow!" I said in mock-astonishment. "It was meant to be."

Charles looked down at the floor and shook his head. "You're making fun of me, but you know that famous actor and director Edward Burns?"

I had never heard of him and told Charles so. Cal asked if he was kin to George Burns.

"Sorry, I forgot," said Charles. "We insiders assume everyone is familiar with the business and its luminaries. Anyway, take my word, Edward Burns is a biggie."

Cal smiled. "I'll add that to my assumption list."

"Good," said Charles without hesitating. "Mr. Burns's leap to fame began when he was working as a gofer. He slipped a film script that he'd written to Robert Redford. Fame followed."

He looked at Cal and then over at me. "You *have* heard of Robert Redford, haven't you?"

Cal nodded, and I smiled.

"You'll remember us little folks once you become famous, won't you?" asked Cal. He tried to hold back a grin but failed.

Charles finally used up all he had to share about his career change and asked again what in "blue blazes" had happened in Cal's. Cal and I then told Charles in detail, excruciating detail, all about it—not once, but twice.

Each of the who's, what's, when's, and where's were shared and repeated until Charles was comfortable—no simple task.

"Why" remained a mystery.

CHAPTER 2

MELINDA BEALE, CHARLES'S AUNT, HAD dropped in out of the blue last August—more accurately, out of a blue and gray Greyhound bus. Charles hadn't seen his only living relative since he left Detroit for a life of premature retirement. The charming, quirky newcomer had revealed within minutes of her arrival that she had terminal cancer and had only days, weeks, maybe months to live. Charles's life hadn't been the same since then.

Now seven months later, Melinda continued to defy the fatalistic predictions of her doctors. She had celebrated her eighty-first birthday a week ago with Charles and a handful of his friends. Before she had blown out the lone candle in the center of her cake—Charles didn't want to chance fate or fire by adding the other eighty—Charles's girlfriend, Heather, had asked Melinda what her secret was to living so long. She had blown out the candle, looked around the room, said a silent prayer, and then given an answer that would have made gerontologists the world over salivate: "I suppose I just forgot to die."

Events like her birthday and coming face-to-face with a killer her first month here had drained her energy for a few days, and Charles had been convinced she was taking her last breaths. He was now hundreds of thousands of breaths wrong.

Charles and I sat in Melinda's small efficiency apartment in a run-down former bed-and-breakfast. Her living space, small by most standards, met her needs, and she didn't have to go far to reach anything. She had said before that it was much larger than her coffin would be. Her sense of humor and approach to life were refreshing and had made her imminent death much easier on her nephew and the other friends she had accumulated during her short time on Folly.

Melinda was finishing her third can of Budweiser, and Charles was telling her about his new career as a gofer. She was struggling to figure out how that differed from what he had been doing since he moved to the beach decades ago. He explained that other than his nonpaying career as a private detective, he had helped his friends over the years. Sometimes he delivered goods from the surf shop for Dude, cleaned understaffed restaurants, or helped builders who needed an extra set of hands. But those weren't careers. His primary career, as he explained it, was as pro bono executive sales manager at Landrum Gallery, a small, financially unsuccessful gallery featuring photos taken by yours truly, hence the egocentric name on the storefront.

Melinda then asked him if he meant that his career was a nonpaying gig at a gallery that really didn't need the extra help to not sell photos. Her lips formed a sly grin as she asked, and I sat back and watched him squirm.

"You could put it that way," he said and offered to get her another beer and refill my wine glass.

I wondered what other way it could have been spun and said that another drink was a good idea. Charles quickly figured that he wasn't garnering quite the level of awe that he had expected from his announcement and rushed the five paces to Melinda's minikitchen. He returned and began telling her about the accident at Cal's.

Melinda had been feeling "puny" the last few days, so she hadn't been as inquisitive as I knew she could be about the movie and what was going on with it.

"Why, pray tell, did the movie folk choose Folly Beach?" she asked.

"Glad you asked," said Charles, who then went into Wikipedia mode. "Over the years, there have been several films with scenes in the Charleston area. Stars like Elizabeth Taylor and Mel Gibson have been captured on film in the area. Some television shows and movies were actually set on Folly."

"Like *Harry Potter*?" she asked.

"Not quite," he said and then smiled. "In 2010, there was *Angel Camouflaged*, and a decade earlier one called *Folly Island*."

"Never heard of them," she said.

"Not many have," I added. "They were low-budget efforts with what they politely call a *limited audience*."

"Is that like no one went to see them?" she said with a smile.

Charles apparently didn't like the direction of the conversation. "*Army Wives*, the TV series, often shoots here."

"That I've heard of," said Melinda.

Charles nodded like he had finally succeeded. "More than forty films have been shot around Charleston."

"Because it's so pretty?" asked Melinda. She then took another sip of beer.

"That's one reason," I said. "Another is because South Carolina offers generous tax incentives. It's harder in other parts of the country."

"Makes sense," she said and then studied the side of her beer can. "What's the movie about?"

I was pleased to see that Melinda had regained some strength and was taking an interest in the film. I smiled and said, "It's about a couple—"

"About Haney and Rodney something," interrupted Charles. "They're the mayor's cousins in a make-believe town called Oceanside, Georgia."

"Is that what Folly is in the movie?" asked Melinda.

Charles nodded. "It's supposed to be near Jekyll Island. The two cousins—"

"Why didn't they just call it Folly?" Melinda interrupted. "Wouldn't that have been easier?"

Charles scratched his chin and looked at me.

I was a bit taken back that Charles didn't have a ready answer, so I gave it my best shot. "A bunch of bad stuff is going to happen in the movie, and they didn't want to get in trouble with the city fathers and good citizens who are helping with the project."

"What kind of bad stuff?" she asked.

"There's corruption, sex and drugs, and a murder or two," I said.

"Yeah," said Charles. "Apparently some bad guys smuggle drugs from across the Mexican border and fly more into Florida and then truck them to Oceanside. Then other bad guys in Oceanside cut the drugs, and—"

"Cut the drugs?" said Melinda.

"Dilute them so they'll go farther," said Charles. "Then they ship them up north to Ohio, Pennsylvania, and New York."

"None of which would be good for our image," I added.

"Oh," said Melinda. "There's enough of that real stuff here. Don't need to add make-believe bad things happening."

I'd worked hard the last six months to block out memories of a serial killer that Charles and I had caught last summer. Melinda's comment dredged up those memories. I took a deep breath and decided that I could handle some fictional murders.

And then Melinda got my stomach churning again when she said, "I don't think it was an accident."

I looked at Charles. He took a sip of his second or maybe third beer and scratched his chin. "Now, Aunt M., why'd you think that? It was an accident. It's just a shame that the poor actor was under it when it fell."

And thankful that Dude wasn't under it, I thought.

"A crew member told me that accidents happen all the time on sets," I added. "Everything is temporary and built quickly, sometimes not very well. Many of the sets are facades with nothing structurally sound behind them. All ingredients for accidents."

"Uh hum," she said. "Seems fishy." She rubbed her temple. "Who was standing by the big thing that fell?" She glanced my way and then turned to Charles.

"Don't know," he said. "I wasn't there, remember?"

She nodded and then turned to me. "Well?" she said.

"I don't know either," I said. "I was outside. The people I talked to who had been in the bar said it must not have been braced well. Someone could've accidently bumped it. It looked like an accident to me."

Melinda pointed to me and then turned her attention to Charles. "Seems to me that it must've been too big for gravity to just have grabbed it and yanked it down. It's about time the two of you found out who *pushed* it down." She sat back and folded her arms across her chest.

I didn't think what had happened at Cal's was anything but an accident, and I started to point that out to her again. I also knew that once Melinda got something in her mind, it'd take more than a titanium crowbar to pry it out. This certainly wouldn't be the last we'd hear from her about the attempted murder at Cal's. Perhaps we could humor her and see who had been there when the accident—or whatever—occurred.

"We'll ask around," I said.

"Good," said Melinda. She held up her empty beer can. "Charles, let's celebrate with another."

He looked at the collection of empty cans in front of her. "But—"

"It's Bud, Charles, not *but*."

He took a deep breath and stood. "On my way."

Until last summer, Charles had only a couple of phone conversations with his aunt over the last thirty years, but from what he had known before leaving Detroit, she was a serious consumer of alcohol. Charles's grandmother, a teetotaler who had raised him, had said that Melinda was an alcoholic. I didn't know about that, but I knew that during the brief time I'd known her, she was quite fond of beer and other adult beverages. Alcohol was the least of her worries considering her cancer, and neither Charles nor I was overly concerned about her drinking.

Through Charles's admirable efforts and the increasing influence of alcohol, Melinda's train of thought about the event in Cal's was derailed. Charles appeared pleased that the conversation had taken a more positive direction until Melinda asked him when he and Heather were getting hitched.

I grinned, sat back, and waited for his answer. Charles had dated Heather Lee for three years. If the phrase "made for each other" hadn't already existed, it would have been coined to describe the lovebirds. She was a massage therapist by day and plied her trade at Millie's Salon. Heather's free time was devoted to being a psychic and a self-proclaimed country music singer. Her psychic abilities were questionable at best, but there was no question about her crooning. She sucked. Her total lack of musical talent didn't keep her from appearing at open mike night each week at Cal's bar and anywhere else in the area that provided a venue for amateur musicians to show their talents.

I overlooked her lack of talent when I saw how perfect she was for my friend. She laughed at his humor, and she told him he was full of processed meat when he said something stupid. In a word, she made him happy, and she was as quirky as he was—okay, almost as quirky.

Charles looked at Melinda and then over to me. His expression screamed *help*. I tilted my head and smiled, clearly not what he was looking for. He then asked Melinda if he could get her anything else. She said no. Also not what he was looking for. Over the next ten minutes, he performed a tightrope act that the Flying Wallendas could have only dreamt about.

He explained in tedious detail how they had met, how Heather had had several traumatic experiences with relationships that had ventured toward matrimony, how their "complex" lives didn't lend themselves to the "intricacies" of marriage, how they were perfectly satisfied being "significant others," and how she had shared some of her psychic vibes with him, and they didn't vibrate positively when the M-word entered the picture.

When he got to the psychic vibe, Melinda raised her hand over her head and said, "Whoa! Stop!"

In a moment of wisdom, Charles did exactly that.

"My dear nephew, you do know that I've given up my life-long propensity toward profanity—right?"

Charles nodded, and I leaned forward.

Melinda lowered her hand and stared at her *dear nephew*. "To honor my commitment, I will resist saying what came to mind somewhere in the middle of that malarkey you've been spouting. But I must share that what you just rambled on about was a supersized pile of pachyderm poop."

"Now, Aunt M.—"

She shoved the palm of her hand in Charles's direction. "I'm much older than you and should be the one forgetting stuff. But—"

"You're not that old—"

"Not my point, Charles." She shook her head and then continued, "Have you forgotten that dear, sweet Heather lives right there?" Melinda pointed across the hall toward Heather's apartment. "In your male, messed-up mind, do you think the two of us don't talk to each other? Do you for a second think we never talk about the idiot men in our lives and why they're so stubborn about things that involve matters of the heart?"

"Of course not—"

"Charles, Charles, Charles," interrupted Melinda. "I'm two sips of beer and about fifty words away from going to bed, so listen carefully. There are three things dear, sweet Heather wants in life. Two of them she'll never get: a hit record and an appearance on the Grand Ole Opry. No way, not ever, never. The third thing's in the hands of one person in this room, and it ain't Chris." She turned and pointed at me and then returned her stare at Charles. "Heather's a hankerin' to have her last name changed to Fowler."

"Aunt M., I don't—"

Her hand was back in Charles's face. "Beddy-bye time. Charles, figure it out."

Murder and matrimony—where had the night gone astray?

CHAPTER 3

POLICE CHIEF BRIAN NEWMAN AND I were having lunch at the Lost Dog Café. Brian had been Folly's chief for more years than teenagers have been alive and had been my friend for a half dozen of them. We had occasionally butted heads when I had stumbled on a murder or two and had, in his mind, interfered with police business. For the past three years, I had also been in the precarious position of dating his daughter, Karen.

We were sipping cups of steaming coffee, eating oatmeal, and talking about how strange it was to see the movie-set sign over the window-sized opening to the kitchen saying it was the *Blue Dog Café* rather than *Lost Dog*. The name was different, but everything else was the same—a comforting environment for each of us.

Things got less comforting when Marc Salmon sidled up to the table and looked down at us from his six-foot-tall frame. "Laurel's going to make it," said Marc. "Afraid he's going to lose an arm though."

One of Folly's quirks that I had become accustomed to was that greetings like "good morning," or "how are you," or other customarily accepted social pleasantries were apparently banned on the island.

Marc was a longtime member of the Folly Beach City Council and handsome enough to have a starring role in the movie, with his short, black hair and endearing smile. He was also one of the city's more prolific gossips. He and another member of the council, Houston, met almost daily in the Dog and discussed the business of running the city and the island's latest happenings, real or imagined. He was also a good guy and had occasionally shared critical information with me—once, information that saved my life.

Usually Marc would share a dollop of gossip or an occasional fact and then move to the next group of diners to enlighten them about whatever he was spreading. Today he stood at the table and stared at the empty chair like an English pointer locking in on its prey. Brian, being police-chief perceptive, asked Marc if he wanted to join us.

Marc thanked the chief and then sat. He gave us a more detailed health update about the injured actor and a rumor about a cook at one of the local restaurants who was fired for substituting snake meat for chicken in an irritating customer's meal. He then looked around the restaurant to see who was nearby while his hands fiddled with the salt shaker.

"Chief," he finally said, "there's something I'd like to talk to you about when you have time."

Brian looked at me and then sideways at Marc. "What?"

Amber, one of the Dog's waitresses, one of the first people I'd met when I arrived on Folly, and someone I had dated for a time, took Marc's order for coffee and toast. Marc continued to play with the salt shaker and look around the room. "Umm, this isn't something I want to bother Chris with." He looked at me and gave an uncomfortable smile.

Brian looked over at me and gave a quick nod. "I haven't found there's much that Chris doesn't like to be bothered with."

Brian then turned back to Marc. "Whatever it is, you can talk about it in front of him. Besides, he'll find out anyway; he's nosy like that, you know."

Marc wasn't happy with me being there, and the courteous thing for me to do would have been to excuse myself, but now I was interested. It was in Marc's court.

"Umm," said Marc, "it can't leave this table. Okay?"

I nodded but was confident that if it left the table, it would be from the lips of the council member.

Marc again looked around the room. Not seeing any shotgun microphones pointed at him or nearby diners paying attention to us, he leaned closer to Brian. "We have a special election coming up in May to fill the unexpired term of Mayor Lally."

Mayor Joshua Lally abruptly resigned a few months into his reign last summer. The official reason given was that he had to move to California to care for his ailing mother-in-law. His reason wasn't terribly credible since his mother-in-law had resided in a Sacramento cemetery for the last five years. Most citizens didn't care, but a handful of us knew the real reason for his quick departure. To understate our pleasure, we were thrilled.

"I know," said Brian.

"What you don't know," said Marc, "is that three council members have asked me to talk to you about throwing your hat in the ring."

Brian ran his hand through his short, gray hair and tilted his head toward Marc. "You've got to be kidding," he said. "I don't know anything about being mayor. I've been a cop all my life. Besides, why would I want the headaches?"

Marc shook his head. "Chief, you know as much about Folly Beach as anyone. At least anyone on the right side of sane. You know the politics, you have a good working relationship with

Charleston County, and you're well-respected by the business owners. I've even heard," Marc laughed, "that most of the townies you've arrested know you're fair."

"Eli Jacobs is doing a good job, isn't he? Won't he run?" I asked.

Eli Jacobs had been a member of the council and was appointed interim mayor until the special election. Eli had been on Folly for a decade and was an accountant for a large auto parts distributor on James Island. The scuttlebutt was that he was appointed because he would be a benign leader and wouldn't rock any boats. I thought he had the personality of a jellyfish and that he was almost as articulate, but no one asked my opinion.

"Eli is doing exactly what we wanted him to do," continued Marc. "He's avoided controversy. He's looked like the mayor of Folly Beach with his long, flowing, gray hair and casual attire."

"Then what's the problem?" I asked.

Marc smiled. "Eli's perfect at doing nothing. After Lally stirred up every pot he came near, alienated all but the wealthiest residents, and in general screwed up our fair city, Eli's doing nothing was exactly what we needed. He's filler."

"So much of nothing gets nothing done," I shared, and then smiled at my profound statement.

Marc pointed his index finger at me. "You've got it, Mr. Citizen."

"I get that," said Brian. "But why me?"

Marc blinked a couple of times and nervously looked around the room again. "Simple. No one wants Eli for a full term, and no one else on the council has interest in the job."

"So," said Brian, "I get the nod because no one else wants it."

"I wouldn't put it like that," said Marc. "But I see your point. There'll be others who aren't on the council who'll run.

I know two right now and wouldn't be surprised if the list didn't increase unless a strong candidate steps up and scares others out."

"And that strong candidate would be me?" said Brian.

"You got it."

I hadn't thought about Brian as mayor, but he would be a great choice. He knew the island and all its quirks, character, and characters. He was levelheaded, knew the importance of vacationers to the small slice of heaven, and could balance the needs—real and perceived—of the varying constituencies.

Amber returned and asked if we wanted anything else. Refills on our coffee would do, so she left to get the pot.

Brian watched her walk away and then turned back to Marc. "Who are the three members?"

"This is a little touchy," said Marc. "They don't want to be identified."

"Why not?" I asked.

"It's complicated," said Marc. "If the chief announces that he's running, they'll come out and publicly support him. But if he doesn't run, they'll have to back someone else. They don't want it to get out that the other candidate wasn't their first choice."

"How would it get out?" I asked. Was he saying that neither the chief nor I could be trusted not to tell anyone?

"It's politics. Secrets are about as hard to keep as, well … I don't know what, but really hard to keep."

Brian and I nodded at that explanation from the analogy-challenged council member, but I seriously doubted either one of us understood what he meant.

"Marc," said Brian, "this comes out of the blue. My first reaction is no way." He smiled. "That's also my second reaction. But, for you, I'll give it serious consideration."

"That's all we can ask," said Marc. "The election's a few months away, but we'll need your answer in a couple of weeks. Remember, the sooner you jump in, the better the chance of squeezing out any competition."

"I understand," said Brian.

"Then I'd better head out while you're still in the mood to think about it," said Marc. He laughed, shook my hand and Brian's, and headed toward the door.

"Mayor Newman," I said. "It's got a nice ring to it."

"Some days it's better not getting out of bed," said Brian. He stared at the door that closed behind Marc.

CHAPTER 4

GEOFFREY CROWN, KNOWN TO HIS friends as Geoff, was one of the actors who migrated to Folly with the production. My first contact with the thespian was as I stood outside Cal's and watched him on the sidewalk holding court with a group of middle-aged female vacationers who had apparently never seen a real "movie star" up close. Geoff played the part well. He was in his early fifties, six foot three, square jawed, and looked like an actor from the 1940s. His stage-honed voice was clear, powerful, and British. His smile was quick, and his sky-blue eyes oozed charm. I'd heard from Charles, the gofer, that the Brit was even quicker to drop names of famous actors and directors he claimed to have worked with during his illustrious career. Charles had made it clear that he wasn't a fan of Mr. Crown.

The more Geoff flirted with the women, the more they inched closer to him. He was dressed like a small-town police chief, the role he was playing in *Final Cut*. His long-sleeve tan uniform shirt was sweat-soaked and sticking to his back, and the women were more beach-appropriate, dressed in bikinis with mesh cover-ups and wide-brimmed straw hats. They weren't fazed by the heat as they cell-phone photographed one another with the actor. I was about ten feet behind the group when Geoff spotted me. He looked over a redhead who had put her arm around him and said in my direction, "Ready to go?"

I glanced behind me at the empty sidewalk and realized he was talking to me. He gave a quick nod, and I took the hint.

"Yes," I said. "We're going to be late."

He looked down at the adoring fans who reminded me of a pride of lions surrounding a hapless antelope and said, "Sorry, ladies. I would love to talk longer, but the bloody schedule, you know."

He gave each lady a quick hug and walked up to me. I asked him where he wanted to go.

"Damned near anywhere that's air-conditioned."

I took his elbow and escorted him around the corner to my SUV. My introduction to the "famous" actor was as I drove him around Folly Beach pointing out the various spots of interest. The Infiniti's air conditioner was in fine working order, and my passenger appeared content to sit back and see the sights of my community. He was slightly stuck on himself and spent a good portion of the time trying to convince me that he was the greatest actor who had ever appeared on the big screen.

Despite his best efforts to convince me otherwise, I saw glimmers of a middle-aged, insecure actor who, in reality, was relegated to a minor role in a low-budget "project," as he called the movie. He was also twenty-five hundred miles from his "place" in Los Angeles and thousands of miles from his native country. With his not-quite-starring role, he had to share a second-row-from-the-beach, three-bedroom house with two other actors. I asked him twice during the tour where I could drop him, and he said he was finished shooting for the day and was between calls from his agent and his business manager. My gut told me that he had absolutely nothing to do or anywhere to go. We ended up sharing a bar-height table at Snapper Jack's where he said a lot of words but revealed little. He finally thanked me for saving him from heatstroke and the groupies. I assumed that he went home; at least he walked in that direction.

***

Charles, Cal, and I were in Cal's. It was late afternoon, and the film crew had moved to the Lost Dog Café for late-afternoon and evening shooting. The scenes were timed so filming could take place during the lulls in business: Cal's was used in late morning and early afternoon; the Dog, in late afternoon and evenings; and Bert's Market from about three in the morning until ten.

Cal slowly walked over to his jukebox. He bypassed the coin slot and punched in several numbers. The distinct voice of Merle Haggard bemoaned that the good times might be over for good. Cal then returned to the table and finished telling us how many takes were needed for the star, Wynn James, to tell the bartender played by Dude that he wanted a beer.

"I've been around the block a few thousand times and have a fairly good sniffer when it comes to someone touched by the mind-altering world of drink and drugs," said Cal. "Wynn had a lot more words to say than Dude, which was exactly zero. All Dude had to do was nod. The boy's good at noddin'. But I reckon a professional actor, such as Wynn, could have managed saying 'Bud, and quick' in fewer than seven takes." Cal put his foot on the chair next to him. "Hell's bells, I memorized the line after the second time, and I wasn't anywhere near the cameras."

Before Charles or I could ask more about Wynn, the side door opened, and Geoff stuck his head in. "Anyone in here?" he asked.

"This is the whole posse, England," said Cal.

"Mind if I join you?" said Geoff.

Charles looked at me and rolled his eyes; he had no use for the actor. I had asked him why after I had told him about Geoff's guided tour of Folly.

He'd said, "Not certain, just don't like him."

"Come in and sit a spell," said Cal.

Geoff nodded to Charles and smiled at me before taking the remaining seat at the table. He then looked around the room and said to Cal, "Got those Samuel Smiths?"

"Nope," said Cal.

"How about the Newcastle Brown?"

"Nope," repeated Cal.

By now, Charles, the trivia collector, had to ask, "What's a Samuel Smith and a Newcastle Brown?"

"Best beers in the universe," said Geoff. "British, of course."

"Of course," said Charles in his most sarcastic voice.

"When will they arrive?" asked Geoff. He turned and looked at the door leading outside like he expected someone to walk in carrying a case of the British brew.

"Don't know," said Cal. He hesitated and then grinned. "Probably after I order them."

The world traveler and famous actor probably assumed that since Cal owned a bar, he had mastered the art of ordering various beers. Cal was competent in ordering Budweiser, Miller High Life, red, white, and pink wine; beyond that, he was outside his comfort zone.

Geoff blinked, looked at Charles and then at me, and then back to Cal. "Could you order them soon?"

"Reckon so," said Cal.

"What's wrong with the beer here?" asked Charles, pointing his cane at the bar.

"Old chap, those bloody American beers taste like llama piss."

"You drink a lot of llama piss?" snarled Charles. He balled his fists, started to say something else, but then showed something that he'd been working on the last couple of years: restraint.

Cal saw Charles about to explode and walked behind the bar. "How about wine?"

Geoff ignored me. "Bring it on, old chap."

Charles followed Cal to the bar and mumbled along the way, "I'll take some of that llama piss, Cal."

The pissing contest had begun.

Drinks were on the table. Geoff and Charles traded a couple of less-than-good-natured barbs, Cal provided generous refills, and I simply watched my best friend and my newest friend go at it. They finally agreed to disagree about most everything and progressed into a civilized conversation about the movie. Charles had been on the set during the early-morning shooting at Bert's and late last night at the Dog, so he and Geoff has something to discuss without World War III erupting.

I remembered what Melinda had said about the falling lights not being an accident and asked Geoff if he'd been there when it happened.

"I most certainly was, old chap. I'd exited the khazi when all haides exploded."

"The what?" blurted Charles.

"The loo, of course, old chap," said Geoff, unfazed by Charles snarkiness.

After six years, I had begun to figure out Dude's surfing terms. Now I was going to have to learn British.

I waved my hand around the room. "Who else was here?"

"Let's see, mate," said Geoff. He looked at the ceiling where the near-deadly beam had been replaced and then over at the bar where gravity had taken it. "Of course, the chap it landed on was here." He pointed at Cal. "You were too. And so was that funny, little, hippie bloke with the peace symbol shirt, long hair, and short words."

"Dude," said Charles.

"That's him," said Geoff. "Let's see, oh yeah, Krista Hill was over in that corner by the rubbish container." He pointed to the front of the bar beside the women's loo.

"Who's she?" I asked.

"Actress," said Geoff. "Young, wet-behind-the-ears, but a quick study. She plays a waitress."

"Is that it?" I asked.

"No, no, no," said Geoff. "The director."

"Talon Hall," said Charles.

"Of course, he was directing," said Geoff. "Then we had the terribly untalented, overrated, lead actor Wynn James and his trampy, main squeeze."

"Donna Lancaster," said Charles, filling in the blanks.

"The slut," said Geoff.

I didn't take that as a term of endearment even in British. "Anyone else?" I asked.

He closed his eyes and turned his head to the left and the right. I assumed he was playing back the scene where the light support fell. "Don't remember names well," he said. "There had to be five or six other people. The cameraman, Ben—I think that's his name. The cute sound chick with some *y* sounding like an *e* name: Brittany, Tiffany, Candy, Holly." He snapped his fingers. "And a couple of production assistants. I never learn their names—never even know what they're supposed to do. I remember how my good friend Harrison Ford often made fun of them." He looked at Cal and laughed.

By now, Cal had become bored with the conversation. He leaned back in his chair and began singing "I Just Came Home to Count the Memories" along with John Anderson on the jukebox.

Charles looked away, smirked, and then returned his gaze to Geoff. "Anyone else?"

"Let's see, unless I'm badly mistaken, those two who are financing the film were in the room—Robert Gaddy and Becky Hilton, I believe."

"Is it normal for people financing the film to be around the set?" I asked.

Geoff nodded. "Yes, especially early in the production when they think moviemaking is glamorous." He shook his head. "They'll usually tire of the monotony and stop showing up." He looked around the room and then motioned for us to come closer. Unnecessary, I thought, since we were the only people there. He whispered, "It's a low-budget project, and most of the money comes out of their pockets. They want to make sure it's not wasted." He pulled his neck back. "On the many big-budget projects I've starred in, funding was from deep-pocket companies. They didn't feel the need to be on set after the first few days."

He continued. "I shouldn't be telling you this …" He paused and closed his eyes.

Once he said that he shouldn't be telling us something, the inevitable happened. Charles leaned to within inches of Geoff's face. "That's okay. You're among friends," said Charles.

I hoped that Geoff didn't remember that Charles was snarling at him moments earlier.

"My understanding is that the preliminary budget for the project was calculated on five people fronting the project. Contracts were signed, talent hired, and the equipment, cameras, and editing paraphernalia rented. Then the shite hit the proverbial fan."

Charles was now even closer to the actor. "What happened?"

"Sources who would know said three of the deep pockets had an enormous blowout with the other two. They told them where they could put their project and pulled out." He shook his head. "Something like that happened a few years back when I was starring in one of Woody's films. A bloody mess, it was."

I ignored his comment about Woody and thought I'd better change the subject before Charles exploded. "That's another reason why the two financiers are here?" I asked.

"Suspect so," said Geoff.

"Do they have enough money to finance it all?" I asked.

"Don't know," said Geoff. "But I do know that there are a lot of expenses and many people working on the project who'll be hurt in the pocketbook if there are delays or unusual expenses." He turned to Cal, and then Charles, and then back to me. "And delays and extraordinary expenses are as common on these projects as flies on shite."

CHAPTER 5

*F*INAL CUT MAY HAVE BECOME a low-budget movie, but that wasn't apparent to the untrained eye. Evidence of the invasion was everywhere. A large banner welcoming *Final Cut* was draped on the wooden fence beside the Sand Dollar, and smaller welcome signs were visible in the windows of most businesses. "*Final Cut*, Welcome to the Edge of America" had been painted in red on the side of the Folly Boat, a leftover from Hurricane Hugo that had devastated the area in 1989. The boat had become a makeshift billboard for anyone with creativity, cans of paint, and the need to share something with the community. The Folly Boat welcome lasted exactly seven hours until it was replaced with "I Love You, Gretchen!"

The production company had rented a vacant lot across from Bert's to use as a staging area. It was home to a semitrailer that served as equipment storage, wardrobe, and no telling what else. There were also three luxury motor homes staged on the lot. Two were the home-away-from-home for the "stars," Wynn James and Shannon Moore, with the third vehicle reserved for the director. There was also a smaller trailer that served as the production's office. Lesser-known actors were housed in a few large homes scattered around the island, and the rest of the crew packed into cheaper rentals off-island.

BILL NOEL

A smaller, vacant lot beside Cal's had been commandeered to feed the cast and crew. According to Charles, craft services was the most appreciated group on a movie set; it was the department that provided food for those working on the production. Food can conquer most problems associated with moviemaking. The erratic filming schedule made it difficult for them to eat at regular hours, and it wasn't unusual to see groups eating breakfast at three in the morning. At least that's what I'd heard. I took great pride in not being up at that ungodly hour.

A twenty-five-foot-long, white Wyss catering truck was parked in the lot closest to Cal's. Water and electric lines snaked from the truck into the side door of the bar. In case there was any doubt about the purpose for the vehicle, ProCatering was painted in bright red along both sides of the truck. Cal had shared that the truck was out of Atlanta and catered primarily to movie companies filming in the southeastern states.

A thirty-by-forty-foot tent covered much of the remaining space in the lot. Under the tent were seven aluminum picnic tables and three heavy-duty card tables. Two seven-foot-high, portable light stands were in the corner opposite the catering truck to provide illumination for after-dark feedings.

Charles had wanted to talk to me about Melinda's deteriorating condition and asked me to meet him at the tent. He was on the clock but appeared to have little to go for when I found him standing under a shady corner and leaning against his handmade wooden cane. His Tilley hat was cocked slightly on his head, and he had on a long-sleeve, white, University of Georgia T-shirt. It wasn't lost on me that the shirt represented the state where the fictional city of Oceanside was located. I wouldn't let him know that I thought it was a good touch.

In addition to two people working in the catering truck, Wynn James, the lead actor whom I'd only met by reputation, was at one of the tables talking to two women I didn't recognize. Dude was talking to one of the cooks standing by the large side panel of the truck that was propped open. And according to Charles, a woman sitting by herself at the far table sipping on a Styrofoam cup of coffee was Becky Hilton, one of the financiers.

I looked at Charles, who was staring into space and, from what I could tell, doing absolutely nothing. He was overpaid.

"Able to break away from your taxing duties for coffee?" I asked with a straight face.

"Believe I can work that into my schedule," he said with an equally serious gaze.

Food and beverage from the catering truck was reserved for the cast and crew, but rules were only loose guidelines to my friend. He walked to the stainless steel coffee urn on a table beside the truck, pointed at me, and said something to the catering manager. The man laughed, and Charles filled two cups. He returned and handed one to me.

"I think assistant gofer is an honorable title, don't you?" he said.

Not particularly, I thought, but I enthusiastically told him yes and took a sip.

"Doesn't matter," he said. "Mitch liked it." Charles tilted his head in the direction of the catering truck. "You're now one of us. Wear your title proudly; it'll get you free food."

It's always an adventure when visiting Charles's World. Most of my life had been spent working in the large, bureaucratic, and often boring world of the human resources department of an international health-care company. Its policy and procedures manual approached the size of the *Encyclopedia Britannica* but wasn't nearly as interesting or as well organized. Creativity was often rewarded with scorn and occasionally termination. Black and white were absolutes, and gray was only acceptable in men's suits—and then, only dark gray. On Folly Beach, and especially in Charles's World, absolutes evaporated at the bridge separating the island from reality.

Nothing appeared to be happening at Cal's, which was unusual since it was time for shooting to be taking place there. "Where is everyone?" I asked as we sat at the table closest to the street.

"Old coast guard property," said Charles. "They wanted the lighthouse in the background."

The decommissioned coast guard station was on the east end of the island and overlooked the historic Morris Island lighthouse. The lighthouse had once been the beacon to the area for approaching vessels, but because of inevitable erosion, it was now stranded on a sandy base and at times was surrounded by the sea. It was replaced some fifty years ago by the black and white, famous-architect-designed, triangular—and in my nonnautical opinion, ugly—Charleston Light. It was known by the locals as the Sullivan Island lighthouse, which was located, yep, on Sullivan's Island.

The coast guard property was perfect for filming because it was isolated from traffic, had a nice, wide beach at low tide, had a perfect view of the iconic lighthouse, and most important to the production company, it was cheap.

"Is Oceanside supposed to have a lighthouse?" I asked. "Won't some people recognize the lighthouse in the film and know where it is?"

Charles glanced at the tent and then in the direction of the lighthouse. "Good question. Maybe that's why they're shooting now, so the sun will be behind the lighthouse and it won't be recognizable." He squinted like he was trying to picture the backlit icon. "Probably doesn't matter. Don't think many people will be going to the movie."

It was a weak answer, but I wasn't that interested anyway.

"They didn't need their chief gofer?" I asked.

Charles shook his head. "Didn't need his assistant gofer either. That's why we're here." He took another sip.

Charles had taken me on as a project years ago, and I had made much progress toward the world of irresponsibility and *gray*, but I still had to overcome six decades of conditioning.

"What's up with Melinda?" I asked, to steer the conversation back to sensible.

Charles looked down in his Styrofoam cup. "She's getting weaker, forgetting things."

From what Melinda told us when she had arrived on Folly, it was a miracle that she was still alive. I knew Charles understood that intellectually, but since his aunt had been here, he had shown emotions and shared memories that I hadn't seen or heard before. He loved her deeply, and I dreaded the day that she was no longer in his—and to be honest, my—life.

I took the cowardly way out and didn't remind him that the end was probably closer than he wanted to admit. "She's been through a lot and probably needs her rest," I said. "You know, she keeps bouncing back."

Charles finally looked up from his cup. "Maybe you're right," he said. "I don't know what I would do if I lost her." His eyes dropped back to looking in the cup.

Perhaps it was perspiration, but a drop of water rolled down his left cheek.

Then someone screamed.

CHAPTER 6

THE YELL CAME FROM BEHIND us and near the catering truck. I was first around the truck, Charles a step behind me. There were three picnic tables between the catering vehicle and the back of Cal's. Most of the actors preferred to sit at these tables so they could eat in peace away from the curious eyes of vacationers and starstruck locals.

Carla, one of the young production assistants, had her arm wrapped around the back of someone who was doubled over a table.

"Help me," she said.

I moved beside her and saw that she was comforting Wynn James, the movie's lead actor. He looked anything but like someone who had starred in soap operas and three feature films. His face was milk-white, and a low, guttural moan came from his mouth as he leaned over a puddle of vomit. The sight and the stench were unsettling.

Mitch Abbot, the caterer, moved closer. I asked him to get a wet towel and then handed Charles my phone and told him to call 911. He said it would take too long and then sprinted across the street to the fire department.

Carla and I unwrapped Wynn from his grip on the bench and slowly lowered him to the sandy soil.

"What happened?" I asked the assistant.

Her hands were shaking. "Don't know," she said. "We were finishing lunch, and Mr. James turned pale. He looked at me, opened his mouth, and then put his hand in front of his face and …" She stopped and pointed to the puddle seeping into the sandy soil.

Mitch returned with a wet and a dry towel. I handed the assistant the wet one, and she began to wipe the puke off Wynn's face. She put her other hand on his forehead. "He's burning up," she said.

"Help's on the way," I said and put my arm around her shoulder.

Wynn's eyes began to focus, and he glanced around. "Pull me up," he said.

"Just relax," I said. "Stay where you are."

"I need to—"

He started to retch and pushed himself up with his elbow. He vomited again.

I gagged at the smell and turned away. Fortunately, an EMT rushed across the lot and exhibited an air of confidence that all of us needed to see.

Carla and I stepped a few feet back to allow the expert to do his thing and, I suspected, to get away from the nauseating odor. Charles joined us and asked what he'd missed. I told him that it was nothing that he wanted to know about. A second EMT arrived, conferred with his colleague, and then came over to us and said that an ambulance was on its way.

The paramedic looked at the three of us and asked, "Who knows what happened?"

Charles and I turned to the production assistant, who tentatively raised her hand like a teacher had just called on her. In a soft, almost indecipherable voice, she said that she had been with Mr. James since he went through the buffet line and then sat with him while he ate. The EMT asked her name, and she told him.

"Carla, do you know if he's on any medications or illegal substances?" said the first responder.

She looked at the ground and then over to where the other paramedic was helping Wynn to a seated position. "I don't know about medications," she slowly said. "He looks healthy to me." She stopped and looked at the EMT. He returned her gaze but didn't say anything.

Carla looked at Charles like he could bail her out and then turned back to the EMT. "I haven't seen him taking anything illegal."

The EMT nodded. I thought she had given an excellent nonanswer, one that screamed *yes* without saying so.

The EMT returned to his colleague and Wynn. The two medical professionals conferred and asked Wynn some questions that we couldn't decipher, and then the one who had been talking to us called the caterer over. I heard him saying something about shutting the operation down.

I asked Carla if she had eaten the same food as Wynn, and she said no. She had eaten a large breakfast in town and wasn't hungry, so she only had tea. I asked if anyone else had been eating when Wynn got his food. She said that there were several people standing around, but the only one she noticed filling a plate was that "funny hippie who has trouble stringing words together."

Dude was the only person on Folly, and possibly in the continental Unites States, who fit that description. I looked around but didn't see him.

"Did you see what Dude had to eat?" I asked.

"Is that the hippie's name?"

I nodded.

"Sure fits, doesn't it?"

I nodded again.

"Don't know for sure, but his plate was chock-full."

I looked around. "Do you know where he went?"

Carla smiled for the first time. Her two front teeth were wide apart, but she still had an attractive smile. "No, but he said something like 'gotta boogie, push boards,' whatever that meant."

Carla probably didn't know that Dude owned the surf shop, so I understood her confusion. "Did he have more scenes today?"

"Doubt it," she said. "After the lighthouse shoot, everything'll be at the Dog." She snapped her fingers. "He put one of those plastic tops on his pile of food. Must've been heading somewhere."

The medic came over and said it appeared that the actor had food poisoning. He would probably be okay in a day or so, but they wouldn't know for sure until they got him to the hospital, got him on an IV, and ran tests. I asked if someone could get food poisoning that soon after eating. He said it usually took longer but guessed it was possible. He said that if the actor had eaten more, it could have been much worse. I heard the faint sound of an ambulance's siren approaching the island.

If he'd eaten more, it could have been much worse reverberated in my head. Carla had said that Dude fixed a plate full of food. I said that we had to be going and waved for Charles to follow me.

The surf shop, with the name all lower case for reasons known only to Dude, was two blocks away, but my car was closer, so we drove. Other than the Atlantic Ocean, the surf shop was the epicenter of the universe for surfers on Folly Beach. To someone like me from the middle of the country, the products Dude sold and the preponderance of his unusual customers were as familiar to me as the native language of the

| 45 |

groundhog. The long, narrow shop was filled—cluttered—with surf paraphernalia and clothing.

Dude had two full-time employees who had no more use for me than they would have had for Mormon missionaries. At their friendliest, they greeted me with a snarl, and today was no exception. One of Dude's charmers waited on a man with a shaved head and chest hair sprouting out his open-collared shirt. The customer's left arm had a sleeve tattoo that resembled a war between a consortium of octopuses and three Martians, but it was no match for Dude's two tat-covered workers.

I made eye contact with the other employee, who appeared to be doing absolutely nothing. He looked away. I took that as a sign that he wanted to talk, so I stepped closer.

"Where's Dude?" I asked and looked around the store.

"Why?" said the more-friendly-than-usual chap, as Geoff would say.

"It's important," I said.

Instead of answering, he jerked his head toward the back of the shop and then abruptly turned his back to me.

I loosely interpreted that as, "Why he's in his office, Mr. Landrum. You're more than welcome to go back. Is there anything else I can do for you this lovely day?"

I waved for Charles to follow, and we weaved our way around surfboards, wetsuits, and many things whose function I had no clue about. Dude's small office was in the back of the store, but his door, covered in surf-product decals, was closed. That was unusual since he normally liked to see everything that was going on in the shop.

I knocked.

Dude coughed and then yelled, "Scram!"

I knocked again and then turned the knob. The door was unlocked, so I pushed it open.

A plastic food container was on the desk, and it didn't look like much food was missing. Dude was slumped over the small, cluttered desk. His face was death-white. He raised his head to see who had invaded his space. He looked at Charles and me, rolled his eyes, and said, "Assquake."

I started to speak, shut my mouth, and looked at Charles.

"Diarrhea," said Charles. He often served as my translator when I was around Dude.

"Bad?" I asked in Dude's direction.

"Woe, world be spinnin'," he said before his head slumped and hit the desk.

I remembered what the EMT had said about how it could have been much worse if Wynn had eaten more. I didn't know how much lunch Dude had eaten, but he looked anything but well.

"Let's get him to the hospital," I said to Charles as I started to clear a path from the desk to the back door.

Charles looked down at Dude and then back at me. "Shouldn't we call 911?"

"He's worse than the actor," I said. "It'll take too long for an ambulance to get here. The car's not that far."

As if to reinforce what I had said, Dude lifted his head, made a guttural sound, and then puked. Charles grabbed a half-empty trash can from beside the desk and put it under Dude's head—better late than never. Charles then went to the small bathroom outside the office and grabbed a handful of paper towels. The two workers were in the front and oblivious to what we were doing, which I suspected was a regular occurrence.

Dude moaned and then tried to stand. I held him back and said for him to stay in the chair and that we'd take care of everything. He wiped his chin and said, "Dirty licking."

I hoped he didn't mean it literally.

"Means bad wipeout," said Charles.

I told him to stay with Dude, and I headed out the back door to bring the SUV around. I was back in less than a minute and rushed in to help Dude.

The aging surfer was mumbling, and Charles was bent over him trying to keep him still. I got on Dude's left, Charles got on his right, and we slowly walked him to the car. His arm was hot, and I realized he had a fever. Was taking him to the hospital the right thing to do? Calling for help would have been safer, but the added time couldn't be good.

We fastened Dude's seat belt, and Charles went back in the shop to get the trash can. The distance from Folly Beach to Charleston's Roper Hospital was just shy of twelve miles, but the time it took to make the trip varied dramatically. With luck, little traffic, and the shortage of police patrolling the area, I could make it in fewer than twenty minutes. It could take more than twice that long in heavy congestion.

Traffic was relatively light as I left the island, and we were making good time. Dude began to moan louder, and Charles, who was next to him in the rear seat, kept repeating, "He's burning up."

Our good luck came to a screeching halt as we turned off Folly Road and merged onto the James Island Connector about three miles short of the hospital. There were flashing emergency lights in the distance and stopped traffic. People were out of their vehicles and walking around to see what was going on.

Dude moaned and grabbed his stomach, Charles repeated that he was burning up, and I opened the door and told Charles to stay with him. We were stopped on the bridge that crossed the Ashley River with nowhere to get off. Traffic had us pinned, so we couldn't turn back, and clearly we weren't going anywhere.

I jogged toward the front of the line of traffic. About thirty vehicles in front of us, a minivan was flipped onto its roof. Window glass and parts of its grill were scattered on the pavement, and just past the minivan was a late-model Camry pushed into the concrete wall on the right with its trunk smashed into the rear seat. Three ambulances and I don't know how many police vehicles surrounded the wreckage. We weren't going to be moving soon, and Dude needed immediate attention.

Four Charleston police officers were standing near two patrol cars off to the side of the wreck. I was about fifteen feet from them when one of the officers waved for me to return to my car. I ignored his not-so-subtle hint and continued toward the group. The officer broke away from the others, gave me an impressive police frown, and headed my way. It was probably my imagination, but I thought he moved his right hand closer to his firearm.

"Sir, please return to your vehicle," he said without a bit of friendliness.

I ignored his "request" and began telling him about Dude. He realized that I was serious and listened. He then looked around and called one of the other officers over. They huddled briefly, and then one of them said something about making the vehicles in front of us move to the right so we could follow him in the narrow pull-off area to the left. He said for me to return to my car. He would follow in his marked Mustang.

I jogged back to the SUV and gave Charles an abbreviated version of the plan. Dude moaned and then went into a coughing fit. The Mustang, with lights flashing and siren blaring, pulled beside us and carefully made a U-turn. He then waved for the two cars in front of us to pull up as far us as they could so we could get out of the line of traffic.

A minute later, we were tailgating the Mustang in the emergency lane on the James Island Connector before we gracefully merged back into the driving lane as we passed the wreck.

We pulled up to the emergency room entrance, and the police officer helped Charles and me move Dude from the car to the door. A gurney waited for Dude, and a nurse took over. She politely but firmly pushed us aside, pointed to where we needed to fill out paperwork, and rolled him away. I was grateful. The helpful officer wished us luck and left.

I had spent more time in emergency rooms since moving to Folly than I had my entire first sixty years. Off the top of my head, I could remember being the patient on three occasions. More times than I could remember, I had come to visit friends. Hospitals deal with the living, but I believe I'm more comfortable visiting funeral homes.

Our first half hour was spent with an intake clerk who was doing her job but was running into a blank wall pulling the appropriate information she needed from Charles and me. Dude had left his wallet at the surf shop, and all we could tell her was his name, his approximate age, and on what street he lived. As hard as it may be to believe, the insurance company and hospital felt that that dearth of information was inadequate. Charles had tried to be helpful by offering that he was sure Dude would be "more than happy" to stay and wash bedpans to pay his bill once he was discharged. The scowl on her face said she wasn't a regular at comedy clubs.

The excitement of registering Dude was out of the way, and the next two hours were past boring. Finally, a harried ER doctor pushed open the stainless-steel door to who-knows-where and looked around the room. There were a dozen other people waiting on information, but the doctor walked directly to us.

"Mr. Landrum, Mr. Fowler," he said.

We nodded.

He ushered us to an empty corner of the room and spoke in a low voice. "Mr. Sloan said that it was all right if I reported on his condition, or I think that's what he meant. It appears to be a bad strain of salmonellae, probably from something he ate. He was troublesomely dehydrated before he ate whatever made him sick, which made everything worse. Mr. Sloan also has bronchitis that's bordering on pneumonia. If you didn't get him here when you did, it may not have turned out this well."

"What kind of food? What caused it?" asked Charles.

"Something uncooked—eggs, poultry, seafood, maybe dairy products. Mr. Sloan said he had food off a catering truck. Food that could have been sitting outside too long."

"He just ate an hour or so ago," I said. "Could it come on that quickly?"

"Unlikely," said the doctor. "It usually takes four or more hours before the symptoms appear."

"What now?" asked Charles.

"He's still dehydrated and on an IV, and we're loading him with heavy-duty antibiotics. I'd like to keep him a couple of days, but he said something that I think meant he was leaving tomorrow." The doc shrugged. "We have a crotchety, old hospital administrator who says we can't hog-tie patients to keep them here; we'll have to wait and see."

"Can we see him?" I asked.

"He'll be moved to a room in a few minutes, and you can see him there." He pointed toward the information desk. "She'll be able to tell you what room, but give her some time for it to get in the system."

We thanked the doctor and realized that we were hungry, so we got in line at the hospital cafeteria for a quick bite. A friend of mine had a bar and grille a couple of blocks away that served the best cheeseburgers in Charleston. I would have preferred to go there but knew it would take too long.

As I stood in line, I focused on everything that looked undercooked. I wondered what Dude had done to be nearly beheaded by the light bar and now almost done in by food poisoning. Merely a coincidence—or was it?

***

"Me be noodled," said the weak, raspy voice of Jim "Dude" Sloan.

Charles leaned toward me as we moved closer to Dude's bed. We had just walked in, and I was struck by the vague smell of disinfectants. "Think it means exhausted," said my friend and Dude-speak translator. He leaned closer and said, "Or he's hallucinating and thinks he's pasta."

Dude was on the far side of a pea-green curtain in a room he was sharing with an elderly lady who looked like she had gone head-to-head with a gorilla. Her scalp was wrapped, her nose covered with gauze and tape, and her right arm in a cast. I suspected that she had an interesting story to tell, but she was asleep, and I would have to hear an abbreviated version later from Dude.

On the other hand and the other side of the curtain, Dude didn't have any obvious signs of injury, and a lone IV bag provided him nourishment and antibiotics. The head of the bed was elevated at a forty-five-degree angle, and his long, gray, curly hair was spread out on the pillow. He had dark circles under his eyes, and his arms looked anorexic.

"When are you going to break out of this joint?" asked Charles. He grinned, walked over to the bed, and patted Dude's leg.

"*Manana*, Angel of Mercy Chuckster," said Dude in a weaker-than-usual voice. "Tried to scat today. Docster say no way, Jose-Dudester."

"It's better that you stay, maybe even longer than tomorrow," I said, remembering the doctor's wishes. "How're you feeling?"

"Step above dead," he said. "But see light at end of barrel."

"Inside a wave," whispered Charles in my ear.

"When did you start feeling bad?" I asked, still confused about how the illness had come on so quickly after lunch.

"Right before I skedaddled to the head with the runs," Dude said and took a deep breath. "Made it by a follicle."

"Was that after you ate lunch?" I asked.

"Sort of," said Dude.

"What's that mean?" asked Charles.

Dude slowly turned away from me and looked at Charles, who was on the other side of the bed. "Took three nibbles, stomach screamed, squirts be comin'.'"

Charles looked at me and mouthed *diarrhea*. I nodded understanding but didn't understand how Charles knew that.

"So lunch didn't make you sick," I said, stating the obvious.

"Not unless exotic, quick-acting squirt stuff be added," he said.

I asked when he had eaten before lunch. He pondered the question like I'd asked him for the square root of 213 and then said it was about four hours earlier. He had breakfast at the food truck before rehearsing two scenes in Cal's. He said that he had eaten eggs, fruit, and three helpings of grits.

"Who else was eating then?" asked Charles.

"Bunch-o-peeps," he said.

"Could you narrow it down?" asked Charles.

"No be knowing all," said Dude. He looked at Charles for direction—I assumed. Getting none, he continued. "Geoff be there, so be bird claw-foot guy, and—"

"Talon Hall," interrupted Charles.

"What I said. Pay attention, Chuckster."

"Who else?" I asked.

"Billy B.," continued Dude.

"That's Billy Robinson," said Charles for my benefit. "He's that five-year-old-looking assistant director."

Dude raised his non-IV'd arm and stared at Charles. "You be telling story or me?"

Charles opened his mouth—to offer a smart remark, I suspected—and then closed it and smiled. "Your story, Dude."

"Money woman be there. Becky something."

I wasn't certain why it mattered, but I was curious how many of the others, if any, had gotten sick. Dude's list would make it easy to check. That was until he answered Charles's next question.

"Anyone else?"

Dude shook his head and then slowly nodded. "Yep. More actors I didn't know. 'Bout six crew peeps. Couple of suits. Some others, career paths unknown to Dude."

Great! That narrowed it down.

"That all?" asked Charles.

"Be thinking so."

"What about Wynn?" I asked, since he was the other person I definitely knew had gotten sick.

Dude's eyes were closed. I didn't know what meds he had taken, but he appeared to be drifting away. He opened his right eye and whispered, "Wynn, yep," and then fell asleep.

CHAPTER 7

THE SUN ASCENDED THE NEXT morning as if nothing unusual had happened the day before. Charles thought that getting his aunt out of her tiny apartment would be good for her morale—and good for his as well. I would have picked her up, but instead Charles had borrowed the phone at the Lost Dog Café to call and tell me that he and Melinda had made the three-block walk and were now wondering why I wasn't there yet. He said I was late. I told him I didn't know anything about the rendezvous, so I couldn't imagine how I could have been late. Of course my words were wasted, and I agreed to do better next time. I asked him to save me a seat, and he said that he already had.

The restaurant was busy, so I parked a block away. The spring air had a crisp feel, and Charles and Melinda were seated on the front covered patio. The faint, sweet fragrance of spring flowers from the small community park beside the restaurant hinted at the warmer weather to come. Melinda smiled as I walked to the far end of the patio and stepped around a silver water bowl provided for thirsty canines. Charles frowned and looked at his bare wrist to let me know that I was late. His watch was imaginary, as was the fact that I was tardy.

"How's Dude?" asked Melinda, instead of saying something radical like, "Good morning."

I told her that I didn't know any more about him than Charles did and that we were going to pick him up this afternoon unless the medical staff could convince him to spend another night. She asked what the odds on that were. Charles said, "Zero." Then, more importantly, I asked how she was feeling.

"Would be better if my gall-darned nephew hadn't dragged me out of my comfortable apartment and made me walk three miles here." She glared at Charles and then grinned and took a sip from her mug.

The common gene thread ensured that both Charles and Melinda wouldn't let facts get in the way of a good story. After all, *three miles* and *three blocks* each had a three in them.

She looked better than the last time I had seen her, but Charles was still convinced that her health was deteriorating rapidly, and I had noticed swings in her energy level. She had good color, was aware of what was going on, and maintained her charming sense of humor.

Amber peeked around the door that led to the dining room and saw the new addition to the table. She positioned her hand like she was holding a mug and then raised it to her mouth. I nodded, and she went back inside.

A car pulled out of one of the prime parking spots in front of the restaurant, and the space was quickly filled by an ocean-liner-long 1971 Cadillac Eldorado, captained by Cal Ballew. The coupe's door was so wide that Cal had to squeeze through the narrow gap between the door and the Ford Explorer that was nestled beside it. The task wasn't nearly as difficult for Cal as it would have been for me since he was tissue-paper thin. He made up for his lack of depth by his height, and his trademark Stetson added another six inches. The temperature hadn't reached hot, so Cal had on his rhinestone coat that he had worn in front of audiences throughout the South for the last forty-plus years.

The country crooner saw Melinda and broke into his patented wide grin. "Yo, Ms. Detroit, it's a pleasure to see you." He removed his off-white hat and gave a stage bow.

Melinda gave an equally large smile and turned to Charles. "Now that's a move that you and Chris should work on."

"And hey to you, Kentucky and Michigan," added Cal. He had already returned his hat to his long, gray head of hair and didn't honor us with a bow.

Charles pointed to the fourth chair at our table and invited him to join us.

Cal looked around to see who else was there—or for a better offer. Finding none, he walked over to Melinda and planted a kiss on her stubbles of gray hair. She had worn a wig when she arrived on Folly, but terrifying events a few months ago convinced her to trash it. Besides, several people had told her how good she looked with her nearly bald head. That was all it took for her to stick with the less-is-more look.

Amber returned with my coffee and asked Cal if he wanted anything. He said coffee would be perfect and told her that she was "as cute as a bug's ear" this morning.

My mind wandered momentarily as I wondered which bug that old expression referred to. I couldn't recall any insect that I would consider cute. But then again, I couldn't recall ever noticing a bug's ear, either. I also knew not to share my thoughts with Charles. The last thing I wanted this morning was a lecture on bugs, their origin, Latin names, and probably what cultures considered them a culinary delicacy.

The film crew was shooting at Cal's, so I asked why he wasn't there. He was usually in the bar when they were so that he could make sure nothing got damaged or purloined. After the first day of shooting, he'd told me that, with so many mangy-looking folks, there had to be a thief or two in the bunch. He now explained that today there was only a skeleton crew shooting close-ups of a scene that had been shot yesterday, and he trusted the crew that was there.

"Trust them more than I trust that danged Mitch Abbot," said Cal. He took his Stetson off and carefully placed it on the deck.

"Who's Mitch Abbot?" asked Melinda.

"Guy who owns the food truck," answered Charles before Cal could.

"What's wrong with him?" she asked.

Instead of answering, Charles turned to Cal.

Cal frowned and turned his beaked nose toward Melinda. "Nothing, I guess. Just irritates the snot out of me that the danged production company had to hire some blasted caterer all the way from Atlanta to feed their prima donnas."

"Doesn't seem right," said Melinda.

"Ain't no chow they fix that Cal's couldn't provide," stammered Cal.

Unless the cast and crew had a hankering for hamburgers, hot dogs, and chicken fingers each meal, Cal's couldn't possibly provide twenty-four-seven food for the production. However, nothing would have been gained by me pointing that out.

Amber returned with Cal's coffee and abruptly shook her head. Her long auburn hair was tied back in a ponytail and swung from side to side. "You're not the first to think that," she said. "The Dog could have done just as well—"

"Better!" interrupted Charles.

"Or better," added Amber. "I've heard grumblings that other restaurant owners are more than pissed—excuse me, Melinda—about ProCatering. Somebody said that they wouldn't be surprised if that guy who has that minirestaurant he runs out of an Airstream over on East Ashley didn't poison the food."

"Folly Fries & More?" asked Charles.

"That's it," said Amber.

Charles laughed. "Hear that the *More* means heartburn."

Before we all turned into food critics, Marc Salmon rounded the corner, most likely on his way to have his daily powwow with fellow council member Houston. He headed our way when he saw more than one person gathered in a group that could include voters.

"Morning, my favorite latecomer from Motor City, my favorite singer, my favorite waitress, and Charles and Chris," said the council member as he turned to face each of us.

"Aren't Chris and I your favorite anything?" asked Charles.

Marc smiled. "Of course you are." He turned back to Amber. "Is Houston here?"

She shook her head.

Marc grabbed a chair from a nearby table and slid it between Cal and Charles. "How's Dude?"

I was surprised that he knew about Dude, but then again, I shouldn't have been since it was way back yesterday when he took ill. "How'd you hear about it?" I asked.

He rubbed his chin. "Let's see," he said. "Millie called me last night. She wanted to talk about some city business but also wanted to share what had happened to my good surfer buddy."

"How'd she hear about him?" asked Charles.

Marc smiled. "Well, seems that your main squeeze told her. Heather said you told her yesterday. So, I learned about it from you, Charles. Funny, isn't it?"

It didn't take long for rumors and an occasional fact to bounce around the tiny island. Marc usually caught the rumor on its first bounce.

Charles gave Marc a faux smile. "Hilarious."

This was a good time to take advantage of Marc's talent of collecting information. "Have you heard how the actor's doing?"

"Fine, I think," said Marc. "They didn't take him to the hospital after all. Told him to get some rest, drink plenty of liquids." Marc paused, looked around the patio, and leaned closer to the table. "By liquids, they didn't mean the alcoholic kind." He leaned even closer. "He's got a serious drinking problem, you know."

I didn't know but had heard rumors—and not from Marc. I also heard that his bad habits didn't end with alcohol. Drugs had been a large part of his past, and I suspected that was why he was in the low-budget flick instead of more mega-million-dollar productions like those on his resume.

Marc leaned back in his chair after sharing his inside scoop. "Just glad Dude and the actor are okay. It'd be bad PR for the city if they weren't."

"It's getting to be a heaping helping of accidents," said Cal. "First, that poor director getting himself drowned." He looked down at the table. "And then the lights smashing up that guy in my bar. Now, two people with food poisoning."

Marc pointed at Cal. "Some folks are starting to call it snake-bit productions."

I hoped it wasn't a deadly reptile.

CHAPTER 8

CHARLES AND I WALKED MELINDA to her tiny apartment. I was surprised how spry she was after I'd listened to Charles bemoaning her deteriorating condition the last couple of days. She did say she needed a nap, but I thought that I might need one too. I definitely didn't see that as a sign of rushing to the grave.

"How about a visit to Mitch Abbot?" Charles suggested after we left Melinda's and arrived at the spot in the road where we had to choose a direction.

"Why not," I said. Besides, I was starting to like watching the moviemaking. As a photographer, I appreciated the various cinematographic challenges those who worked in the movies faced with each setup.

The tables in the covered picnic area closest to the catering truck were full. They had finished shooting inside Cal's, and most of those gathered had piled their plates and were shoveling food into their mouths. No one appeared worried about salmonellae.

"Hey, Charles!" yelled a young man dressed in cargo shorts, ratty tennis shoes, and a sleeveless T-shirt with the logo from *The Hunger Games* on the front. He was seated at the table farthest from the truck and pointed to a space wide enough for two on the bench. "Got room if you want." He was chewing on gum so much that I had to concentrate on what he was saying.

Charles waved and said that we'd be right over. Mitch Abbot had his hands full at the truck with feeding a dozen starving crew members, so we filled our glasses with ice tea from the large stainless-steel dispenser, and I followed Charles to the empty spots beside the stranger.

Charles slipped his legs over the bench and set his cup on the table. He then turned to me. "Chris, this is Billy B. Robinson." He patted Billy on the back. "He's the assistant director." He turned to Billy. "This is my best friend, Chris."

Billy, who probably was in his late twenties but appeared younger, reached behind Charles and shook my hand. Between a mouth full of food and his jaws working overtime on his gum, I believe I caught, "Nice to meet you."

Charles said that Billy was a surfer, so I asked if he knew Dude.

He said, "Sure, the old hippie with few words. Some of them sort of make sense. Seems like a good guy." He paused and took a gulp of soft drink. "How's he doing? I hear he got sick yesterday."

I thought that was a good description of Dude. I said that the hippie was in the hospital but should be fine. I also told him how good a surfer Dude was, and Billy said that he was glad he was okay and that he might talk Dude into a lesson or two.

Charles looked around the crowded tables and then turned back to Billy. "Anybody else get sick?"

"You know about Wynn?" said Billy.

Charles said yes.

Billy continued. "Other than him and the surfer, don't think so."

"Hear what caused it?" I asked.

Billy looked toward the food truck and said, "Can't imagine anything Mr. Abbot fixes could've made them sick. He's such a nice man. The food's always top drawer."

Billy paused and stuffed another stick of gum in his mouth.

"What do you think happened?" asked Charles.

"A big coincidence," said Billy between chews. "I'm glad they're okay. Especially Wynn, after what happened with him and Donna."

Charles's antennae poked straight up. "What happened?"

Billy looked down at his near-empty plate. "I don't like to gossip, you know. Well anyway, she came all the way from California to be with Wynn. She even left her two teenage kids back in LA with their father, who, truth be told, is an addle-brained louse. Wynn's a wonderful guy, but he hasn't been happy since she arrived."

He stopped and looked at Charles like "That's all."

My friend would have none of that. "So what happened?"

"Geez, I hate talking bad about people," said Billy. He tilted his head to the left and then the right. "Oh well, story is a couple of nights ago they had a knockdown, drag-out at the big house the company rented for Wynn. Someone called the police to calm things down. They're both really nice people, but I guess something just wasn't clicking. That happens at times, you know."

Billy abruptly jumped up, shook my hand, and repeated that it was nice to meet me. He patted Charles on the back and then told us he had to get in Cal's and clean up after the morning shoot. I now knew what an assistant director did.

"Is there anyone he doesn't like?" I asked after Billy was outside hearing range.

"Other than Donna's addle-brained louse of an ex, I think liking everyone's his kiss-ass plan to move to the top." Charles nodded. "Think Donna poisoned Wynn?"

"Seems unlikely," I said. "If she wanted to do him in, she could have flattened his head with a frying pan and claimed self-defense."

Charles nodded. "Or a rolling pin."

"Or a six-speed blender," I added.

I was thankful that no one had recorded the conversations Charles and I had. My college degree was in psychology, which gave me enough knowledge to be dangerous. It also gave me enough insight to know that it would take a decade or so of psychoanalysis to uncover why Charles and I had become best friends. Phrases like "night and day," "oil and water," "black and white" popped up in conversations when others talked about us.

Regardless, I wouldn't trade it for the world.

The line of hungry crew members had finally diminished, and Charles waved for Mitch to join us. The truck's owner whispered something to one of his assistants, removed his heavy-duty, red and blue striped apron, and walked over to our table. Mitch was a commanding figure with his shaved head, six-foot-four and three-foot-wide frame, and ghost-pale skin. I wouldn't have wanted to meet him in a dark alley.

He reached the table and patted Charles on the back, apparently a common moviemaking gesture. "How's the funny-talking surfer doing?" asked Mitch.

Charles gave a concerned nod. "*Dude* is going to be okay."

"Dude, yeah," said Mitch. "I hear he went to the hospital. Did the docs say why he got so sick? It couldn't have been the food." He waved toward his truck.

"He'd been feeling poorly for a few days. Bronchitis," said Charles. "He was already dehydrated, and the food poisoning made it worse."

"Why do you think the food couldn't have made him sick?" I asked.

Mitch turned my way. "You're Chris, right?"

I nodded.

"Thought so," he said. "I've heard about you."

Before I could get up the courage to ask what he had heard about me and how he had heard about Dude going to the hospital, Charles interrupted. "Did anyone test the food after Dude and Wynn got sick?"

Mitch's eyes narrowed. His left hand balled into a fist. "Why would they?" he said. "Wynn was the only person around here who started feeling bad, and the medics said it couldn't have been anything he just ate. It came on too quick, they said. Nobody knew about the weird surfer, I mean Dude, until later."

"Anybody else get sick?" said Charles.

He shook his head.

"Didn't the EMTs shut down the line?" asked Charles.

Mitch started to speak and then hesitated. He wiped some toast crumbs off the table and then turned to Charles. "Wouldn't say shut down. They said that I might want to throw away what was left. Of course, I did what they suggested. Routine, I'd say."

I thought about what the doctor had said about taking a few hours before setting in. "What about breakfast?"

Mitch tilted his head. "What about it?" His hand was still in a fist, and he started fidgeting.

"Were Wynn and Dude here at breakfast?" I asked.

"Yeah," he said. "They came later than the rush. The rest of the crew was setting up for a scene in the bar and ate earlier. Why?"

I glanced at Charles and wondered if Mitch was as dense as he was acting or was hiding something.

Charles gave me a quick nod and said, "Maybe they both ate something at breakfast and didn't get sick until lunch. That would be around the time the doc said it would've hit them."

Mitch's fist loosened. "We'll never know. I threw out all the food and sanitized the serving trays and utensils."

"Seems like a waste of good food," said Charles. "You always do that?"

Mitch looked back at the truck. "Umm, sure. Gotta get back to work." With that, he abruptly turned and walked around behind the truck.

Charles watched him round the corner. "Not a convincing 'sure,' was it?"

"No," I said, "but if it was something in the food that morning, why didn't anyone else get sick? Think there's any truth to the story that a local restaurant may have tainted the food?"

Charles looked at the top of the tent and then back at the food truck. "Nah ... umm, probably not ... hmm." He shrugged. "Maybe."

"Glad you clarified that," I said.

"Yep."

I interrupted our enlightening conversation when I saw a familiar face coming around Cal's. I nodded my head in his direction. "Isn't that the director?" I asked.

Charles twisted around to see. "Talon Hall."

"Think so," I said. "I've seen him but haven't met him."

That's all it took. Charles hopped up and waved in Hall's direction. "Yo, Talon!"

The director turned and looked at Charles, tilted his head, frowned like he didn't recognize who had yelled, and then broke into a smile. He headed our way, so I assumed he finally recognized Charles.

Talon reached his hand out to Charles. "Hi, umm, Chuck. How—"

"It's Charles," interrupted my friend. Charles had always been sensitive about his name. He corrected those who had the audacity to call him Charlie or Chuck. Only Heather, and occasionally Dude, could get away with something other than Charles. After the correction, he shook Talon's hand. "Meet my friend, Chris Landrum."

Talon smiled and gave my hand a politician's shake.

"Oh yeah," he said, smiling. "I've heard of you." Something more and more people had in common.

Talon was my height at five foot ten. He wasn't nearly as imposing as Mitch, so I asked, "What have you heard?"

"Not sure exactly," he said. "Something about you helping catch a killer last year. Good job, I hear."

Charles leaned close to Talon. "Yes, Chris and I managed to take a raving lunatic off the streets."

"You'll have your hands full now," said Talon as he continued to smile.

"Why?" asked Charles.

Talon laughed. "At last count, we had twenty-seven actors on this project. That's twenty-seven raving lunatics." He continued to laugh and held out his arms.

Charles smiled and said, "How about crew?"

Talon stopped laughing but continued to smile. "And directors and assistant directors and financiers and ..." He paused and waved his arms around. "And no telling who else's hooked up with the project." He paused again. "Actually, we're only lunatics. We leave the raving to the actors—God love them."

I nodded. "Spoken like a true director, I'd say."

"You've got that right," he said.

After we finished categorizing the various groups of lunatics, Talon got a cup of tea and joined us at the table. He shared that production had been halted for the day because of something related to the grips having problems with the camera dolly and electrical service at the Dog. Charles and I nodded like we understood. I didn't, and I suspected that Charles shared my level of knowledge. I did figure out that grips were lighting and rigging technicians and that unless they were happy with everything, not much happened on the set. Talon bemoaned that if this had been a larger-budget production, the problems they were having would have never occurred. Then he joked that one of the actors probably sabotaged the set so he could go to the beach.

When he said that, I could almost see the wheels turning in Charles's head. He looked in the direction of the beach and then back at Talon. "Were you here at breakfast yesterday?"

Talon's smile faded. "Yeah, why?"

"Just wondering if you got sick like Wynn and our friend Dude."

"Oh," said Talon. "No. Felt fine all day."

"Hear of anyone else coming down with anything?"

"Umm, don't think so. Nobody said anything to me. Why would you think they got sick from eating here? Aren't they the only two who felt puny?"

Felt puny was quite an understatement since Dude could have died. "Just wondering," I said. "We heard a rumor that someone may've put something in the food to make it look bad on ProCatering."

Talon's eyes widened. "Who would've done that? Why?"

"Only a rumor," said Charles. "Small town, big movie comes around, something to gossip about."

"Hope that's it," said Talon. "Don't want anything else bad to happen with the movie. I feel bad enough about what happened to poor Cesar. That was terrible; he was so good."

"Did you know him well?" I asked.

"As well as you can know anyone in this business," he said and shook his head. "He and I worked on a couple of projects a few years ago. We were both aspiring screenwriters."

"Any luck with that?" asked Charles.

Talon laughed. "Not really. I've written two scripts that have made their way to the bottom of my underwear drawer. Poor Cesar said he'd penned one. We spent hours talking about how we were going to hit it big with our movies. Most of us in the business have such dreams—fantasies really."

"You never know," said Charles, the optimist.

Talon looked around the tent and strummed an imaginary guitar. "I've written some songs too." He smiled. "While I'm fantasizing, might as well become a fifty-five-year-old rock star and songwriter." He air strummed some more and then laughed.

Charles pointed to Cal's. "You ought to talk to Cal. He wrote and performed a hit record back in his day."

Talon looked back at the bar. "Someone else told me that. Might talk to him." He continued to smile but put his imaginary guitar down. "Thanks. It's nice talking to someone around here who isn't a raving lunatic."

Talon said that he needed to get back to the "zoo" and invited me to stop by the shooting tonight. He said they would be on Center Street, the center of Folly Beach where most of the businesses, restaurants, and bars were located. He said they wanted to capture some of the character for the movie's fictional Oceanside, Georgia. I said he could definitely capture character after dark on Center Street.

CHAPTER 9

T HE SUN HAD DISAPPEARED BEHIND the marsh, but the temperature was still in the seventies with a light breeze off the ocean—a perfect night for shooting. I had walked the short distance from the house to Center Street, and it didn't take a movie buff to see where the sets were being readied. Three blocks of the street were blockaded, from the front of the Avocet Realty building to the town's only stoplight at Ashley Avenue. Yellow barriers and blue lights from two Folly Beach patrol cars made it clear that traffic had to find alternate routes through town.

Cindy LaMond was directing traffic at the Ashley Avenue barrier. There was little traffic at that time of night, and she waved when she saw me. I hollered and asked if she had seen Charles. She growled at the driver of a yellow Volvo and told him she didn't care how much he thought he should be able to drive up the blocked-off street. She then recommended that he take the detour or he'd have to wash his hands several times to get the fingerprint ink off. He wisely took her suggestion.

She yelled back to me that Charles had left with a cinematographer. She thought they were headed to an upper floor at the Tides. The nine-story hotel was at the ocean end of Center Street, and with open corridors that led to each guest room, it presented an excellent bird's-eye view of the main drag.

I thanked her and wished her well with traffic control. She said it was more fun than any cop should have.

The crew was still placing the artificial lights in strategic spots on the sidewalk, so I figured it would be awhile before shooting began. I headed to the Tides to see what gofer Charles and the cameraman had planned.

Jay greeted me as I entered the front door and facetiously asked what I was doing out so late. I had known the personable bellhop, expert on everything Folly, and one-man welcoming committee for several years. I joked that I must be walking in my sleep, and he agreed, pointing out that I seldom was out this late.

I asked if he had seen Charles, and he pointed toward the ceiling of the nautically appointed lobby. "He and Laramie, the cameraman, headed up to get a shot of Center Street. Come on, let's find them."

I told him that he didn't have to go up and that I only had eight options where they might be. He said one of his jobs was to help the film crew with any needs they might have. He said that getting me to Charles without me pestering his paying guests fell under his umbrella of responsibility.

"Charles would be a bigger pest to the guests than I would be," I said.

Jay laughed. "That's really why I need to find them."

We started on the top floor where I thought they'd have the best view of downtown. We struck out and walked down a flight of stairs to the next floor.

Charles was standing next to a gentleman I assumed was Laramie, situating his heavy-duty tripod close to the elevator core where he would have an unobstructed view of Center Street. Charles was holding a two-way radio and pointing to what he thought Laramie needed to focus on. To Laramie's credit, he was ignoring the gofer.

Jay told us not to jump off the building, not to throw the camera over the railing, and not to break into any rooms. He then headed to the elevator and laughed as he pushed the down button.

Charles introduced Laramie and told him that I owned the photo gallery on Center Street. The cameraman must have been in awe because all he could say was, "Whatever." I wrote it off as his loss and asked him what he was hoping to get. The director wanted an overview of the area where the bars were located, and he and another cameraman would be getting street-level shots later. I had taken night photos from the Tides vantage point over the years, capturing interplay among the lights from the cars, the streetlights reflecting off the palmetto trees that lined the road, and the colorful signage on the businesses.

Laramie told Charles to radio to the street and have the police turn off their emergency lights so they didn't show in the shot. This was the first thing I had seen gofer Charles asked to do. A minute later, the strobes were extinguished, and Laramie spent the next twenty minutes shooting the street. Live rock music from Rita's and the upper deck at Snapper Jack's began to fill the air. I had enough trouble understanding the words to contemporary rock, so when it was coming from two venues at the same time, I was lost. Laramie was finally satisfied with what he had recorded and pointed for Charles to fold the legs of the camera-laden tripod and lug it to the elevator. Now I had seen Charles do two tasks to earn gofer pay.

***

"Cut!" yelled Talon. "Do it again."

I was standing with Charles in front of the City Hall. We were watching a scene across the street on the sidewalk in front of Mr. John's Beach Store, one of Folly's iconic retail establishments.

The two-story, concrete-block and weathered-wood building that had originally been a restaurant now sold most everything beach vacationers wanted but seldom truly needed: giant floats, T-shirts, rafts, squirt guns in all shapes and sizes, and enough toys to stock a large day-care center. It was classic Folly.

The scene being shot involved the two cousins meeting a character who looked like he had answered the casting call for a drug-dealing, terrorist vampire. Charles said that he was supposed to be the cousin's drug connection from Florida and all-around sleazy business partner. He looked the part, although he didn't look much different from several members of the crew.

The cousins had walked back around the corner from Mr. John's and were ready to step back in the scene. Off to the left of the auxiliary lights, Geoff and Wynn were standing toe-to-toe with their faces nearly touching and their arms animatedly punctuating each word. Geoff tried to step away, and Wynn grabbed his arm and yanked him around. Geoff then pushed Wynn in the chest and backpedaled out of Wynn's range.

Wynn wasn't going to let Geoff go; he inched closer to him. His right hand was fisted, and he lunged at Geoff. By now, several onlookers who had been following the staged action in front of Mr. John's turned to watch the more interesting interaction between Geoff and Wynn.

Robert Gaddy, one of the financiers, was standing behind the camera and noticed the off-set commotion. He rushed over to the actors, put his arm behind Wynn, and whispered something to the aggressor. Wynn pushed Robert's arm away and said something to Geoff before stomping away from the gathered crowd.

"Think they were making dinner plans?" said Charles.

"Couldn't decide between Asian and Italian," I said.

"That'll do it every time," said Charles.

"Raving lunatics," I said.

CHAPTER 10

THE CHARLES AND CHRIS TAXI picked Dude up at the hospital the next morning. His color, what little he normally had, was back, but he moved sluggishly. He grumbled the entire trip back to Folly about how the doctor had repeatedly tried to kidnap him for another day. Failing that, the doctor told him to drink plenty of liquids, treating him like a baby. The doctor didn't know Dude, so I understood why he had treated him that way. Dude did say that he was "stoked" about "paddlin' out of Sick Hotel."

He lived in a small, elevated, pre-Hugo house on a street midway between the ocean and the marsh. Dude's rusting 1970 Chevrolet El Camino was parked under the house, which surprised me since we'd taken Dude directly from the surf shop to the hospital. He said that one of his employees drove it to its "nest" so it would be there when he returned. The borderline-evil worker doing something nice threw me.

We helped Dude in the house, and I said we'd check on him in a couple of days. Dude told us to check at the surf shop because that's where he'd be. We didn't argue; it would have been futile.

Filming was taking place at Cal's, and Charles had to be on the set to do whatever gofers do—very little in Charles's case.

It appeared that those higher on the food chain liked to have gofers around in case they wanted something to drink or an errand to run or a multitude of other menial tasks. Regardless, Charles was excited to be part of the "industry," as he continually referred to it.

I asked him to find out what the Geoff-Wynn spat was about, and he said it was his number-one priority. No surprise there.

The duct-taped light on Cal's side door was illuminated, and Charles held his index finger to his lips as he slowly opened the door. I added silencing interlopers to his list of duties. Actors, crew, and official hangers-on were gathered around the bar. Geoff was in a police uniform. I was amused at how the movie portrayed the chief as compared to the Tommy Bahama, colorful, camp shirt and gray slacks that was Brian Newman's typical uniform.

The scene had Geoffrey arguing with Wynn James, who was playing the mayor, about the increasing supply of drugs being smuggled into Oceanside. I considered that the two may have been rehearsing the scene last night but then dismissed the thought when the two actors stared at each other like two boxers at center ring before the bell. Talon was between the two. He wore all black clothes and a black ball cap with the logo of a strip of movie celluloid and *Director* on it. He looked like an actor playing a director rather than the real thing. I wondered what— if anything—was real in the magical world of moviemaking.

Charles moved beside his new friend Billy B. Robinson, who stood behind Talon. Cal was on the other side of the building, as far from the action as he could be while still being inside. He wore his Stetson but had substituted a faded, gold golf shirt for his rhinestone jacket, and tan shorts for his aged Levis. The look was weird, but weird had a far-different meaning on Folly and had tempered my critique of proper attire and behavior. At times, it was no simple task. The country singer saw me and started to wave but then pointed to the exit and motioned for me to follow.

"How about a saunter?" said Cal as he carefully closed the door so as not to disturb the action in the bar.

I should add language to my list of Folly's quirks that I had adjusted to. Over the years that I had known Cal, we had never suggested a walk much less a saunter, so I was intrigued by the idea and quickly agreed.

Cal led me toward one of the island's residential areas. We made small talk about the weather and the expected influx of vacationers over the coming weeks. Three blocks from the bar, he took off his Stetson, waved it in his face, and placed it back on his long, gray hair.

I did the same with my Tilley. Hat waving is like yawning; when one does it, all do.

"What do a Ping-Pong ball and a check from Cassie Productions have in common?" asked Cal as he looked back toward the bar.

I suspected that I knew, but I didn't want to spoil his story. "What?"

"The damned things bounce like a kangaroo on a pogo stick."

"Sorry to hear that," I said.

"I'm losing a cornfield full of business being shut down days for that movie," said Cal. He started walking again. "The rent they're paying me—*supposed* to be paying me—would make up most of it. Then their danged Ping-Pong ball check bounced."

"Have you talked to them?"

"Danged right, I did," said Cal. He walked faster with each word. "Soon as the bank jolted me out of my financial well-being, I zipped over to Ms. Movie Moneybags."

"Becky Hilton?"

Cal nodded.

"What'd she say?"

Cal stopped abruptly and then took a couple of steps toward the shade of a large oak near the side of the street. "You ready for this?" he asked. He took off his hat again and ran his hand through his hair.

I said that I was.

"I told her that my bud Kris Kristofferson may have written about that Bobby McGee chick being 'Busted flat in Baton Rouge,' but by God, this here Cal wasn't going to get busted on Folly Beach because of her freakin' kangaroo checks."

I choked back a giggle and said, "Her response?"

"The slimy con artist tried to snow me with some cock-and-bull story about the money coming from an offshore bank and something about the float and dropping interest rates because of blah, blah, blah." Cal kicked the sandy berm with his well-worn tennis shoe. "I know rotting malarkey when I hear it and told her that it wasn't my first rodeo and get to the finish line."

I smiled. Cal had spent much of his life around musical bookers and promoters; most, as he had told me before, were out to screw singers out of a fair price for their appearances. Malarkey detection was one of his strengths. "And?"

Cal frowned. "The manure deepened. Hilton said she was offering me a 'deal of a lifetime.' She said that she wouldn't do it for just anyone, but because I was such a 'good friend,' she was offering me a back-end deal where I would get points and profit participation. Said it could be worth millions." Cal's frown turned to a smile. "Millions of chiggers from my way of thinking."

"To someone who's supposed to stay outside when the red light's on, what's all that mean?" I asked.

Cal shook his head. "Dummin' it down, it don't mean squat." He looked over his shoulder toward town. "Hilton made her offer of a lifetime, and I looked at her and said, 'Can I pay my beer bill with those back-assed points? How about paying my rent with a profit-participation note?'"

I nodded. "Did she say yes?"

"Humph," said Cal. "She said I would get money once the film was released, had become a blockbuster hit, and the zillions started rolling in. I told her that I was going to offer her a *deal of a lifetime.* I said she could keep all those zillions, and in trade, if I didn't have my rent in some nonbounceable form by noon tomorrow, I was going to throw her entire rhumba of rattlesnakes out of Cal's, talk to my *good friend* the police chief about the drugs her cast and crew had been sneaking around with, and make a call to my connected friends in Chicago."

"Get her attention?" I said.

Cal smiled. "Ms. Moneybags said she'd have my money and asked if cash was okay."

"Didn't know you had connected friends in Chicago," I said.

Cal smiled. "Don't, but she danged sure don't know it. Between you and me, my sniffer says the production is flat-out pennies away from pooped. They're broke. I'd bet my gold teeth on it."

I wished him luck collecting his rent. He said he'd better get back to the bar before they started stealing his tables, chairs, and toilet paper.

CHAPTER 11

MY EXPOSURE TO HIGH FINANCE was limited to how much I was losing each month at the gallery. I wasn't wealthy, but by living frugally, I should have enough money to live out the rest of my days. I didn't have any outstanding debt, owned my cottage outright, and through the good luck of working for the company that I had given decades of my life to, had health insurance to meet any unexpected catastrophe. I knew little about the movie industry and even less about movie finance. My eyes glazed as Cal talked about points, profit participation, and back-end deals. I was concerned about him getting taken by the sharks of the industry.

Sean Aker was one of Folly's four attorneys and a friend. I had met him my first year on the island when he did some legal mumbo jumbo to help me get the gallery open. He had also provided me invaluable information in catching a killer, and then Charles and I reciprocated when we proved him innocent after he had been accused of murdering his law partner and torching his own office building. Our interactions had been relatively few, but on the intensity scale, off the charts.

Sean would know more about movie financing than all my friends combined, so the next morning I headed to his rebuilt, second-story law office. Mornings weren't usually a busy time in Sean's office, and we shared coffee and a couple of muffins I'd picked up from the Dog on the way. Food was an effective bribe with my friends.

Sean looked the part of a successful beach attorney with his short, curly hair, trim build, light blue Ben Silver polo shirt, and tan, linen slacks. His attire was in stark contrast to the bow tie, navy blazer group in the downtown Charleston law firms. Sean accurately accused me of feeding him for some reason other than his waistline, so I told him about my conversation with Cal and my skepticism about Cassie Productions. He confessed that he knew little about movie finance but had a law-school colleague in his scuba-diving club who specialized in entertainment law at one of Charleston's large firms. I asked Sean if he thought a muffin would get some information from his contact. He said not unless it was on a silver platter in a private jet flying to Los Angeles. Sean then smiled and said that he had a few valuable nuggets from law school, memories that his buddy would pay dearly not to have resurrected.

Sean stubbornly refused to disclose what he had on his classmate. He was more concerned about what it would say about him than about his colleague. After all, he had been there during whatever his classmate would want long forgotten. We spent the next half hour developing a list of questions for Sean to ask. Proof that there was more than one way to skin a corporate attorney.

The vacation season was just around the corner, and in addition to the movie-related influx of visitors to the island, there seemed to be an unusually large number of vacationers walking the streets. I had only opened the gallery Friday through Sunday the last few months. I suppose I was a slow learner, but I finally realized that being retired shouldn't mean having to work nearly every day.

Ten o'clock was the normal opening time, but before Charles took on the highly prestigious job of gofer, he was my highly underpaid "executive sales manager." He was usually on the job no later than nine thirty and chided me for "being late" if I arrived near opening time. I smiled as I unlocked the door at 10:10, knowing that he wouldn't be there to point out my terrible indiscretion. I didn't have to push my way through a mad rush of customers to get to the door.

No sooner had I had turned on the coffeemaker in the back room than the bell over the front door clinked. I heard Geoff's familiar voice. "Yoo-hoo, old chap, are you entertaining customers?"

I went out on a limb and figured he was asking if the gallery was open. "Welcome," I said and walked to the showroom.

Geoff was smiling and had a black fedora on his head. Instead of his faux police chief uniform, he wore a black, sleeveless T-shirt and black jeans. He looked around the room and then walked over to one of the large, framed photos of the Morris Island lighthouse. "The color is splendid," he said, rubbing his chin. "These are all your images?"

I said yes.

"Quite nice, quite nice," he said. "This is my first time in. Reminds me of some of the quaint shops in Stratford-upon-Avon."

I wasn't a big reader but knew that Stratford-upon-Avon was the birthplace of that writer chap, Shakespeare, and I took Geoff's comment as a compliment. "Thank you," I said. "Join me for coffee?"

He smiled and looked around again. "Have tea?"

"No," I said.

"Then coffee will be splendid."

I would never have called coffee splendid, but I'd never been to England. I waved him toward the back room.

"Aren't you working this morning?" I asked as I fished through the cabinet over the coffeemaker and found two fairly clean Lost Dog Café mugs.

"Not for a couple of hours," he said. "They're transitioning from overnight work at your Brat's Market to the pub."

"Bert's Market," I corrected.

"Ah yes," he said. "Like my good friend Burt Reynolds. I've worked with him on numerous projects. Great chap."

An advantage of being in my sixties was that I'd observed all kinds of people, including many with overinflated egos. Some of them had good reason to think highly of themselves, but many were only masking deep-seated insecurities. I'd been able to get along with most of those in the latter category by feeding the ego when needed, but by also letting them know in small ways that it's okay to suffer the same disease of the human condition as does most everyone else, insecurity.

I suspected Geoff was masking more insecurity than confidence in his abilities. "You must have come into contact with countless famous actors during your illustrious career," I said.

"I've been quite fortuitous to have shared many a Klieg light with some of the best," he said and then smiled. "Meryl, Harrison, Mia, stunning Kathleen." He laughed. "Oh, the stories I could tell." He paused and looked back toward the small refrigerator. "Have any cream, possibly a scone?"

I shook my head. "No and no."

Perhaps I'll have to get some if he starts bringing Meryl, Harrison, Mia, and stunning Kathleen with him.

"That's fine," he said. "I remember filming near a mountain stream in Montana. The chow wagon, as they called it there, only had black coffee and burnt toast." He smiled. "I survived."

That reminded me. "Hear of anyone else getting sick the other day?"

He took a sip of the cream-less coffee and shook his head. "Ah, that was a bloody mess. But all who suffered were that talentless arse Wynn and your friend what's-his-name."

"Dude," I said.

"Yes, he of words, funny and few," said Geoff. He set his mug on the table and looked around. "I don't see any ash receptacles. May I smoke?"

"Sorry, no," I said. "You can go out back if you like." I nodded toward the rear exit.

He blinked twice and smiled. "I can wait. I remember once shooting in Utah. Smoking was—"

The bell over the front door interrupted what was to be, I'm sure, a fascinating story. A few seconds later, Charles bopped into the room, his homemade cane tapping the wooden floor with every step. He wore a cardinal red, long-sleeve T-shirt with Willamette Bearcats in gold block letters on the front, cutoff jeans, and his Tilley. I'd left my Tilley at the house and felt almost naked with my exposed, thinning head of hair while my two visitors' heads were covered.

"Oh, hi, Geoff," said Charles. He tried to hide the beginnings of a frown, but I knew he wasn't happy to see the actor. Charles still hadn't warmed to the egotistical thespian.

"Please join us," said Geoff, who then waved his right arm in a wide arc, a move that would have made any stage director proud.

Charles opened his mouth but shut it as quickly and walked over to the coffeemaker and poured a cup. He knew there wasn't cream or a scone within a half mile and didn't ask.

"How come you're not at work?" I asked as he put his Tilley on the edge of the table.

"Wynn was supposed to be in a scene at Bert's, but his girlfriend—"

"The whore," interrupted Geoff. "Oh sorry, old chap, please continue."

Charles looked at Geoff and squinted. He then turned toward me. "As I was saying, his girlfriend came in and told Talon that Wynn was 'under the weather' and was unable to make it. We were finishing at Bert's, so Talon ranted, raved, and called Wynn everything but a star and said we would begin this afternoon at Cal's."

"Speaking of Wynn," I said, "it looked like the two of you nearly came to blows last night."

Geoff took a long sip of coffee and then grinned. "Ah, you witnessed that. Was merely a bit of creative disagreement. No big deal." He quickly looked toward the showroom. "How long have you been open?"

I gave a brief answer and asked again about Wynn. He repeated "no big deal," and I gave up—for the moment.

Geoff stood and walked to the coffeepot, poured a refill, and returned to the table with the carafe. "Like more?" he asked.

Charles said no, making no attempt to hide his surprise about Geoff's kind gesture. I let him pour more in my mug.

"You know, Wynn's erratic behavior is because he's a drug addict," said Geoff as he returned the carafe to the coffeemaker.

Charles, the ultimate trivia collector, jumped on Geoff's comment like spaghetti sauce on a clean, white shirt. "Don't believe we were aware of that," he said, speaking for both of us even though he had no idea if I had known.

"Ah yes," said Geoff, standing straighter and walking around the room. He was center stage and in his element. "Don't suppose everyone knows. Mr. James's acting fame came early, and for the life of me, I don't comprehend why. He's talentless, boorish, and all-things-unbecoming about my industry." Geoff raised his chin and shook his head. "Neither here nor there.

He'd starred in a couple of daytime soaps. Now, there's nothing wrong with soaps. In fact, my good friend Demi's career began that way. But that's another story."

"Back to Wynn," said Charles.

Geoff turned to Charles. "Yes, old chap. Worthless Wynn, as I've heard him referred to—behind his back, of course. He had a promising career ahead of him, although I can't speculate why. Then drugs led him down the pebbly path to oblivion."

Geoff paused. I couldn't tell if he was waiting for applause or trying to decide how much to confide in strangers. I also wondered if he realized that the person whom he was sending down the path to oblivion was now starring in a movie, and Geoff, the actor who had rubbed shoulders with and become friends with film legends, had a minor role in the same production.

"And?" said Charles, always uncomfortable with silence.

Geoff seemed to realize that he was the only person in the room standing and slowly lowered himself in his chair. "Acting in a soap is gruesome," said Geoff. "Production can run six, seven days a week. Often, actors don't receive their scripts until the night before taping. A superb memory is a must. Distractions have ruined many a career."

"Drugs can be a huge distraction," I said.

"Exactly, old friend," said Geoff with a stage nod. "What little talent Wynn James had—and I emphasize little—he lost when drugs became his mistress." He coughed and looked around again. "Sure I can't smoke in here?"

"Yes," said Charles.

Geoff looked at the back door, huffed, and then continued, "Then that bloody bint got ahold of him."

"Bint?" interrupted Charles.

"Um, scubber, loose morals, a pimp short of a prostitute," said Geoff.

"Oh," said Charles. "Go ahead."

"Anyway, little Miss Donna Lancaster got her fangs in him. She has two offspring she dumped back in LA with their father. Followed Wynn out here to make sure he doesn't stray, and I'd wager, to stay close to his supply of coke—and that's not cola, you know."

Charles asked Geoff if he wanted more coffee. Either Charles was warming to the Brit or wanted to pump him for more information. Geoff said he was fine, and I did too even though he didn't ask if I wanted more.

"Funny you say that about Wynn," said Charles after he refilled his mug. "I heard him telling one of the stagehands that you were a nice guy and a good actor."

Geoff laughed. "Let me tell you about actors. They earn their keep by lying. They play roles. They live in a world of make believe. You can't believe a word they say."

"You included?" asked Charles.

Geoff smiled. "You bet, old chap."

Charles pumped Geoff for more gossip but gave up after a couple more questions. Since Geoff was an actor and, according to him, all actors lied, I wasn't certain how much credence to put into what he'd said. And besides, he said he had to get to the set. Charles said that if he was going to earn his humongous paycheck—his words, not mine—he should follow Geoff to Cal's. I couldn't tell how much my friend had warmed to Geoff, but they left the gallery together—not arm in arm but side by side.

Three potential customers drifted in over the next hour, and I sold a large, framed print to one of them. I often went days without a high-end sale, so I was pleased with the morning's take. Brian Newman held the door open for the customer carrying the framed print, nodded to me, and then walked to the back room.

"Nice to see one of your photos walking out," he said and smiled.

I agreed and said that I could close for the rest of the week and live off the profits. He said that I must overcharge and then asked if I could spare a cup of coffee. I said sure, since he'd already taken a mug from the cabinet and poured a cup. We both moved to the table, and I pushed a pile of paperwork out of the way for his mug.

"What brings you to Folly's best and only photo gallery this fine morning?" I asked as I poured myself more coffee.

He blew across the cup, took a sip, and said, "Just thought I'd stop by to say hi."

That may have been true, but I knew there was more and nodded.

He looked toward the gallery. "Think I should run?"

I sat back in the wobbly, wooden chair. "What do you think?"

He smiled. "What do you think that I think you think, or what do I think about running?"

I resisted my innate smart-aleck tendency to say yes and instead said, "What do you think about running?"

Brian stared in his mug and finally said, "Chris, you know that I've been in law enforcement my entire adult life. I'm not perfect, but in my sphere, I know what I'm doing. I think I'm good at it."

"You are," I said.

"There's politics involved in policing, for sure," he said. "Any chief would be an idiot and most likely out of work if he didn't pay heed to the wishes of his bosses, the mayor, and council."

I nodded.

Brian returned my nod and continued, "But overall, the rules are black and white. We have laws, we have ordinances, we have regulations. As a sworn law enforcement official, I'm obligated to follow the rules." He looked back into his mug. "I grew up in that world. I'm comfortable there."

The carafe was nearly empty, and I asked him if he wanted me to make more. He said no. I turned back to him and said, "But as mayor?"

He leaned toward me and put his elbows on the table. "I know mayors have rules. They have stuff they're supposed to follow. But from what I've observed over my nineteen years as chief, those rules are like Jell-O. From a distance, they look firm, appear solid, but the closer you get, the mushier they become. The mayor is often stuck in the middle. This constituent wants this. Another constituent wants that. Developers want to develop. Environmentalists want things to stay the same or change at molasses's speed."

Brian was on a roll. He stood and walked to the door leading to the showroom and then back to the table.

"Remember the huge issue over drinking on the beach a few years back?" he asked.

"Hard to forget."

How could I have forgotten? Until two years ago, Folly Beach was the only community in the state that allowed alcoholic beverages on the beach. It seemed that every year there was an incident or two where someone abused the privilege, and finally after a Fourth of July melee, the city fathers had enough. They followed the lead of every other community on the coast and banned the possession of alcoholic beverages on the beach. While they were in the process of making that decision, the council members and the mayor were inundated with calls, e-mails, and personal confrontations from both sides. Some residents hated the ban; some loved it. Some businesses hated the ban; some loved it. And there were good, valid points to each side. Brian had his opinion, but his job was to enforce the law.

"I had a front-row seat in city hall for the debate. Discussions—using the term politely—were as heated as I'd ever seen inside those coral-colored walls. Some of the officials involved should have had their pictures in the dictionary under *two-faced*. 'Oh yes, Citizen Fred, I fully support the ban. Oh yes, Citizen Jane, you can count on me to oppose the overreaching governmental control.' On and on."

If Charles had been here, I suspect he would have had a presidential quote about it.

"Brian, I wasn't that close to it, but I know what you mean. The naysayers would say, 'That's politics.'"

Brian plopped down in the chair. "Exactly. That's my point. I don't know if I want to enter the fray."

I pointed to his coffee cup, and he shook his head. "You asked what I thought about you running," I said. "I know the system's not perfect, and it never will be. I also don't know a person on Folly Beach who could do the job as well as you could. Would you make mistakes? Of course. Would you make enemies? You bet. Would you be frustrated to the point of hightailing it out of town? Most likely. But, in my humble opinion, you'd be great for the city."

He smiled. "Thanks, I think. But my point is why would I want to make mistakes, make enemies, and be frustrated at this stage of my life?"

"Good questions," I said. "My first response is because you care. But regardless, it's a decision you'll have to make. For what it's worth, you have my support either way."

"Thanks, again," he said. "Now I have one more question before I leave to save the city from the evils of the world.

If—and it's only an *if*—I do decide to run, and something strange happens, and I win, I'll have to name my replacement."

"True," I said. Clearly he'd given the race more thought than he had been letting on.

"What do you think of Cindy LaMond as chief?"

That was a surprise. Cindy would be the first female chief. She didn't take lip from anyone, she was irreverent at times, she had a great sense of humor, and from what I could tell, her policing style was opposite of Brian's.

"She'd be fantastic," I said. "Why her?"

Brian laughed. "First, it'd irritate the hell out of many of the old guard. Nobody'd accuse me of putting a clone of myself in the job. And I think it's time for a change, a big change."

I smiled. "That'd do it."

Brian then frowned. "Trouble is that she'd be promoted over some officers with more seniority and rank. It'd be tough for her."

"She can handle it," I said.

Brian slowly pushed back from the table and walked to the door. "Thanks for the coffee and ear," he said. "Please keep this conversation confidential. That means from Charles too."

"Sure," I said.

Interesting, I thought.

CHAPTER 12

THE NEXT TWO DAYS WERE uneventful. Charles was off doing whatever gofers do, and I spent several hours doing what struggling shop owners do. That included paying insurance and utility bills and some tax preparation—frustrating, expensive, boring.

Things got less boring when Charles called to tell me they were shooting a night scene on the beach. He wanted to know if I wanted to go. According to the gofer and film-explainer, the scene was centered around a huge bonfire at the edge of the water. There would be a wild party hosted by two cousins played by Haney Lawrence and Rodney Able. Both were in their early thirties with black hair that looked like it had been styled by a grease-covered auto mechanic. Every time I'd seen them on a set, they wore black T-shirts with the sleeves ripped out, black jeans, and three-day-old beards. Rodney seemed to have some sense, but Haney kept telling everyone that he was a gunslinger in an earlier life and that they'd better stay out of his way. They played drug runners from south Florida and looked the part from a mile away. Typecasting at its best.

Charles also explained that there was to be a confrontation between their uncle, Wynn James, and the cousins when he learned that they were on the wrong side of the law. All this was to take place around the bonfire, surrounded by thirty or so twenty-something-year-olds, played by a handful of professional actors, and the rest by partiers recruited from the local bars. The crowd would be enjoying the fire, free booze, and drugs supplied by the cousins.

A little before sunset, I walked a block east on Arctic Avenue away from Center Street to where the set was being prepared. It was one of the few places on Folly where there was easy beach access from the street for the various vehicles and cumbersome portable lighting units needed for the shoot. Even though Charles had made me an assistant gofer, duties yet to be determined, this would be only my second outdoor shoot. And quite a spectacle it appeared to be.

One lane of Arctic Avenue was blocked by two Folly Beach Department of Public Safety vehicles, their blue LED lights filling the air and reflecting off the windows of nearby beach condos. A fire engine was parked just past the police vehicles. The sand-covered beach access opened to the wide section of beach where a huge pile of wood stood on the edge of the high-tide mark.

The structure was roughly eight feet high and once engulfed in flames should be a great visual. To save wood and so the set could be constructed quickly, the logs on the back side of it were stacked at right angles like they would be in a log cabin. The side that would face the cameras was piled to look like a traditional bonfire with logs, old palmetto trunks, and branches from nearby trees. The structure truly looked like a movie set—realistic from the camera's view yet only a facade. The lighting crew was setting the portable lights so they could work their magic by lighting a night scene enough to see the action without appearing to be artificially illuminated.

Charles was at the far side of the set barking orders to two locals he had apparently designated as assistant gofers. I wasn't jealous of his new helpers; it beat me having to pick up wood and do physical labor. Twenty yards in front of the pyre, three of Folly's finest were standing around one of the city's ATVs normally reserved for beach emergencies. A dozen or so extras were gathered around Billy B. Robinson, who was flailing his arms around, his jaws chomping on gum in time with his arms. Each gesture was carefully watched by the soon-to-be famous actors whose day jobs included maintenance at the Tides, bartending at Planet Follywood, and studying at the College of Charleston.

I was startled when someone tapped me on the shoulder.

"Evening, old chap," said Geoff. "Sorry to frighten you."

He was in his chief's costume. "Just surprised me," I said. "I was watching my friend ordering around his helpers."

Geoff looked toward Charles and then at Talon, the director. He was in deep conversation with Wynn James, who was dressed in a short-sleeve, starched, white dress shirt and gray slacks. He was as out of place on the beach as a giraffe at a morticians' convention.

"Lots of bossing around on a movie set," he said.

I looked at his shirt and then down at his uniform slacks. "In this scene?"

"Call sheet says so," he said.

I had no idea what a call sheet was, and Charles wasn't nearby to translate, so I asked Geoff what he would be doing.

He pointed three fingers like a pistol at Wynn and Talon, who were still in deep conversation. "Worthless actor over there will get in a fight with his cousins, and then the best actor on the production, yours truly, will come in and help break up the fisticuffs." He hesitated and shook his head. "Hardly a scene worth me getting out of my dressing room for."

One of the stagehands walked around the large pile of wood and ignited it with a device that looked like a flamethrower.

He was followed by another member of the crew carrying a fire extinguisher. Billy had arranged his extras in groups around the bonfire, and Talon and Wynn were joined by two actors playing the cousins.

"Excuse me a moment, old chap," said Geoff, who then walked toward the surf and around behind the wooden structure.

Billy, his chest puffed out and his head held high, moved to the center of the set and yelled, "Lock it up!"

Geoff returned, and we moved closer to the set. I glanced over at him, and he leaned close. "Means shooting is to commence," he said. "It's an antiquated phrase that means lock all the equipment down so it won't make any noise during the shoot." He waved around the area where the crew was standing. "See any bloody blokes locking anything?"

I shook my head. "Thanks. Do you need to be over there?" I pointed toward the gaggle of actors to the left of the set, rehearsing their lines.

"No, old chap. I won't be on for a while."

The combination of the flamethrower and the dry, fan-leafed branches from the palmetto trees turned the pile of wood into a flaming inferno in seconds. Talon jumped out of his director's chair and yelled for Billy and another member of the crew to get things moving. He appeared surprised at how quickly the fire had progressed. The cloudless sky was darker than light but not nearly as dark as the director had hoped.

"Action background!" yelled Billy.

The extras quickly went from standing around looking bored to a festive group of young people drinking beer, giving each other high-fives, and having, as Geoff would say, a jolly old time around the raging fire.

"Roll sound," were Billy's next words, followed ten seconds later with, "Picture's up!"

Two soundmen stood outside camera range and hoisted their large boom microphones over the action but out of sight of the cameras. Another man holding an old-fashioned clapper board shouted, "Marker!" and then slapped the guillotine top down.

Geoff laughed and said, "Guy's called a clapper."

I nodded, afraid to say anything since we were only ten feet from the action. I didn't want to be accused of not *locking it up*.

Talon waved his arms. "Cut!" he screamed. "Do it again." He looked at the cameraman holding the handheld unit and told him to move more to the left and get a close-up shot of the "busty, bouncy, babe in the bikini." He gave the clapper a dirty look. "Hurry!"

The whole process began again, and Geoff leaned over to me. "Directors and especially the bean counters hate night scenes. The weather seldom cooperates, extra equipment needs to be rented, and then a bloody truck, or boat, or aircraft blasts by and ruins the shot. Costs shoot out the roof."

Talon must have been happier with the second take. He nodded to one of the cameramen and said, "Cut. Let's get the A team in there."

Wynn and the actors playing the cousins appeared out of nowhere and moved to positions outside camera range. Talon called for Billy to get on with it, and he started the process of getting things going.

The cameras began rolling, and the two cousins entered the scene from stage left—a bit of movie lingo I had picked up— and Wynn from stage right.

Wynn immediately got in the face of one of the cousins, and the two began a well-scripted shoving match. Wynn and Geoff's confrontation the other night was more convincing.

"Cut, cut!" yelled Talon, who then jogged over to the two actors. I didn't hear all he said but caught "move closer … fire" and "shove harder."

Talon waved for Billy to do his thing. The fire was rapidly spreading to the remaining part of the pile. Flames shot high into the air, and the Folly Beach firefighters inched closer without stepping into camera range. The heat from the inferno was so intense that I took several steps back.

Action resumed, and the two actors played their parts to the hilt. Wynn shoved Haney. He stumbled and hit the ground hard. He pushed himself up quickly and attacked Wynn. That moment, the section of the pyre that had been constructed like a log cabin burned through two of the logs, and the top half of the pyre tumbled toward the actors.

Wynn tripped over the first burning log, and Haney stumbled over Wynn's left leg. Talon screamed, "Keep rolling!" Two extras closest to Wynn and Haney ignored Talon's command and ran out of the scene. One of the others pointed at Wynn and screamed for someone to help. The firefighters rushed toward the actors from the other side of the set.

Talon yelled, "Cut, damn it!"

Haney had jumped up and was trying to pull Wynn away from the burning logs. The right sleeve of his dress shirt was in flames, and he was trying to rip it off. I was closer to Wynn than anyone other than Haney. Flames had now jumped to Haney's shirt, and he fell away from Wynn. I took three steps toward Wynn, pulled him back down to the beach, and rolled him in the sand. The flames scorched my wrist, but I somehow managed to rip off what was left of his smoldering shirt.

Haney was on the other side of Wynn and screaming like someone had cut his hand off. The first firefighter hit Haney with the extinguisher's spray and then turned to Wynn. The sand had extinguished the flames, but the firefighter sprayed the shirt to be safe. The second firefighter arrived with the medical kit, and Talon lugged his director's chair closer for Wynn to sit on.

The firefighter asked if I was okay. I glanced down at my wrist; it stung but didn't appear to be the worse for wear. I told him I was fine, and he turned his attention to the other two who were being tended to by the other medic. Charles stepped in, and he and some of the extras kicked the burning logs back to the main fire, which was still burning intensely.

Wynn's girlfriend, Donna, came from somewhere behind the fire, gave me a hug, and thanked me for "saving his life." She then comforted the actor, who had minor burns on his arm but basked in the attention nonetheless. After all, he was the star, the center of attention.

Geoff and I moved to the background and out of the way of the emergency responders. The crew made sure the sound and video equipment and the portable lighting were secured. One of the firefighters stood near the burning wood and spread his arms to shoo away anyone getting too close. No efforts had been made to extinguish the bonfire since no one was now in danger.

Geoff said, "Bloody good job, my friend," and patted me on the back. He then turned toward the crowd that had gathered and kicked the sand with his polished uniform shoes. "But there went another blasted night. Look over there."

I turned and saw Robert Gaddy and Becky Hilton, the financiers. Their heads almost touched. Becky was waving both arms at the outdoor set, and Robert shook his head. Becky turned to walk away but hesitated. She glanced at the bonfire and then glared at Robert and gave him a shove reminiscent of the one in the scene that had rapidly turned to a near disaster.

"Not happy campers?" I said.

"They see currency going up in flames," said Geoff in a conspiratorial tone. "Each day this drags on, they get more irritated and downright surly. Wouldn't be surprised if the funds are drying up."

I understood how each extra day would be a serious drain on the limited budget, but what I didn't understand was what I saw directly behind the financiers. Parked on the side of the road was Charleston's TV4 news van. A cameraman walked toward the fire and was followed by a young, blonde reporter who was dressed more like she was going to a prom than to the beach.

How could they have gotten there so quickly?

CHAPTER 13

CHARLES, MELINDA, AND I WERE in my favorite booth at the Lost Dog Café. Melinda had a burst of energy and wanted to have a good breakfast instead of her regular bowl of cereal in her apartment. I had gladly offered to pick her up and take her to breakfast. Besides, I wanted to hear the gossip that I was certain would be bandied around after last night's accident.

We had ordered our food, and Melinda turned toward me and patted my hand. "I hear you saved that poor actor's life."

"Hardly," I said. "The firefighters would've kept him from getting too badly hurt."

She patted my hand again. "Oh so modest, you lifesaver you."

I blushed, and Melinda was distracted by what was being said at the table beside us. Gossip was being spread like jam on toast. Over the next ten minutes, we heard that locals had coined Wynn the Torched Thespian and were joking about how great it was that lowly ole Folly now had such a "hot" actor in its midst.

Melinda was getting as bad as Charles—and yes, me—about soaking in the latest rumors. She leaned around the corner of the booth to where Marc Salmon and Houston were holding their unofficial city council meeting and asked Marc what the latest was on Wynn's condition. Next to getting reelected, Marc got the most satisfaction out of being asked anything about his city and especially something that only he would be privy to. He sat up straighter and proceeded to tell Melinda that Wynn only had a minor burn and would be as good as new. He then proceeded in one breath to share that he had heard that the film was in financial trouble, Wynn's girlfriend was mad at him, and one of Folly's restaurants was about to close. And with that— whew—I stopped listening.

Before Melinda could ask more, Cindy LaMond entered and looked around. She spotted us and started our way before stopping to glance at the front page of the Charleston newspaper sitting on the counter. She finally made it to us, and I asked if she had time to sit. She nodded, so I moved over. She was in uniform, so Melinda asked if she was working. She said no and that she had just gotten off and had stopped to get Larry breakfast to go. He had been restocking the hardware store since early morning, and she wanted to be a good "homemaking" wife and take him some food.

Melinda smiled. "Back in the good old days, homemaking meant cooking the food."

Cindy returned the smile. "That's why I decided not to be born in the good old days. If Larry ever caught me fixin' food with a contraption other than the microwave, he'd scream to high heaven and swear that I'd been possessed by Paula Deen."

"You hooked a good one," said Melinda. "Don't let him get away."

Cindy laughed. "Don't intend to." She looked down at the table, and her smile slowly turned to a frown. "Let me bounce something off you guys."

"Bounce away," said Charles.

"I'm not big on coincidences," she said. "Does it seem strange that since the movie folks arrived, the director went and got himself drowned?" She held up her index finger. "Then the scaffolding fell and nearly killed someone." The middle finger then joined the index finger in the air. "And that big-shot actor and Dude got food poisoned." Her ring finger then went up. "And now last night the bonfire gets out of control and nearly cremated that same big-shot actor."

Amber brought coffee for Cindy and asked if the rest of us needed anything else. We said no, so she moved on to Marc and Houston.

I had been thinking the same thing but couldn't see how they were connected. "Does something make you think they weren't accidents?" I asked.

"Not really," she said and then sipped her drink.

"Was there anyone around at all the accidents?" I asked.

"Wynn, of course," said Cindy.

"Are you sure he was on the boat?" I asked.

"Think so, but I'll check."

"Anyone other than Wynn?" asked Charles.

"Was Geoff there last night?" asked Cindy.

I was quick to say yes since I'd spent most of my time talking to him.

"Then he must have left before I got there. He was at every accident. Let's see, so were those sleazy, LA-looking money people and the director and that kid who's assistant director—"

"Billy B.," interrupted Charles.

"Yeah," said Cindy. "The one who's about as old as my bra."

That was an image I wasn't ready for.

"Anyone else?" asked Charles.

"There could have been others. The crew eats at the food truck, and most of them are on the sets. There are a handful of bit-part actors and friends of friends of people in the production."

"But they weren't on the boat," I said.

"True," said Cindy. "There were only two other actors and, of course, the worst captain since *Gilligan's Island*."

Melinda looked at Cindy and then turned to Charles. "Cindy's 100 percent right," she said. "Don't know how someone made them look like accidents, but where there's this much stink, there's camel crap."

Melinda had verbalized what was becoming clear to me. I didn't know how they were created or who was behind them, but they weren't accidents, and I wanted to get Cindy's take. I also didn't want to give Melinda's analogy any more thought than I did to Cindy's bra, so I said, "Cindy, have you shared this with anyone?"

"Only Larry," she said.

"What's he think?"

Larry spent many of his formative years engaged in the age-old practice of second-story burglary until the state of Georgia provided him with eight years of free room and board in Coastal State Prison. During those years, he wisely decided that the price of room and board was quite favorable, but the lack of freedom wasn't to his liking. Even after turning his life around, he was familiar with the shady side of the law. I trusted his judgment.

"He said that I didn't have enough evidence to convict anyone of sneezing much less killing a director and trying to kill anyone else."

Melinda tapped her palm on the table. "I think I've got this figured out," she said.

We turned toward her.

She looked around the room and leaned over the table. We leaned closer.

"Y'all said the movie was probably in money trouble." She paused and looked at each of us.

We nodded to keep her talking. She did. "Cindy said those finance folks were at each 'accident,'" she said, raising her hand and making an air quote.

Again, we nodded.

"I had a ringside seat to the auto industry when I was in Detroit. In the old days, not only were housewives cooking," she paused and winked at Cindy, "but most of the cars in this great country were made in Detroit. General Motors, Ford, and Chrysler meant something then. Government bailouts, bankruptcy, imports, offshore whatevers weren't on anyone's lips." She paused and took a sip of coffee.

"The good old days," interjected Charles.

"Anyway," continued Melinda. "Every year in the fall when the new and improved models were released, the auto giants would stage a humongous publicity stunt like parachuting a new car out of some big-ass airplane or hiring some hot model—chick model, not car model—to sit on the hood of a bright-red convertible and then plaster a picture of her and the car all over the newspaper." She shook her head. "For the life of me, I never understood what good it would do to know that a new car could fall out of an airplane without getting smushed." She looked at me. "Did you ever worry that you'd be peacefully sitting in your car minding your own business and then—holy moly—it fell out of an airplane?"

I hadn't and suspected that neither had Charles or Cindy.

"The stunts got everyone talking about the new car," continued Melinda. "I suppose buying a bunch of them. Otherwise, they'd stop dropping them and polishing the hood with some hot chick's butt."

"I agree, Melinda. Don't know if they were for publicity, but someone staged the accidents," I said.

Melinda gave a big nod and once again tapped her hand on the table. "I'm sure they're for publicity."

Cindy cocked her head sideways. "Would someone resort to killing people for publicity?"

"There're millions at stake on movies, even cheap ones like *Final Cut*," I said. "People have been killed for less."

Melinda's comments reminded me of something, and I turned to Cindy. "Was the Channel 4 van still around when you got there last night?"

"Humph, sure was and blocked Ashley Avenue. Had to ask them to move. Why?"

"Because it got there immediately after the accident."

Charles looked at me and then at Cindy. "How'd it get there that fast?"

My question exactly.

"Don't know," said Cindy. "The guy toting the camera told me that they were almost done and to give him a couple more minutes." Cindy smiled. "He was sort of cute if you like the chunky, bearded type, so I gave him some grief but figured two more minutes wouldn't hurt anything. The on-air gal was talking to one of the actors and kept looking back at the camera guy and me. Guess she thought I was going to shoot him or something."

"He say anything else?" I asked.

Cindy nodded. "One of our off-duty officers working security told me that the TV truck got there when all the ruckus was going on. I asked beard boy how they learned about the accident. It usually takes a half hour or so for TV crews to get to Folly. He said he didn't know for sure, but that the smiling, toothy, on-air lass got a call from the station, and here they were."

"Did he say where they were when she got the call?" I asked.

"No," said Cindy. "No reason to ask, but I doubt they were anywhere near—no other news was going on in this neck of the woods."

"Publicity," said Melinda. "*Car dropping out of the sky* publicity."

Charles nodded. "Oscar Wilde said, 'The only thing worse than being talked about is not being talked about.'"

I was impressed. Oscar Wilde had never won a presidential election.

Melinda leaned back in the booth. "So now that I've figured out the motive for you amateur detectives and lovely police lady, who would benefit from the extra publicity?"

"Who wouldn't?" I said. "Everyone involved has something to gain. If the film's a success, the actors could get bigger roles, the director's status would elevate, and the financiers would make a profit."

"How about who would benefit the most?" said Melinda.

"The folks with the checkbook, period," said Charles.

Two ringing cell phones interrupted—Cindy's and mine.

Larry was calling to ask Cindy where his food was. Something about him starving to death, and if she didn't get there quickly, he was going to turn to dust and blow away. Cindy said something about Larry needing to be in films because of his sense of drama, but then said she'd better go. She headed to the counter to place his order.

My call was from Sean Aker, who said that he'd talked to his friend about movie finance and had something that I might be interested in. Even though Cal had called me yesterday and said that he'd received his rent in "clean, crisp, noncounterfeit c-notes," I was definitely interested in what Sean had learned. Melinda said that she felt just fine and if her "dear, sweet, beloved" nephew would walk her home, she'd be near perfect. The look on Charles's face said that he would rather go with me but didn't want to endanger his "dear, sweet, beloved" status. He agreed to escort her to her apartment.

***

Sean was on the phone when I entered his office suite a little before noon. Marlene, his receptionist, wasn't at her desk, but Sean's door was open, so I stood in the entry until he waved me in.

He finished his call with a laugh and a promise to whomever was on the other end that they would plan a scuba trip soon.

"Chris, this is your lucky day," he said and then stood, walked around his desk, and shook my hand. He pointed to one of the two side chairs in front of his desk. I sat, and he took the other chair.

"My fine University of Alabama law school training continues to pay off," he said. "I learned all the legal mumbo jumbo that keeps the untrained citizens such as yourself in the dark, so you have to pay me more than I'm worth to solve your problems that were created by other lawyers. And more importantly to you, I learned to remember and keep notes on all the unsavory activities of my law-school buddies." He hesitated and looked at his cell phone on the desk. "Imagine what the world would be like now if we had phones with video cameras back in the day."

I gave it a brief thought, shuddered, and then smiled. "Your professors would be proud."

Sean laughed. "My criminal law professor's motto was, 'Whatever it takes.' That's about all I remember from him other than that he was fired after being arrested for a couple of acts involving members of a traveling carnival. I'll share that another time, maybe."

I nodded and told him that I looked forward to hearing it. If Charles had been with me, I would be listening to the story now.

Sean looked down at a legal pad on the corner of his desk. "Back to why you're here," he continued. "Cassie Productions is owned by Robert L. Gaddy and Becky Hilton, both listed from

Torrance, California. You can tell Charles that the company was named after Gaddy's daughter. I know how much he likes trivia crap."

I said that I would, but I wouldn't.

"There was another partner who bailed a few months ago. My friend did a little more digging and found that Mr. Gaddy's family is in the horse-racing business. His father owns a training facility, and his brother is deeply involved in running it. Apparently, Robert is the black sheep in the horse business— yes, I know that I'm mixing my whatever those word things are called."

"That's interesting," I said and smiled.

Satisfied, Sean continued, "Robert is in hock up to his hairspray. He's borrowed on his family's name, and unless Cassie Productions turns a profit, he'll be mucking stalls for dear old dad the rest of his life—unless dad kills him first."

Sean hesitated and took a sip of bottled water from a table beside his chair and belatedly offered me a bottle. I declined, and he screwed the top back on his bottle and turned back to his notes. "Dear Becky is another story. It's a story that's full of blank pages. My friend is exceptional at digging up information on people, but not about Becky. There is apparently nothing to show where her money comes from. It's as if she just appeared on this earth from another planet."

"How's that possible?" I asked.

"Not easily," said Sean. "My friend's theory is that she's in witness protection or involved with the mob."

"Mafia?"

"Ah, Chris, my out-of-touch friend, no one uses that term anymore. The rumor is that Ms. Hilton is loosely affiliated with a group of gentlemen who make a significant contribution to the economy by allowing citizens to exercise their God-given right to play games of chance, or enjoy the pleasures of the opposite sex without the tedious binds of holy matrimony, or experience the wonders that chemical and organic substances can achieve."

"So," I said, "if the movie fails, Ms. Hilton may experience a seriously unpleasant outcome?"

"You catch on quickly," said Sean. "Bottom line is unless *Final Cut*, which happens to be Cassie Productions' only project, turns a significant profit, both Mr. Gaddy and Ms. Hilton are in—as my Latin teacher once said—seriously deep Shetland shit."

"They would benefit from any extra publicity the movie could garner?" I said.

"They're betting their life on it," said Sean.

CHAPTER 14

I WAS SITTING ON THE ocean end of the thousand-plus-foot-long Edwin S. Taylor Fishing Pier. From the diamond-shaped elevated deck at the end, I could see the shoreline along much of the island. The Tides Hotel and the Charleston Oceanfront Villas, a large condo complex, dominated much of the nearby view, but dozens of beach houses, large and small, dotted the remaining miles. It was my favorite spot to sit, think, and occasionally nap.

The pier received heavy foot traffic during vacation season, but it wasn't heavily populated the rest of the year. A few optimistic fishermen spent hours watching their fiberglass rods in hopes of hooking the one to brag about. Today it was nearly empty, and the only sounds came from waves gently rippling to shore and the occasional circling seagull complaining about the shortage of food.

What Sean had learned about Hilton and Gaddy were powerful reasons for them to create publicity for the *Final Cut*, but it also raised questions. First, despite my strong suspicions, there was no evidence that the incidents were anything but accidents. If intentional, how could they have caused the boat to capsize, or the structure holding the lights to fall, or the food poisoning, or for the bonfire to collapse? If they were so concerned about the budget, why would they create accidents that would result in expensive delays, especially since the movie was nowhere near complete, with weeks of shooting ahead and then months in postproduction before it ever saw a big screen? How would publicity this early in the process benefit the film at the box office months down the road?

Were Charles, Melinda, and now Cindy and I chasing something that didn't exist? Accidents were not uncommon on movie sets, so no one with the production appeared surprised about them. Cindy was right though. Four accidents in a short period was an extraordinary coincidence. Regardless, despite Charles's job as gofer, the few cast and crew that I'd become acquainted with, and Dude's serious illness, none of it involved me. For that, I was thankful.

Somewhere between me pondering the accidents and falling asleep in the shade of the roof, I heard, "Hey, old chap, is that you?"

Geoff was about twenty feet from the steps to the upper deck where I was comfortably leaning against the back of the bench. I waved, and he headed up.

"Thought I recognized your red shirt and follicle-challenged head," he said and then chuckled.

"Funny," I said. "Have a seat. What brings you to the edge of *The Edge of America*?"

He joined me on the bench and then waved in the direction where the film trucks and trailers were staged. "Hanging around film blokes is quite tiring. I prefer mixing with the locals and picking up the quirks of the area, the distinct language of the Lowcountry in this case. Besides, I don't have to be on the set until late afternoon at the Blue Dog, your fine Lost Dog Café."

I commented on how nice the weather was, and he shared that he hoped it stayed that way so they could get the outdoor scenes shot and he could move on to "other projects." I asked him what he was doing next, and he mumbled something about the projects being in the "development stage." It sounded a lot like he didn't have anything once *Final Cut* wrapped.

I had a captive audience, so I thought I'd see what he knew about the film's finances. "I hear money may be running low."

He gave me a sideways glance and made a wave motion with his right hand. "Hollywood accounting, old chap."

"What's that?" I asked. I didn't remember Sean using the term and knew Charles hadn't or he would have spent ten minutes explaining it.

He pulled his shoulders back and sat straighter on the bench. "Only about 5 percent of films show a net profit."

"I thought it'd be much higher."

"Did you know that *Rainman*, *Forrest Gump*, and even *Batman* lost money?"

"Weren't they hits?"

"Yes and no," he said.

I held my palm out to him—explanation, please.

"Hollywood accounting," he said. "Blooming Hollywood accountants sit on their bums and mix a recipe of fictional overhead expenses—"

"Whoa," I interrupted. "Explain?"

An elderly man carrying binoculars walked past us on his way to the rail. Geoff waited until he was out of hearing range and then continued. "I'll try, but it's more complicated than this old actor can understand. Here goes." He paused again, took a deep breath, and exhaled. "A film project has real costs like paying the actors, crew, renting the equipment, licenses, paying off-duty police for security, housing, costumes, transportation. Think everything that a check has to be written for."

"Got it," I said.

"That's where it gets complicated. The overhead that goes on the books is calculated on a percentage of the production cost, regardless of how much it actually is. In other words, the true overhead costs may be thousands and even hundreds of thousands less than the reported cost. When all is said and done, it often appears that the production was more expensive than it actually was. Not only is production figured that way, so is distribution and marketing overhead." He shook his head. "It's more complex than that, but when the final numbers are figured, investors could lose millions even if the film is a box-office smash."

"Is that what's happening here?" I asked.

"That's part of it, but I think it's worse. There are only two investors, Robert and Becky. Rumor is that neither has money to lose. Some have hinted that the bloody funds have been borrowed from blokes you don't want to fail to repay."

"That's why they're here all the time?"

"Yes," said Geoff. "It gets worse because the people who've loaned them the money think it's doing better than it is. They think the book-cooking is going on and there will be much more cash left after it's finished regardless of what the accountants say. I hear that's not the case. I was chin wagging with one of the equipment blokes yesterday who said that three rental checks have bounced, and one company actually came and retrieved its lighting." He stopped and smiled. "They confiscated Wynn's motor home, and he had to move to a smelly, moldy, old house."

The check they had written to Cal bounced, but I didn't mention it.

He slowly stood and stretched out his arms. "Got to get ready for my scenes this afternoon. Good talking with you." He started to walk away and turned back. "Perhaps someday I'll be able to live somewhere like here. Everyone is so sane and kind."

If he thought that about Folly, I now knew what Talon had meant about all actors being raving lunatics.

Geoff headed down the steps, waved back at me, and said, "Cheerio!"

CHAPTER 15

CHARLES STOPPED AT THE HOUSE after a day of gofering and said that he'd had it up to the crown of his Tilley with whining actors, directors, and sound techs. He was ready for some good old nutty, quirky, and oddball Follyites. I said that it takes one to know one, and he asked what was wrong with that.

I shared what Geoff had told me about the finances and what Sean had gleaned from blackmailing his classmate.

"I don't know what you see in Geoff," said Charles as he pulled a Budweiser out of my refrigerator.

"Why?" I asked.

"Can't put my finger on it," he said. "He seems to be a shallow, foreign blowhard. Yesterday he was telling Billy that he thought he spotted his *good friend* Angelina Jolie on the—get this—*porte cochere* at the Tides. Imagine someone using that language on Folly? Plus, I don't trust him."

I shook my head in mock disgust and wondered if it was Jolie. Charles's problems with Geoff still confounded me. He always found the good in everyone, even blowhards, and I knew he was more tolerant of unique characters than I was. I liked Geoff and told Charles so. He said "whatever" and went back to what I had learned.

"I know what you mean about the finance peeps," he said. "Everyone on the set avoids them, and when they're stuck talking to them, they're guarded about what they say. Even Billy B. who sucks up to everyone struggles with kind words to spread on their bagels."

"Regardless," I said, "even if they're out of money or are connected to folks you wouldn't want to climb in bed with, I don't know how they would've staged the accidents."

"I agree," said Charles. He looked down at the beer can and then snapped his finger. "Guess what?"

I hate it when someone asks me to guess.

"They've stopped making M&Ms," I responded with a straight face and a sliver of revenge.

Charles raised his hand to his mouth. "Really?"

I smiled. "No."

"Why'd you say it?" asked Charles. In an odd way, he appeared relieved.

"You asked me to guess." I shrugged. "So I did."

He sighed. "And you think I'm strange."

"So what was I supposed to guess?"

He looked back at the beer can. "I forgot."

I said I'd get him another beer while he figured it out. He thought that was, in Geoff-speak, a bloody good idea.

I returned, and so had Charles's memory. "I was talking with Marc Salmon last night, and he said that he'd been doing some politicin' for Brian and was 'almost positively, probably, near certain that he'd win.'"

I wouldn't want to take those odds to Vegas, but from Marc, they were encouraging. I still had mixed feelings about the chief running. Local politics, be it Folly or any of the thousands of other small cities in the country, was a world of frustration, backstabbing, and no-win situations. Feelings would be hurt. It became extremely personal. Nevertheless, if Brian ran, I would be his biggest supporter.

"Glad to hear it," I said. "Although I can't see why he would want to."

"He thinks he can make a difference, more than he makes now," said Charles. "I hope he runs. Abraham Lincoln said, 'To sin by silence when they should protest makes cowards of men.'"

Charles finished his second beer and said that that was enough political talk for a day and probably a week. He was not a fan of politics, a fact I found interesting since he had a propensity for quoting presidents. He said he was heading to the library. I asked him if, as inconceivable as it may seem, they had a book that he didn't already own or hadn't read. He said that he doubted it, but he was going to do some research on a certain British blowhard.

When Charles was on a mission, he was like a pit bull with a rabbit clamped in its jaws. Nothing short of a bolt of lightning would get him to let go.

Geoff had told me that his next big scene was going to be on the patio at the Dog. He and that "half-arsed, moronic-actor Wynn" were going to have a confrontation where Geoff's character was going to tell Wynn's character that he had to either get his cousins in check or be prepared to spend several years locked up with them. He was excited about the shoot, so excited that he had invited me to watch. I couldn't tell if he was more pleased that he finally had a pivotal scene or that he was getting to yell at the moronic actor. Either way, I said I'd be there.

Shooting should have been in full swing when I arrived. Instead, artificial fill-lighting was strategically arranged around the patio, a cluster of crew members stood off to one side, and absolutely nothing was happening at the table where the actors should have been walking through the scene.

The fact that nothing was happening didn't stop a steady stream of cars from slowly rolling by the restaurant. Vacationers and several locals made it a daily routine to check on the movie's progress. Cindy was in the small parking area in front of the Dog, making sure vehicles kept moving.

I weaved my way between two slowly moving SUVs and stood behind Cindy.

She twisted her head in my direction while she waved her arms for the traffic to keep moving. "See how exciting police work is?" she said. She nearly smiled.

I did smile and said, "Maintaining law and order never ends."

She took her right hand out of traffic-waving mode and pointed toward the empty patio. "The gawkers are sure getting their fill of movie magic this morning."

"What's going on?" I asked. "Geoff told me they would be shooting on the patio."

"There's a big powwow inside," she said, returning both arms to traffic control. "Seems that Donna Lancaster got an e-mail this morning from her heartthrob saying something like he couldn't take the pressure and that the drugs were controlling his life again. He apologized to everyone but had left the state and checked into rehab."

Not the publicity the finance duo would want. "Did Donna know about it before he left?"

"Don't think so," said Cindy. "She acted shocked when she got here this morning to tell Talon and the others."

"Anyone know where he went?"

"I forgot to mention," said Cindy. "The e-mail said that he didn't want anyone to try to contact him."

"Does anyone know where he went?" I repeated.

Cindy smiled. "I heard Donna telling Talon that she thought it was a rehab center in either California or Montana."

I rubbed my chin. "That narrows it down."

Cindy giggled. "Yeah, if Donna wants to stand by her man, she'll have to do a heap of huntin' to find him."

You could take Cindy out of the mountains, but you couldn't take East Tennessee out of Cindy.

"Does it make sense to you that Donna wouldn't have known where Wynn went for rehab?" I asked.

"Unlikely," she said. "But rumor is that they've been fighting. Maybe she's part of the reason he fell off the wagon."

"Could be," I said, "but it stills strikes me as strange. And why's she still here since her family's in California and there's no telling how long Wynn'll be gone?"

Cindy shrugged.

"What're they going to do?" I asked. "I'm not an expert on movies, but I think the star is fairly important."

Cindy continued to wave her arms to keep traffic moving. "You're not going to believe this," she said. "The big brains behind this production—and I'm using *big* generously—didn't have the smarts to invite me into their what-the-hell-are-we-going-to-do meeting that's been going on for an hour."

I'd love to see Cindy as police chief, I thought. "Who's in there?" I asked.

"They were doing a lighting check on the patio when Donna arrived. Talon sent the lighting, sound, and camera guys away, as well as the actress who was playing the waitress. The two money people were here since they've been sticking to the shooting like moss on a tree. They're inside. Of course Donna and Talon are still here." She paused and gave a big move-it wave to a Honda Civic that had stopped. "Okay, where was I?" she said. "There was a lot of yelling and a couple of tables kicked. They were throwing out words like breach of contract and zillion-dollar lawsuits. Oh yeah, I forgot, Billy's in there, and so is Geoff since he was supposed to be sitting on the other side of the table from Wynn. Think that's it."

I looked around. The line of traffic was backed up to Center Street, a block away. "I'll let you get back to your serving and protecting," I said and left her standing in the street waving her arms at a carload of vacationers from West Virginia.

I walked away from the Dog and wondered what could possibly happen next to *snake-bit production*. My phone rang before I could speculate more.

***

"Chris," said Charles. "I'm at Melinda's. Could you come over?"

No smart remark, no nonsensical comment, no presidential quote. Something was wrong.

"I'm on my way."

Her apartment was in the back of the building, but Charles was in the corridor pacing when I arrived.

"What's wrong?" I asked.

"She's worse," he said. "I stopped by to see if she was up to a walk. I haven't seen her much since I've been working. It took her a long time to answer the door. She looked terrible—all slumped over, head bowed."

He walked to the front door of the building, looked out, and then returned to her door. "She said this was the first time she'd been out of bed in two days." He paused. "Chris, why didn't I check on her yesterday?"

"I'm sorry." What else could I say?

"I told her you might be stopping by, and she said to give her a few minutes to get presentable."

"I don't have to come in—don't want her feeling uncomfortable," I said.

"Don't be silly," said Charles. "She wants to see you."

Charles opened her door and waved for me to go in first. Melinda was perched on an old, flowery couch. She leaned to the right and was supported by a green pillow that Goodwill would reject. Her Walmart blouse that fit her well a few months earlier was loose on her shoulders. The skin on her face sagged. Despite all that, she broke into a smile when she saw me.

"Hallelujah," she squealed like a little girl. "It's good to see someone who can say something good." She looked at Charles and frowned. "Old worrywart here keeps talking about me going to a doctor or the hospital. Think the dear, sweet boy thinks I'm ready for a fitting at Coffins 'R' Us."

I glanced at Charles, who rolled his eyes and said, "I'm just worried about you, Aunt M."

"I'm fine, Charles. Just a little under the weather. Probably a cold. All I need is a bottle of Maker's Mark to kill the germs."

"We'll see what we can do about that," I said.

I knew that despite Charles's efforts and cajoling, Melinda would never go to the hospital. She had told us before that she had made peace with the Lord, had thoroughly enjoyed her life, and was going to leave on her terms. She knew her cancer was terminal, and she had already lived longer than the doctors had predicted. I also knew it was tearing Charles up. He felt helpless and didn't handle it well.

"Good," she said. "Now what're the latest movie shenanigans? More 'accidents'? Publicity stunts?" She leaned back on the couch, her head held higher.

I shared the latest from the set. Melinda listened carefully, and Charles huffed and asked when I was going to tell him. I told him that I just did. He said that I knew what he meant. I did, but I didn't give him the satisfaction of admitting it.

"Are they sure he went to rehab?" asked Melinda.

"They don't know where he is," I said. "Just what the e-mail said. Why?"

Melinda looked at Charles, who stood in the corner still peeved because I hadn't told him first about Wynn's departure, and then back to me. "Sounds fishy," she said. "Sounds rotten, stinky, fishy."

CHAPTER 16

"SHE'S WORSE NO MATTER WHAT she says," said Charles. We were walking from Melinda's apartment to Folly Liquors. The weather was near perfect with lower-than-average temperatures and low humidity. Charles needed to vent, so the walk was for more than a bottle of bourbon.

"I know she is," I said. "More than anything, she needs you to support her—no doctors, no hospital. She's not mixing misery and Maker's. She's content, Charles. Let her savor it. Being here for her is the best gift you can give."

Charles kicked the sand and gravel on the side of the road. "I know, I know. It's just hard. I don't want her to suffer."

Charles needed a distraction. "Did you see signs that Wynn was on drugs?" I asked. "Distracted? Hyper?"

I remembered what Geoff had said about Wynn and his using drugs, but I had discounted most of it because of his bias against the star.

"Nothing," he said. "In fact, I heard him talking to Billy B., and he was saying how good he felt. He mentioned how long it'd been since he had 'taken a snort,' but I didn't hear how long it was."

"Do you agree with Melinda about it being fishy?"

Charles stopped. "Don't seem like there's a reason to think that," he said, "but there's a big number of coincidences piling up."

"Any idea what'll happen with the star AWOL?" I asked. We had reached the liquor store behind Bert's. I opened the door for Charles.

"It's a fine day, my friends," said the cheerful clerk. He seemed pleased to see us, pleased to see anyone, since we were the only customers in the small store.

We acknowledged that it was indeed a fine day and asked for a bottle of Maker's Mark. The clerk managed that task quite well, and we left the store and saw Billy Robinson was jogging toward us. His gum-chewing jaw kept time with his stride.

"Here comes the answer to your question," said Charles, who then reached out and stopped Billy.

"Hey, Billy B., where're you headed with your britches on fire?" asked Charles.

I often suspected that Charles was a chameleon in a previous life. There's no one better at adjusting to the speech, behavior, and mood of the person he's talking to. I watched him put his arm around Billy's shoulder, and anyone watching would have thought they were long-lost brothers.

Billy rolled his eyes. "Mr. Gaddy sent me to get two bottles of the cheapest hooch they sold. He said they'd need it back at the production trailer—and quick."

Charles gave Billy's shoulder another squeeze and said, "Terrible news about Wynn."

"You've got that right," said Billy.

"What'll happen?" I asked.

Billy looked over at me as if he hadn't seen me standing three feet from Charles. "That's why they need the whiskey."

"You're a big honcho with the production," said Charles, the chameleon and suck-up. "What do you think should happen?"

Billy looked at the door to the liquor store and then to the shaded back corner of the building. "They can wait a few more minutes for their booze," he said.

Charles led him around the corner and out of the sun. Despite the mild temperatures, drops of perspiration rolled down Billy's forehead, and his *The Dark Knight Rises* T-shirt was soaked. The three of us sat on steps to the apartments behind the store.

"Don't know what'll happen," said Billy. He wiped the sweat from his cheek and spit out his gum. "We'll be able to use several scenes already in the can, the ones without Wynn. Talon thinks we may be able to save a few where only Wynn's back is shown." He paused and looked down at the ground at his discarded gum.

Oh please, I thought, *don't pick it up and start chewing.*

"What then?" asked Charles.

Billy looked at Charles and slowly shook his head. "Then the argument started."

Charles lived for words like those. He leaned to within inches of Billy and said, "Really?"

"Yeah," said Billy. "Talon wants to bring in an actor friend of his from LA. Said the guy, who I've never heard of, was finishing a blockbuster and would be available in three weeks." Billy laughed. "That's when Becky and Robert went ballistic. Becky jumped up—almost knocked her chair over—and started yelling at Talon. She called him everything in *Profanity for Dummies* and then kicked the table." He smiled. "She had on sandals and hurt her toe but tried not to let it show."

"Then what happened?" asked impatient Charles.

"Robert jumped in and said there was no way they could delay the production that long. Kept screaming 'days are dollars' and that filming couldn't stop. Talon said that they could shoot scenes that didn't involve Wynn while waiting for his actor friend. Then Geoff, who hadn't said a peep the entire time, stood and walked to the window overlooking the patio and then looked at the photos of dogs on the wall. 'I've got it,' he said like he was projecting to the last row in the LA Coliseum. Everyone in the room stopped arguing and looked at him." Billy looked around. "Think they sell gum in Bert's?"

"Nope," said Charles before Billy could head to the store.

I wasn't about to contradict him. "Got what?" I asked.

Billy looked back at the gum on the ground and then at me. "Geoff said that he could replace Wynn. Said that he had way more experience than Wynn, already knew many of the lines, and would give the production the 'star power' it needed. Talon said it wasn't a good idea."

"I agree," interrupted Charles.

Billy paused to see if Charles was going to say anything else. He didn't, so Billy continued, "Talon then said Geoff was too old for the role. Said that they wouldn't be able to use the scenes that had already been shot with Geoff. Geoff interrupted and said there weren't that many scenes that would need to be reshot and that he thought the lead role could use a more *mature* character."

"What did Talon say?" asked Charles.

Billy smiled. "Nothing at first. He looked at Geoff and shook his head and then looked at Becky and Robert and shook his head again. Robert said it wasn't the best idea he'd heard, but it might work. Becky said, 'Maybe.' Talon said, 'Shit.'"

"And then?" asked Charles.

"Talon looked at me and told me to get my ass to the closest liquor store, get two bottles of hooch, and meet them at the production trailer. Speaking of which, I'd better get going."

Billy left Charles and me sitting on the step as he headed around the corner to do what assistant directors do. "Hope he's not worming his way into my job as gofer," said Charles as he watched Billy go.

"I think your job's safe," I said.

"Oh great," said Charles. "Geoff as star."

"What's wrong with that?" I asked. "It sounds better than waiting on someone from California."

"I don't like that man—just don't," said Charles.

"Did you find out anything about him at the library?" I asked.

"Barely got started on the Internet when this lady on the computer next to me asked if I could help her find a website. She made Melinda look like a teenybopper. Course I told her no and that I was as computer literate as a pelican. She grabbed her walker and scooted over to the librarian for help. I nosed in to learn what she was trying to figure out. And then the librarian told me it was closing time."

"So you didn't learn anything?"

"Picked up a couple nuggets of wisdom before the lights were turned out. I learned how to find what the geezerette wanted to learn, so I'm now more computer literate than a pelican." He reached over his shoulder and patted himself on the back.

"What about the second nugget?" I asked after he finished his self-congratulatory ritual.

"Learned that those 'big films' Geoff said he had been in were more than a decade ago, and he wasn't the star. His name was about five sizes smaller than the lead actor on the movie posters I found on the Internet. His 'big' parts the last three years have been on two cable television 'celebrity' reality shows. They were knockoffs of that big-hair guy's show."

"*The Apprentice*?" I said.

"That's it. According to the website, the two shows pulled a Nielsen rating that converted to fifteen viewers, give or take."

"Not quite starring roles," I said.

"Tell you what," said Charles. "That man has more than an inflated opinion of himself. He said that he was between major roles. He's far between. I was getting ready to open another website that gives 'unauthorized bios of the rich and famous, and then some.' They had a G. Crown listed, but I didn't get to see if it was *your* Geoff. Figured if it was him, he may have been in the *and then some* category."

"Think your gofering job is on hold until they figure out what to do?" I asked.

"Suspect so. Said they'd call when they needed me." He stood and wiped the dirt off the back of his shorts and then picked up his cane. "Going to take the bourbon to Melinda and then see if the library's open."

"Starstruck on Geoff?" I asked.

He growled, "Yeah, right," and then walked away, tapping his cane on the sand with his right hand and swinging the bottle of Maker's in his left.

I headed to my computer. I was far from a computer guru, but I knew more than Charles about how to weave my way through the Internet. It took me all of thirty seconds to find the unauthorized bios site that Charles had mentioned. Two minutes later, I was staring at the screen at a couple of facts that my new actor friend had failed to mention, a couple of facts that made sleep difficult.

***

The next morning, I stepped out my front door to a beautiful sunrise smiling at me from over the Atlantic. Then I saw the subject of my Internet search, who looked more like a black rain cloud, approaching from the east. His near-movie-star face looked like he was playing the part of someone who had been stranded on a desert island.

He saw me on the step and squinted. He flinched when he tried to open his eyes wider.

"Morning, mate. That your abode?" he mumbled and then continued without giving me a chance to answer. "I'm right knackered. On my way to find some hair of the dog."

Okay, I was on foreign soil with that one and walked to the street to meet the disheveled actor. The only thing bright about him was his red eyeballs, so I ventured a guess that *knackered* wasn't something that one aspired to achieve. I did know that *hair of the dog* had something to do with a cure for a hangover.

"Headed to Bert's?" I asked, pointing at the store.

"Yes, if they have a cure for someone feeling like shite," he said—at least that's what I thought he said. His mumble hadn't improved with proximity.

I said that I'd go with him. The staff in the iconic store had seen more than their share of knackered customers who needed a cure for brain-splitting hangovers, so I figured they would be more helpful than if he stumbled into a doctor's office.

They didn't disappoint. Eric, the amiable clerk, recommended a concoction in a small package and then offered Geoff a bottle of water. Bert's staff had a soft spot in their hearts for dogs and hungover walk-ins. Geoff said thanks and tried to smile, a feeble effort, but an effort nevertheless.

I was certain that whatever Eric had sold Geoff would work, but it wouldn't be an immediate cure, and with the way he was wobbling, I doubted he would stay vertical on his own. Besides, I had something I wanted to ask him. "Let's go to the house," I suggested. "I can offer coffee and a chair."

"Bee's knees," he said and walked to the door.

I took that as yes or that he had lost it completely and followed him out. He turned left toward the house, and I walked beside him. We reached the grass, and I was relieved that if he fell he would have a softer landing. Against all odds, he made it into the house. I offered him the only comfortable chair and headed to the coffeemaker.

After Eric's hangover cure, two cups of coffee, an hour, and two nod offs, Geoff began to make sense. Apparently the debate about how to proceed didn't end when the clock struck midnight. If Geoff was able to coherently tell the time, the meeting didn't break up until three this morning. He shared that if his agent agreed, he would move into the lead.

"After roughly twenty shots of cheap whiskey, the arsehole director decided that I didn't appear quite as ancient as he thought when he was sober. I could play the mayor." Geoff sat straighter in the chair. "Hate to admit it, but I believe his decision was heightened by the purse-string holders saying that they didn't have a lot of money left, but that they knew they could find another bloody director." He huffed. "That chap's a pile of insensitive. Reluctantly, he saw the light."

"Great," I said. "Speaking of your roles, I have some questions."

"Fire away," said Geoff, and then our peaceful conversation took a rapid turn to the weird with a knock on the door.

I wasn't nearly as surprised to see Charles at the door as I was to see Dude standing beside him.

"Dude and I were headed to the library to check on *your good friend*, Geoff," said Charles to open the conversation. "Want to tag along?"

I raised my palm in front of his face and then pointed my forefinger over my shoulder at my guest slumped down in the chair. Charles waved his hand in front of his mouth like he was erasing the words.

Dude looked at Charles and then at me. "Yo, Chrisster," he said. "Chuckster hijacked me at Bert's. Said fun be had at the book building."

I considered slamming the door in their faces, but being a gentleman, and curious about why Charles wanted me to go, I let them in. Geoff stood, a good sign, and greeted Charles and Dude with a smile and a PR agent's dream handshake. He offered to leave, but I thought it would be more fun for him to stay—male bonding, and all.

I was wrong.

Charles headed to the Mr. Coffee, and Dude asked if I had tea. I said no, and he said, "Me be okay tea-free."

Charles sat on the ottoman on the other side of the room, and Dude plopped down on the floor, his legs crossed yoga style. I offered to bring a kitchen chair into the room, but he said he was used to being on his butt on the floor. I sat in the only other chair in the room.

"Why are you going to the library?" asked Geoff, who had heard Charles say it when I opened the door.

Charles took a sip of coffee and then turned to Geoff. "Umm, a little research, nothing much."

"Oh," said Geoff, who couldn't have known how rare it was for Charles to do research. "Sounds intriguing."

It wouldn't have if he'd known he was going to be the subject of the research.

Geoff then turned back to me. "What did you want to ask me before the other gentlemen arrived?"

"It can wait," I said. "I'm sure Charles and Dude are in a hurry to get to their research."

Charles looked at Geoff and then at me. "No hurry. Go ahead and ask."

Might as well get it out in the open.

"Geoff, does the name Stanley Kleinert ring a bell?"

Geoff's eyes narrowed, and his jaw tensed. "Umm, why?" He looked at me and then down at the floor.

"Who be Stanley?" asked Dude.

"Yeah, who?" said Charles.

Geoff looked up at me and said, "That would be my birth name." He then smiled, the 40-watt variety.

"Me befuddled," said Dude. "Who be Geoff?"

"Yeah, who?" repeated Charles.

"That's the name our friend assumed early in his career," I said.

"Oh," said Dude, "me be Jim, Dude to all but my mom, Sun God rest her soul."

"One more question?" I said.

Geoff's shoulders slumped. "Okay."

"I was looking up some stuff online yesterday when I found Stanley Kleinert's bio, and it said that he was born in Tulsa, Oklahoma. Is that a mistake?"

He sighed. "No, that's accurate. I was born in Oklahoma."

"Faux foreign?" asked Dude.

"Bloody yes," said Geoff, who broke into a smile.

Dude glanced at Geoff and then at the ceiling. "So Stanley be playing Geoff who be playing Joe?"

Geoff smiled. "Who now in your vernacular *be playing* Carlin."

Dude looked at Geoff. "Jim be Dude, be bamboozled."

I told Dude and Charles that as of sometime early this morning, Geoff had been promoted to play Carlin, the star in the film.

Dude said, "Cool."

Charles said, "Let's get back to the past." He looked like he had won the lottery.

Geoff, said, "I need more of that medicine."

I don't remember what I said.

Geoff walked to the kitchen, poured more coffee, and surprised me when he brought the carafe to the living room, asking if Charles or I wanted some. Charles looked at him and nodded. Geoff refilled our cups and took the pot back to the kitchen. He then returned to his chair and asked how Dude was feeling—another bit of kindness that I wouldn't have expected after Charles's revelation. Dude said that he was *boss* and thanked Geoff for asking.

All eyes were on Geoff. The actor in him should have been pleased. He looked at each of us and began. "I grew up in Tulsa and worked the docks at the Port of Catoosa—"

"Good surfin'?" interrupted Dude.

Geoff chuckled. "Surfing's not big on a river."

Charles was now paying rapt attention. The wheels in his head were spinning, and his trivia-collection pot was filling.

I had little interest in river surfing. "How did you get from dock work to acting?"

Geoff turned to me. "I did some acting in a local theater company. One night after a production of *Hamlet*, I got a note backstage. It was from an actor in a touring production traveling through town. He said that I was 'great'—his word, not mine— and that he wanted to introduce me to his agent who was with him. I met them the next morning at a coffee shop near the theater." He paused and took another sip.

"Rest be history?" asked Dude.

"Not quite, old chap." Geoff smiled. "Dude. The agent arranged to attend that night's production and after the curtain closed said that I had potential but needed work. He offered to be my agent but said that I'd have to move to LA."

"Easy decision?" said Charles as he leaned forward.

Geoff smiled again and held out his left hand. "Backbreaking dock work." He held out his right hand. "Famous movie star." He gave a stage nod. "Yep, hard decision; thought about it for three seconds. I was in my nine-year-old Pontiac two days later, on my way to fame and stardom. Or so I thought."

"What happened?" asked Dude.

Geoff stood and went over to a framed photo on the wall and then turned to his attentive audience. "Flat tire in Podunk Burg, Texas. Water pump busted in Albuquerque. And then during my first hour in the City of Angels, my wallet was stolen smack dab on Hollywood Boulevard."

"Wipe out!" said Dude.

"Think I'd change my name by that time," said Charles.

Geoff laughed. "Things looked up from there. My agent, God rest his soul, got me some small parts in cop shows that were big at the time." He laughed even louder. "Learned all sorts of ways to kill people. I made three episodes of *Baretta*, two speaking roles in *The Blue Knight*, and even *Charlie's Angels*— before you ask, my favorite was Kate Jackson. She's a doll." He paused, but apparently since he didn't hear applause, continued. "After three years and a bunch of small parts, a lady friend I was living with suggested that the problem was the name Stanley. To be honest, something we actors have a difficult time doing, I suspected it was my lack of ability rather than my name, but she was a big fan of British actors and loved their accents. She thought Godfrey would be a good name. I thought it was too British and came up with Geoff since most Americans would pronounce it to rhyme with chef. I worked on the bloody accent for years. I'm fairly good at it, if I say so myself."

"Fooled El Dudester," said Dude.

"Did it help you get roles?" I asked.

"Maybe," he said. "I got several, including two *featuring* credits in big-budget projects." He walked back to the photo on the wall and stared at it for a few seconds. He then turned and asked if we wanted more coffee.

We said yes, and he graciously refilled our cups.

"Most actors never get TV or movie roles, do they?" said Charles.

Geoff shrugged. "Not really," he said.

"You must be pretty good," said Charles.

Charles was being sympathetic and supportive. He put honesty high on his value scale, and perhaps subconsciously he knew that Geoff, or Stanley, wasn't being truthful.

"Good, probably," said Geoff. "But probably isn't good enough in the actor-eat-actor world of Hollywood."

Dude snapped his fingers and looked at Geoff. "Get wallet back?"

Geoff laughed, and Charles and I joined him.

Can't slip anything by Dude.

CHAPTER 17

DUDE SAID THAT HE'D LIKE to "linger and jaw" more about movies and how we were planning to find Geoff's wallet since it had been missing for *only* forty years, but he had to get to the surf shop and protect customers from his obnoxious employees. After Dude left and we finished the pot of coffee, Charles asked Geoff who else knew about his past as Stanley from Tulsa.

"Not sure anyone," he said. "Those who knew me then are either dead or haven't had any contact in four decades."

Charles smiled. "Then I don't guess I should be calling you Stanley or humming 'Take Me Back to Tulsa.'"

Geoff looked at him and started to smile but turned serious. "I'd appreciate it."

Charles nodded. "Okay."

Geoff winked at Charles. "Thanks, old chap."

Charles smiled.

With that bit of ancient history out of the way, I wanted to get back to recent events. "Geoff," I said, "did you know Wynn was into drugs?"

Geoff blinked twice, turned to Charles, and then back to me. "We all knew about his history; no secret there," he said. "But here, hard to say." He shrugged. "I thought he was, but he was at every shoot on time. He was a horrid actor, couldn't remember his lines, missed his mark most every other take, and was as high strung as a hummingbird. I couldn't tell if it was because of drugs or ineptitude."

His use of past tense was interesting. "Any idea why he would have left so quickly?"

"Like you said, drugs or because he knew that he was in over his head."

Geoff asked if he could make another pot of coffee. Charles said that he'd get it and left for the kitchen. My house wasn't quite the size of those in *Architectural Digest*; more accurately, it was slightly larger than one that would have been featured in *Dog House Digest*, if there was such a magazine. Unless Geoff or I used sign language, Charles wouldn't miss any of the conversation.

"Why would he have skipped on a starring role even if he felt like he was in over his head?" I asked.

"Let me tell you about actors," said Geoff, who spoke louder for Charles's benefit. "They—we—are emotional volcanoes. We're insecure, hyper, unpredictable; we're simmering bundles of nerves. Our biggest strength is our biggest weakness. We are always playing roles and don't know who we really are. There's nothing to ground us, so it's no coincidence that we're always getting in trouble. Fantasy and reality are so close in our lives that we don't often know where one ends and one begins."

"You blokes are a mess," said Charles from the kitchen.

Geoff laughed. "You've got that one right, my friend. Jane Fonda said, 'Acting is hell. You spend all your time trying to do what they put people in asylums for.'"

I waited for Charles to say something, but he didn't comment. "So," I said, "you don't find it strange that he checked himself into rehab."

"I find nothing strange that an actor does," said Geoff. "Nothing."

"Seem to be a lot of strange things happening with the production," I said.

"Such as?" asked Geoff.

Charles leaned against the doorframe between the living room and the kitchen and responded. "The star checking himself into rehab, the star doing a human-torch imitation, the star getting food poisoned, the scaffold falling, the director getting himself drowned." He paused. "How's that for a start?"

"Ah, I see," he said. "Movies are prone to accidents. There are always far more moving parts on location than the space can reasonably accommodate—actors, crews, equipment, shoddy sets, bystanders, time to kill, heightened tension, frustration, petty arguments, and occasionally a real knock-down, drag-out fisticuffs. Accidents happen."

"You don't believe there've been more than normal?" I said.

He hesitated and then said, "I think not."

Charles said for him to hold that thought and returned to the kitchen for the coffee. He brought the carafe into the living room and poured refills. The soothing smell of fresh coffee filled the room. Charles then returned and sat on the footstool.

"I'm curious," I said. "I've heard different accounts of the boat accident. You were on it, weren't you?"

Geoff frowned. "Yes, and I thank the Lord that I survived."

"When did you realize that the director wasn't with the survivors?" I asked.

"Let's see," he said and started to stand but lowered himself back into the chair. "We were all thrown in the water. I remember it was colder than I thought it would be, and everyone was yelling. The current pushed some of us away from the boat." Geoff stopped and actually shuddered.

"That had to be frightening," said Charles.

"I'm not too big to say that I was scared, terrified actually. I kept waiting for a shark to chomp off my leg, and I'm not a strong swimmer." He smiled in Charles's direction. "Not a lot of swimming in the ocean in Tulsa, you know."

"True," said Charles. "Then what happened?"

"We were flailing about. Cesar and Billy were farthest from the boat. Several of the others had already clamped their arms around the side of the overturned craft. The waves kept rising and falling." He closed his eyes; his grip on the mug tightened. "I kept losing sight of the boat and the others. And then—never mind. We made it back to the boat." He opened his eyes and looked at Charles. "Back to your question, I don't think it was until those coast guard chaps—men—had pulled us out that I noticed Cesar wasn't there. We were more concerned about hanging on with waves slapping us than with taking a head count." He looked at the floor and didn't say anything for several seconds. "It was another hour before they found his body."

"You wore a life jacket?" I said.

"You bet," he said. "Had it on and strapped tight before we left the dock."

"Did Cesar have one on?" asked Charles.

"No," said Geoff. "He was too cocky to wear one. I remember he said something like he didn't look good in orange. Blooming idiot."

"Doesn't sound like you were his biggest fan," I said.

"He didn't want me on the project," said Geoff. "Told Billy that I was a has-been. He had the rep as being a good director, but I didn't shed a tear when he departed this world."

"When will shooting resume?" I asked.

"A couple of days, I think," said Geoff. "Some rewriting will be needed. Several scenes with Wynn will have to be reshot."

He smiled. "And I will have to prove that I was the right choice to take over the role."

"You'll do it," said Charles.

I was pleased that he was encouraging Geoff.

"Thanks," said Geoff. "We'll have to take it day by day."

Charles nodded. "Abraham Lincoln said, 'The best thing about the future is that it comes one day at a time.'"

Lincoln may have been right, but a lot can happen in one day.

CHAPTER 18

GEOFF SPENT THE REST OF the morning at the house. In addition to us learning some amusing movie tales and Geoff rapidly shedding his British accent, he asked about our background, how we had "discovered" Folly, and what we found to do in our spare time.

Charles shared some of our exploits and misadventures while uncovering a few murders. He remembered and spewed each detail of our harrowing experiences—experiences I had worked hard to forget. Geoff said there should be a movie based on our adventures. I said that it would be a horror movie. Charles said it would lean more toward a mystery with a romantic and humorous twist. I said that Charles had completely lost touch with reality, and Geoff added, "That's what movies are all about."

The actor appeared relaxed and wanted to talk about anything but *Final Cut*. Charles continued to warm to him. Finally, Geoff said he had to meet with the writers and discuss how the script needed to be tailored to his distinct talents. We didn't ask what those distinct talents were.

On his way out the door, he said that if he ever planned to kill anyone, he would make sure that Charles and I weren't around. We thanked him for being so thoughtful. Charles had to go gofering. He mumbled something about needing to help Billy B. with rounding up a new batch of extras for when shooting resumed because they had to work at two locations concurrently to make up for lost time.

I thought about how quickly Charles's opinion of Geoff had changed once the actor admitted to his deceptions. I suspected the change was a result of both Geoff's honest answers to Charles and to my friend's true respect and admiration for even the most quirky character on the island. My brief joy of silence and thought was interrupted by the phone.

"Don't have much time, but knew you and your nosy genes would want to know," said the familiar voice of Officer Cindy LaMond.

"What?" I said as I continued to wonder what had happened to words like hi or hello.

"A little after seven hundred this morning, a gentleman who lives off Peas Island Road was peacefully fishing off the dock behind Bowens Island Restaurant."

Bowens Island Restaurant was a glowing example that not everything in the Lowcountry was what it seemed to be. The restaurant was located at the end of a partially paved road a little over a half mile off Folly Road. It was rustic, to put it generously, but it had been dubbed by one restaurant critic as the most unique dining experience in Charleston, which was saying something in such a strong foodie community. In reality, the food and especially its oysters were known as the best around. New York's prestigious James Beard House had classified Bowens Island Restaurant as an American classic.

"Thanks, Cindy," I said. "Just this morning, I was wondering if anyone was out there fishing."

"Hush, smart ass," she said. "There's more."

"Sorry," I said.

"Anyway, the early-morning fisherman caught himself one that he wished had gotten away. Seems he hooked a 190-pound, six-foot-three *Homo sapien*."

I swallowed hard and said, "Wynn James?"

"You sure take the fun out of my story," she said.

"Suicide?" I asked.

"Not unless he found a way to hold a gun behind his back and pull the trigger twice."

"How long's he been dead?"

"Uncertain. A couple of days, they think."

"It happened there?"

"Don't think so," said Cindy. "The body had been in the water a while. Most likely he floated downstream; killed somewhere else and dumped in Folly Creek."

"Anything else?" I asked.

"No. Gotta go," she said.

"Let me know—"

Too late, she'd already hung up. *Another chapter in the snake-bit production*, I thought.

The phone rang again. Maybe Cindy had realized that I wasn't finished and called back.

Wrong. It was Karen Lawson, detective with the Charleston County Sheriff's Office, daughter of Chief Brian Newman, and for the last three years the love of my life—more accurately, *like* of my life for most of that time, now raised to *love*.

"Busy later today?" she asked.

"Let's see," I said. "I have five meetings, going skydiving, one cricket match, and I almost forgot, sailing to the Bahamas."

"Funny," she said, but not in a lighthearted tone.

"I'll cancel it all if you want to do something," I said.

"I'll be over around five," she said. "We can get something to eat."

I said great.

Now I was worried. I'd had more cheerful prerecorded calls from bearers of gloom and doom announcing that the end of the world was near unless I repented and sent twenty bucks to a post office box in Nebraska.

I sat and pondered the phone, Karen's tone, the death—murder—of Wynn, and the role as British actor that Geoff had been playing all those years. Then my mind wandered back to Melinda's death and then to Joan's murder. I felt tightness in my chest and the dark gloom that occasionally seeped into my consciousness. What could I have done differently to prevent Joan's tragic murder and nearly my own death? Did my meddling make things worse?

And now I was faced with another situation. There was no way I could believe that the so-called accidents combined with Wynn's murder weren't related. Was my reluctance to get more involved because of fear? Was I afraid that history would repeat itself and that I would endanger myself and my friends? Could I actually do anything to figure out something that the police couldn't? Maybe not. I took a deep breath and exhaled. But I could try.

I also remembered how irritated Charles had become every time there was a gap between me hearing something and telling him. Instead of sitting around the house all afternoon waiting for and wondering about Karen's visit, I grabbed a Diet Pepsi and headed the short distance to where he was interviewing potential extras.

Charles was easy to spot. He stood on the top step of a two-step ladder and was surrounded by fifty or so locals and a grinning collie. He wore a red University of Cincinnati Bearcats long-sleeve T-shirt, his canvas Tilley, and waved his cane in the air like he was conducting an orchestra. The potential extras were huddled in the shade of a tent much smaller than the catering tent a few blocks away. The lot where they were gathered was the former location of the Edge, a makeshift boardinghouse that had been destroyed by a hurricane a few years ago. It was now owned by the county and was being rented to the film company. I wondered if Cassie Productions had bounced any rent checks to them like they had to Cal.

"Who can be available for 3:00 a.m. calls?" yelled Charles. He was talking into a battered, green-and-white-striped megaphone. The low-tech instrument looked like it had been swiped from a trash dumpster behind a high school gymnasium.

Hands from all but four of those gathered shot up. The dog kept all four paws on the ground, apparently holding out for better hours.

"Okay," bellowed Charles. "Next ques—"

"Whoa!" interrupted a thin, middle-aged gentleman standing close to Charles. "Does that mean sober?"

"Yes," said Charles.

The man looked around the group and then at Charles. "Better take that poll again."

Several guffaws came from the group. After the noise died down, Charles recanvassed, and only a dozen hands slowly rose into the air. Charles then asked the group how many of them would be available for morning scenes at Bert's. He then added "sober" and "by five in the morning."

The number available then dropped to three. Charles rolled his eyes. "Okay, let's stop while we're ahead. If you raised your hand for any of the sober scenes, mosey over to that table and sign the appropriate list. Be sure and leave your phone number so we can get in contact with you." He paused and then yelled into the megaphone, "One more thing. That young man at the table is Mr. Robinson. He's the assistant director, so be nice to him."

Billy B. Robinson beamed, chewed his gum twice, and waved to the gathering. I suspected that this was about as much attention as he'd ever received.

Charles carefully stepped off the ladder and walked through the dispersing crowd to where I was standing. He patted the collie that had remained behind after the others had lined up at Billy's table. The dog then drifted away after figuring out that Charles wasn't going to offer it a part or give it a treat.

"Come to volunteer for the three-ungodly-hour-in-the-morning shoot?" he asked.

He knew my answer, so I ignored the question. "Got a few minutes?" I asked.

"Sure," he said. "Think Billy B. can handle the sign-up sheet; pretty easy once we eliminated drunk from casting requirements."

The weather was nearly perfect, in the midseventies and partly cloudy. I suggested that we walk a hundred yards or so to the beach, away from any wandering ears of those around the production.

"You don't often tempt me with a romantic walk on the beach," he said as we walked through the loose sand to where there was better traction on the sand packed down by the receding tide.

"Cindy called, and I wanted to get to you as quickly as possible," I said.

He looked at me suspiciously and said, "Good, that's how it should be. What?"

"Wynn James never entered rehab," I said. "He was shot in the back and found in the creek behind Bowens Island."

Charles stopped walking and stared at me. "You're kidding."

"Wish I was," I said.

"When? What happened?" asked Charles.

I shared what little I knew.

We were at the steps leading to the pier. We walked part of the way up and sat in the shade at one of the wooden picnic tables under the walkway.

"What in the blue blazes is going on?" he said as he took off his hat, brushed his thinning hair back, and set his cane on the table.

"Don't know," I said. "But there has to be a connection between Wynn's death and the so-called accidents."

"Wait a sec," said Charles. "If Wynn was dead, who sent the e-mail to his girlfriend about him going to rehab?"

"Here's a better question," I said, leaning toward Charles. "Was there really an e-mail? Have you talked to anyone who saw it?"

"Umm, no," said Charles. "I don't think anyone but Donna did. I heard Cindy ask Talon if he'd seen it, and he said, 'That witch deleted it.'"

I looked at the ocean and then back at Charles. "Like Melinda would say, that sounds rotten, stinky fishy."

"About five days in the sun rotten, stinky fishy," said Charles. "What are we going to do about it?"

"We?" I said. "Wynn's murder is in the capable hands of the Charleston County Sheriff's Office."

Charles bowed his head and looked at me with upturned eyes. "Who's investigating it? Not that oaf Detective Burton, I hope."

"Don't know. I'll ask Karen tonight."

The Folly Beach Department of Public Safety provided the local police force for the island, but the island was in Charleston County, and major crimes were investigated by the county sheriff's office. Until three years ago, Karen Lawson handled that duty. Politics reared its ugly head, and she was pulled from cases with connections to the island. Like most political moves, it was an exercise in stupidity. For years, she had had the trust of local law enforcement, the respect of the community, and an excellent close rate on major crimes. Then a new sheriff came into power, a new mayor was elected on Folly, and for some unknown reason, her connection with Folly's chief became a hindrance rather than a help. She was pulled from the cases, and she resented it but continued to do her job. Unfortunately, there was always enough crime to keep her busy.

"You'll ask her and then let me know before you go blabbing it to everyone else?"

I told him I would.

"So," said Charles, "let's say that the sheriff's office needs some local help in solving the murder. Who benefits from Wynn's death?"

Here we go again, I thought. Somewhere in Charles's warped mind, he prided himself in being a private detective. He'd even dubbed his alleged business CDA, Charles Detective Agency.

"The movie-going public would be the biggest beneficiary according to Geoff," I said. "They wouldn't have to watch the terrible actor."

"That'd be a lot of people to shoot him in the back," said Charles. "Can we narrow it down?"

I thought for a second. "Remember what Billy said about Wynn and Donna fighting?"

"Of course."

"If she was mad enough, she could've shot him. And now no one knows if there was really an e-mail."

"Can't the police subpoena her Internet records to see if there was a message?"

"Yes," I said. "But if she shot him, she would have had his smartphone. She could have sent a message from it, and it would look like he sent it."

"If she was smart enough," said Charles.

"True," I said. "It's a stretch, but the financiers will benefit from prerelease publicity. It's already received more attention than a low-budget film can expect to get."

Charles pondered that and then said, "But Wynn's death is causing more delays, and delays cost bundles of dough."

"That's why I said it was a stretch. I still wouldn't eliminate them."

Charles looked out toward the beach. It was low tide, and the beach near the pier was wider than usual. "Let's take a walk out there," he said and pointed to the beach.

We walked to the sand and headed away from the Tides where most of the beachgoers had congregated.

Charles waved at two men walking the other way. They looked familiar, but I didn't know them. "I suppose Talon could have benefited," he said.

"How?" I asked.

"Now he's directing a film that most likely would've gotten a short run, if any, in theaters. Then it'd go to video, DVD, or cable. With all the publicity, it might get him better directing gigs."

"You sound like an expert," I said.

"I've cyphered that one thing this gofer has is a lot of time standing around waiting for someone to ask me to go for something. I listen a lot. Even this warped brain, as you call it, can learn a bunch of movie lingo."

"Can you cypher other reasons Talon would benefit?"

Charles bent down, picked up a shell, and pointed it at me. "Bivalves, you know."

"Looks like a seashell," I said.

"You're a slow student," he said and shook his head. "Made of calcium carbonate. Plop that in your memory bank. Never know when someone will ask."

I smiled. "Anyone asks, I'll say it's a seashell."

Charles threw the conversation piece into the surf and turned back to me. "He could've benefited if he got his friend the lead role to replace Wynn."

Knowing Charles for almost eight years, I had become accustomed to his apparently unrelated transitions, though it did take me a couple of seconds to rewind our conversation to before his lesson on seashells and realize that he was giving another reason why Talon would benefit.

"Yeah," I said. "But he didn't get to hire his friend."

"He didn't know that when Wynn was killed," said Charles.

"True," I said.

Charles picked up another shell, but fortunately he spared me another conchology lesson.

"Think it's time to discuss the shark under the pier?" he asked.

I glanced over at him. "That anything like the elephant in the room?"

"You're not such a slow learner after all," he said. "Just call it an indigenous conversion of a metaphorical idiom."

I stopped walking. "You made that up."

I was impressed but didn't dare tell him.

"Yeah. Anyway, it seems to me that the person who would benefit the most from the untimely demise of Wynn is Stanley, Geoff to the rest of the world."

"Saying that wouldn't have anything to do with you not liking him, would it?" I asked.

"Excellent question, *old chap*," he said and then laughed.

People often underestimated Charles's intelligence. I had learned not to be one of those people. On the other hand, he often overestimated how funny he was.

"Do you have an excellent answer?" I asked.

"I would have agreed with you two days ago. I simply didn't like the man. But he didn't have to tell us the truth about his past, and I never would have guessed that he'd confide in strangers about being insecure. The more he talks, talks American, the more I like him. He's almost one of us."

Charles started to reach for another shell but hesitated and then turned back to me. "The trouble is that he's the one who would benefit the most from Wynn's trip to the great rehab center in the sky."

I stared out to sea and said, "His star would rise from a second-rate role in a low-budget film to the starring role in a film that will benefit from tons of publicity."

Charles stood beside me and looked toward the horizon. "He's lied to the world about who he is," said Charles.

"That means little," I said. "Actors change their names, their age, and some probably change their nationality. Besides, remember he said that all actors are liars."

"Yes," said Charles. "But he was also at the food truck the morning that Wynn and Dude's food was poisoned."

"So were Becky, Billy B., and several others," I said, a bit more defensively than I intended.

"Geoff was also on the boat," said Charles.

"And he caused the storm," I said. "And then after he caused the storm, he made the boat capsize and somehow drowned the wrong person?"

"Okay, okay," said Charles, who picked up another shell and tossed it into the waves. "I'll write the boat off to bad luck, a terrible accident."

Despite being wrong about the boat accident, Charles did have good points about Geoff. Clearly he would benefit the most from Wynn's death.

"I'll bounce it off Karen," I said. "She'll tell me if she thinks we're off base."

"Good," said Charles. "I'll bounce it off Melinda and Heather. Melinda's getting into this detective stuff, and of course Heather will be able to use her psychic powers and tell me if we're right."

I was fairly certain that Charles was pulling my leg—but only fairly certain.

CHAPTER 19

KAREN ARRIVED EARLIER THAN I expected and was at the kitchen table when I stepped out of the shower. She was in her midforties with chestnut-brown hair, and in my opinion, as well as the opinion of many others, lovely. I suspected that wasn't the perception of most of the criminals she cuffed and hauled off to jail.

"I knocked," she said. "Walked around back and heard the shower running, so I let myself in. Hope you don't mind."

I smiled. "That's why I gave you a key."

She was in navy-blue shorts, a white linen top, and sandals. I was in a green, oversized bath towel.

"Give me a few minutes," I said. "Want something to drink?"

"Get dressed. I can figure out where the refrigerator is." She smiled, but the corner of her eyes showed fatigue. "I am a detective, after all."

"How's Joe?" I yelled from the bedroom.

Joe was her twelve-year-old cat that she had named after Joe Friday from the 1960s television series *Dragnet*. Karen had been worried about him. Twelve years was bordering on the life expectancy of a house cat, and she thought he'd been slowing down.

"Seems better," she yelled back. "But that special senior citizen cat chow costs more than my food."

She was sipping Diet Pepsi when I returned. Its zero-calorie benefit was wasted on Karen. She was runner thin, could eat most men under the table, and never gained an ounce. It drove me crazy.

"Where would you like to eat?" I asked.

She wrinkled up her face. "I'm bushed. Could we get something and eat here?"

It was the first time she'd made that suggestion in the years that I'd known her. She enjoyed the Folly restaurants and walks around town.

"That's fine with me, but since you're a detective, you must know that my cupboard's bare."

She grinned. "Bare! That's an understatement."

I smiled and agreed. The kitchen was the most underused room in the house. I handed her a menu that I'd "borrowed" from Planet Follywood and said that they delivered. She started rattling off several items, so I punched in the number and handed her the phone.

After she'd taken care of the order, she walked into the living room and sat on the stool in front of my favorite chair. She pointed for me to take the chair.

"I've got a favor to ask," she said slowly.

She wasn't in a good mood. I couldn't tell if it was work or something else, so I simply nodded.

"You know Dad's considering running for mayor," she said.

I nodded again.

"I don't think he should," she whispered. "He's been in law enforcement his entire adult life. He's good at it—he's better than good." She paused, but I didn't respond. "It's stressful and dangerous, but it's in his comfort zone. After his heart attacks four years ago, he put on a good front. On the outside, he looks like the picture of health, but he's almost seventy, and I worry about him—worry a lot."

"Is there something wrong with him?"

"Nothing specific," she said. "But I can see it in him. The job of mayor is a twenty-four-seven migraine. I'm afraid it'd kill him."

"Have you talked to him about it?"

"Tried to," she said and then shook her head. "It was like talking to this chair. I'm still his little girl, and he'll do anything to protect me from bad news. He swears he's fine and that being mayor will be easier than being chief." She shook her head again. "Don't know if he's trying to convince me or himself."

I was one of Brian Newman's biggest fans and had already told him I'd support him if he decided to run. I dreaded where Karen was going with her conversation but asked anyway.

"What do you want me to do?"

"Dad has respect for you." She smiled. "He thinks you meddle too much in police business, but he still listens to you." She paused, looked down at the floor, and then back up at me. "Will you try to talk him out of running?"

The phrase "between a rock and a hard place" popped into my mind, followed by "between the devil and the deep blue sea." *Now what do I say?* The truth seemed to be the right thing to say but probably not the best thing. I tried it anyway.

"I'm sorry, Karen. I've already told him that I would love to see him as mayor."

Karen glared at me. "Why?"

"Because I would," I said. "He'd be great for the city. He has the admiration of so many residents. They trust him."

"He might," she said. "But I'm thinking of what it would do to him. Don't you care about that?"

She pushed herself up from the stool, walked to the front door, and opened it. Was she going to leave?

She stared at the busy street and then slammed the door and returned to the stool. She looked like she was about to slam me against a wall, cuff me, and read me my rights.

"Karen, I care a great deal about your dad. But I haven't seen anything that makes me think his health would be in danger."

A knock from Planet Follywood's delivery person interrupted us. She huffed. "Okay, forget it."

I paid and carried the bag into the kitchen. She followed without saying a word. She was several bites into the calamari before she spoke.

"It hurts that you won't help," she said, barely above a whisper.

"Not helping is the last thing I want to do," I said. "Let me ask him if he's thought about his health and the job as mayor, and I won't let him know that you mentioned it. Maybe hearing it from someone other than you will help."

"That'll have to do," she said.

She was still angry. We ate the remainder of our meal with a maximum amount of fries and a minimal amount of words.

I started twice to tell her about Charles and my suspicions but quickly realized that she didn't want to hear about it. She did say that a new detective, Michael Callahan, was assigned to the actor's murder and that she thought he had a good head on his shoulders.

We finished our tense meal, and I asked if she wanted a glass of wine or a beer. She said no. I then asked if she wanted to take a walk, something she always enjoyed. I received another negative response. I then asked if she wanted to stay overnight—something that she had been doing with some regularity the last year.

After the third no, I decided not to ask more questions. That was probably the best decision I had made since she arrived.

CHAPTER 20

SLAMMING TRUCK DOORS, MEN SHOUTING orders, and clinking steel on steel awakened me out of a fitful night's sleep. I was usually an early riser, but supper with Karen and worrying about how to broach Brian's health with him made a peaceful night's sleep near impossible.

I peeked out the side window to assure myself that the brouhaha wasn't something I should worry about, like an aerial assault by the marines in my side yard. It was only the film crew preparing to shoot at Bert's. Knowing that I was safe, I took a quick shower and dressed in my usual retirement uniform of a faded green polo shirt, khaki shorts, and canvas Crocs. Since Charles had coroneted me as his assistant gofer, I headed next door to see if I could assist—actually, more to be nosy, a habit that I had learned after constant tutoring from my friend.

Cindy was in the tiny parking area in front of the store. The entire traffic flow consisted of a Fiat heading toward the Washout with a surfboard precariously perched on its roof and two work trucks heading the other direction toward Center Street, probably to jobs off the island. I walked to where she was prepared to direct traffic if any appeared. She said that the most excitement she'd had was when one of the cinematographers dropped a tripod on his foot. That was fine with her since the production company was paying her regardless of how boring the work was. I hoped her paychecks didn't bounce, but I was quite confident she would know exactly where to tell the company to go if a check failed to clear. It would not be a pretty sight. I asked if Charles was around, and she pointed to the store's double glass doors.

I wished her well with her un–crowd control and peeked in to find Charles and see what was going on. The traveling red light was duct-taped to the wall beside the door but wasn't illuminated. The artificial lighting and cameras were situated in the center of the store and pointed at the checkout counter. Billy Robinson was behind the cluttered counter, rearranging cigarette packs on the shelves behind the clerk.

The cameraman waved to Billy and said there was too much glare on a plastic stand. He wanted him to move it. The cinematographer stood stork style with one foot off the ground, so I figured he was the one whose foot came between his tripod and the parking lot.

The aroma of fresh coffee from a container by the wall got my attention, and I circled around behind the camera to reach my morning drug of choice. Charles was beside the coffee urn and was helping Eric move two boxes that were in the way of the soundman holding a boom mike.

Talon was in front of the counter flanked by the actors who played the cousins. He was telling them how to carry the twelve-pack of beer to the counter. Apparently, they were getting stocked up for another beach party. From what I could tell, partying and opening packages of smuggled cocaine and cutting it with baking soda in their dingy beachfront apartment was about all the two did in the movie.

Most everyone in sight was dressed in what I would call slovenly, biker attire, so it was hard to tell who was in costume or in their regular clothes. Charles asked Eric if he needed anything else. When the clerk said everything was under control, Charles leaned over to me and said that he needed some fresh air and headed toward the door.

Bert's lot was filled with production vehicles, so there was little reason for Cindy to stand in front of the store. She said that if traffic got too backed up, she would "amble into the street, toot her whistle, and wave the road-clutterers on down the pike."

No wonder Brian was considering her to replace him if he was mayor. What other candidate for chief could have said it better?

Cindy, Charles, and I walked around the side of the store and stood under the wall-sized likeness of Bert. Cindy faced the street in case she would have to "amble" out, and Charles leaned against his ever-present cane. I didn't carry anything to lean against, so I stood facing them.

"Charles and I have been thinking about Wynn's death," I said.

"Oh, Lord," said Cindy, tapping her palm against her forehead. "Can't you two get a life? A life that doesn't involve butting in police business."

Charles leaned closer to her. "Don't believe so," he said and then smiled.

Cindy looked toward the steady line of cars passing and then turned to Charles. "If I wouldn't have to fill out a danged ream of paperwork, I'd put a bullet in your overstimulated brain and put you out of your misery."

Charles wasn't to be deterred. "That's a kind offer," he said, "but before you waste a bullet, give my assistant gofer and me a listen."

"Could I stop you if I wanted to?" she asked.

Charles said no and then proceeded to tell her about all our suspects, though he spent the most time talking about Geoff. He didn't reveal Geoff's real identity, but his argument in favor of the actor being the murderer didn't need the added details. I let Charles do the heavy lifting. Cindy twiddled her thumbs at one point, but I knew she was listening. Despite her protests, she had already expressed her doubts about the accidents and wanted to hear our thoughts.

"Fellas," she said after Charles finished his presentation, "I know that you have a strong distrust of the detectives from the sheriff's office—other than Karen, of course." She stopped and grinned at me. "And I know you've been burned by them. Let me tell you about Detective Callahan. He's young and takes his job seriously. Did you know that he's already interviewed several of the actors and crew?"

I shook my head. Charles shrugged.

"Didn't think so," said Cindy. "He was here late last night, and I wouldn't be surprised if he showed up this morning. I think he's good. In other words, the case is in good hands." She stared at Charles. "Back home they'd tell you to cram your meddling in a carrot and stick it in the hog trough."

Charles picked up his cane and pointed it at one of the movie vans parked in front of the building. "Cindy, I—"

She reached out and pulled his cane down. "Stifle it," she said. "I know there's not a Popsicle's chance in a pizza oven to stop you. And I'm not saying that you're wrong. Give me a few beers, and I'd be right beside you, but I'm only a lowly Folly Beach cop. Go share your detectively thoughts with Chief Newman."

Screeching tires from the slamming of brakes got Cindy's attention. She sighed and said, "Gotta go do what cops don't get to do too much—speed up the traffic." She waved over her head as she walked back to the street.

"You heard her," said Charles. "She ordered us to continue investigating and to share our findings with the chief."

"Funny," I said. "That wasn't exactly how I interpreted her comments."

"That's okay," said Charles. "As our buddy Cal would croon, 'Don't we all have the right to be wrong now and then.'"

Billy stuck his head around the corner. "There you are," he said and pointed at Charles. "Need you inside."

Charles nodded and pointed his cane at me. "How about my assistant?"

Billy glanced at me and said, "Not this time."

"Good," said Charles to neither one of us in particular before he turned to me. "You'd better do as Cindy ordered and find the chief."

If only that imagination could be put to some positive use, I thought. I told him I'd see what I could do.

Charles returned to gofering, and I returned home. I didn't know anything that would be helpful, but I also didn't want to be harangued by Charles if I didn't talk to Brian, so I called his cell.

Instead of getting his answering machine as I had hoped, the chief answered with a cheerful, "Morning, Chris."

I hate caller ID. I gave an equally cheery response and asked where he was. He said he'd just pulled in front of the Dog and planned on having a peaceful breakfast. I asked if I could join him, and he said only if I was going to be peaceful. I crossed my fingers and agreed.

Amber had already delivered Brian's coffee and told me before I reached his table that she had waited to bring mine since she knew that I preferred it scalding hot. She also whispered for me to be nice to the chief since he could become the next mayor. So much for Brian keeping secret his interest in the job.

The chief was seated at a small, metal table on the front deck, talking on his phone. Only two other tables were occupied, and neither was close to the chief. "Okay," he said as he placed his cell phone on the table before I even had time to sit. "I'm a highly trained and experienced law enforcement official, so I know your call wasn't to tell me that you were going to offer to do my laundry for the next seven years." He sighed. "I'm going to regret this question, but what's up?"

Amber had already returned before I could answer. She looked at the chief. "Is this shady character pestering you, Chief?"

Brian smiled. "Not yet, but I'd wager he will be before I finish my coffee."

Amber tilted her head. "It could be worse. He could've brought some of his worthless friends. You're lucky."

"Excellent point, Ms. Amber," said Brian.

Amber patted him on the shoulder, rubbed the top of my head, and headed inside.

"Well?" said Brian.

"Charles and I were talking about the actor's murder and—"

"Here we go again," interrupted Brian. He shook his head and rubbed his temple with his thumb and forefinger. "Go on."

Not the most encouraging comment, but a glimmer of encouragement nevertheless. I proceeded to share our thoughts about Becky Hilton, Talon, Geoff, and Wynn's girlfriend, Donna, and how each had reasons to kill him. He asked if we had anything other than our amateur suspicions and marginal motives. The way he asked that didn't give me much hope.

I asked him what he knew about the detective on the case. Brian knew that from a previous series of murders on Folly, I had serious doubts about the ability of one member of the sheriff's office.

"I've only met Callahan twice," said Brian. "I've called a colleague in his office and was assured that he's top notch. He's young but good."

His colleague, I assumed, was Karen. Maybe I shouldn't judge members of the Charleston County Sheriff's Office by the actions of my nemesis, Detective Burton.

"In fact," continued Brian, who then pointed at his phone, "that was Callahan. I wanted to see if he had any leads."

I was surprised that Brian had already talked to him and asked him why.

"Did you already forget how good I am at my job?" he said and then smiled. "I knew you didn't call to see what I was having for breakfast. I knew you and meddling Charles would have already been butting in and that you would have come to some far-fetched conclusions and would want to share them. How am I doing so far?"

I shrugged and channeled Charles. "So does Callahan have anything?"

Brian laughed and then took a sip of coffee. "Not really. I know he's talked to everyone you mentioned." He paused and looked around. "And he said that if he had to like someone for the murder, it would be the girlfriend."

"Motive?" I asked.

"Anger, jealousy, love gone bad, age-old reasons, but nothing concrete." Brian paused, blinked, and then gave me his well-honed police stare. "Callahan's a good detective. Why don't you and your posse of pals try a unique approach and leave police work to the police? I know it goes against your grain, especially flies against the genetic makeup of Charles, but try. Please."

I gave a slight nod but didn't commit. I wasn't a highly trained and experienced police officer, but I knew when it was time to change the subject. "Still thinking about running?"

Amber arrived with Brian's healthy breakfast, a fresh fruit parfait, and my, well, less-than-healthy pancakes.

"A lot of people are encouraging me to go for it," he said and then took a bite of granola and yogurt. "Remember I told you that acting Mayor Eli Jacobs wasn't going to run?"

I nodded.

Brian watched a large food delivery truck stop in front of the restaurant. The reek of diesel fuel mixed with the whiff of coffee.

"He's reconsidering," said Brian. "Likes the attention it's getting him."

"That good or bad?" I asked.

"He's definitely a welcome change from his predecessor, but his idea of the best way to run the city is by doing nothing. We can't afford a do-nothing leader. Folly's at a crossroad. If we take the wrong path or don't take any path and wander off into the marsh, we will only go backward."

Brian was beginning to sound like a politician giving a stump speech. "Who else will run if Eli does?"

"I assume you mean other than the current chief of police," he said with a smile.

Again, I nodded.

"Marley Conrad."

"Who's that?" I asked.

"That was my question too," said Brian. "I had to ask around. I'd never heard of him until last week. He's only lived here a couple of years. He lives in one of those newer houses off Sandbar Lane. He's retired, in his late sixties. Now you know everything I know about him."

"Does he have a chance?"

"Normally no, being a relative newcomer, but against do-nothing Eli, he could. People wouldn't be voting for him but against Eli."

That sounded like even more reason for Brian to run, but I had to make Karen's case for him staying out of the race.

"I've been thinking," I said.

"Oh no," said Brian. "Do I want to hear what about?"

"You'd be a great mayor, no doubt," I said. "But I was wondering if you'd thought about how it may affect your health. I worry about you, and the stress of the new job can't be good."

His eyes narrowed. "Did Karen put you up to this?"

I didn't have much time to think but couldn't immediately see an upside to lying to the police chief and father of the lady I'd been dating. But I'd done it before and probably will again.

"Has she talked to you about this?" I asked, garnering as much innocence as possible. There, that wasn't a lie, right?

"Twice," he said. "I know she cares, but I tried to explain that it'd bother me more if I didn't try to make this fantastic city better. I wouldn't consider running if I didn't feel that I'd contribute more, much more, than the other candidates. I appreciate the support you've offered, and the best way you can help me is to reassure my daughter that I'll be okay."

Not only had I failed to do what Karen had asked me, but Brian wanted me to convince her that he should run. What had I gotten myself into?

CHAPTER 21

THE NEXT FOUR DAYS PROVED to be uneventful by Folly standards. The movie kept Charles busy, but he managed to call each day to fill me in on the latest scoop and to report that Melinda's condition was unchanged. That was as good as could be expected, but I didn't say it to him. Most of the interior scenes were shot on-location on Folly, but the production company had rented a vacant warehouse on James Island and had built the interior of a police station that included two jail cells. It was officially called Sound Stage One but dubbed Sound Stage Only by Charles.

Most of the filming the last two days had taken place in the police station, and since assistant gofers weren't needed, I had stayed home. Charles described it as a not-so-classy version of Andy and Barney's jailhouse in Mayberry. Perhaps movie magic could make it look respectable on the big screen.

In addition to gossip from Sound Stage One, Charles told me that there had been a couple of minor accidents on the set. Cell bars had pulled loose from their hastily built mooring and fallen, nearly turning a good day into a terribly bad one for a cameraman. Also, the fake exterior wall with a window and a photo of a street scene behind it had fallen out of its bracing. Fortunately, no one was under the set. Charles said that everyone attributed the accidents to the snake-bit production.

Geoff stopped by the house one evening and said that he was adjusting to his new role. He confided that if it weren't for his superior acting ability, the poor direction of Talon would have ruined any hope of producing anything but a mediocre film. Geoff said it twice during our brief conversation, so I figured he was trying to convince himself more than me. He couldn't hide his enthusiasm about having the lead, which, of course, was a much bigger role than he had signed up for, and he was taking advantage of it. I said that I was sorry that it had to come as a result of Wynn's death. Actors may be good at lying, but he didn't play grieving over the loss of a colleague very well. He reminded me of a dentist with a mega-mortgage, two luxury car payments, and three kids in college who tries to act sad when telling a patient that he needs extensive—a.k.a. expensive—dental work.

Cindy ran into me at Bert's and said that there was a BOLO—be on the lookout—for Donna. She told others on the set that she'd stayed around Folly after Wynn went into rehab because she felt more at home here than back in California. But apparently she had moved out of her rental, and no one knew where she was. Detective Callahan had interviewed her the day before she disappeared and told her not to leave town. Cindy said that while Callahan hadn't told her directly, it was apparent that Donna was his top suspect. Her disappearance had not helped any. I asked if they could trace her cell phone, and she said sure, but not when the phone was turned off, which was now the case—so, no phone, no car, no forwarding address, no Donna.

I visited the surf shop twice to make sure Dude had recovered from the food poisoning and bronchitis and to see if he was eating better. His office was littered with clear plastic bags from Subway, so I figured he wouldn't win any healthy-eating award but was getting plenty of calories. He asked countless questions about the movie, which surprised me since I hadn't figured him for a movie buff. He explained that the reason he was so interested was because he was going to become famous after his minor, extremely minor, role as a bartender. As he put it, he would become as big as "those stoneheads on Mt. Hurryup." While Charles wasn't around to give me the literal translation of that bit of Dude-speak, I surmised that he meant the presidents on Mt. Rushmore. I tuned him out when he said that he'd started drafting his Oscar acceptance speech.

Unfortunately, part of the reason the week had been so uneventful was because I hadn't heard from Karen, my favorite waitresses were off work the two times I had eaten at the Dog, and no one had called to tell me that I had won the South Carolina Lottery.

I also continued to have this nagging feeling that I was missing something about Wynn's death, something that could prove to be extremely helpful to the police or dangerous to me.

What was it?

CHAPTER 22

GEOFF AND TALON WERE IN deep conversation and were the last two customers in the buffet line at ProCatering when I stopped by to see if Cal was at the bar. It had been several days since I'd seen him, and I wanted to know if everything was going okay with the production. Truth be told, I was more curious about if he'd received his rent or had heard anything about the production company's finances. The door was locked, so I couldn't do either.

Geoff saw me walking away from the bar and waved me over. I smiled and went over to the actor and the director. Mitch Abbot was fiddling with the Sterno under one of the warming trays. He smiled, pointed to a plate, and told me to get a "heaping helping of grub." I was still leery of the food and wasn't certain if I wanted a "heaping helping," so I started to decline.

"It won't kill you. I promise," he said and then laughed.

Geoff and Talon were watching to see what I'd do. I decided to live on the edge. I fixed a burger and filled the rest of the plate with sweet-potato fries. How could they kill anyone? Geoff seemed pleased with my choice—as if I should care—and told me to join them. There was only a handful of cast and crew members under the tent, so I asked Talon where everyone was.

"At the beach catching some rays," he said as I sat next to him at the table. "And Billy's directing some B-roll footage of local surfers doing their thing at the Washout."

I knew what the Washout was since it had a reputation in the area for being some of the best surfing around. The B-roll reference threw me, so I asked about it.

"It's footage slipped in the project for effect," he said. "None of the key actors are there, but it adds color and local character to the film. We might use some of it, might not."

I appreciated his explanation when he could have rolled his eyes and treated me like the movie neophyte that I was. "You don't have to be there?" I asked.

"Nah," he said. "Billy can handle it, and it made him feel like a million bucks that I asked him to do it. He actually has a lot of talent and pays attention to every detail. I predict he'll be a good director someday."

Geoff had been looking back and forth at Talon and me. "I doubt he'll ever be as good as you, Talon."

Talon bowed, not an easy maneuver from a seated position.

Geoff then turned to me. "What's the latest on the murder, old chap? I haven't seen anything about it on the telly."

"Thank goodness you're here," added Talon. "He's been asking everyone about that, but you're the first local he's cornered."

"Not much to tell," I said. "The detective has been talking to everyone, but from what I've heard, there aren't any good suspects."

"Oh," said Geoff. "I hope they find the killer soon. It gives me the willies." He nodded and then said, "I remember back home when I was working with Morgan, there had been a terrible auto accident in London, and the bobbies were investigating— terrible, so terrible."

I couldn't figure out what was so terrible except his fake British accent, but Talon appeared to take it all in. I wondered if he knew Geoff's identity.

Talon sipped his tea and then faced Geoff. "Speaking of investigating," he said, "you certainly had no respect for the late Mr. James, did you?"

"No, God rest his soul," said Geoff. He then shook his head and slowly bowed his head. "His acting ability was no better than a flea. His style was not my cup of tea. And his love life was as disjointed as his acting. But those things certainly weren't enough for someone to shoot him."

Talon laughed. "Unless it was that actress he broke up with before coming here. What was her name?"

I had no clue and turned to Geoff.

"Angelis," said Geoff. "I'm not certain that their ties were truly severed."

"Why not?" said Talon.

"Well," said Geoff. He looked around the nearly empty tent. "I hate telling tales about the dead, but I heard Wynn on the telephone on two occasions talking mighty sweetly to her. And that was the second week we were here."

"How did you know it was her?" asked Talon.

"He kept cooing her name," said Geoff.

"Think Donna knew?" I asked.

Talon jumped on that one. "If she did, there'd be hell to pay. She'd put her foot, among other things, down. She said that if she ever heard that he was seeing the wench, she'd kill him." He raised his hand to his mouth. "Ah, umm, she didn't mean it, of course."

And he knew that how, I wondered. And if it was accurate, the police were justified in focusing on the missing Ms. Donna Lancaster.

"Where was Angelis?" I asked.

"Suppose she's back west somewhere. She lives in Long Beach," said Talon. "Donna found out about her in Denver, I believe. Wynn made the mistake of taking Donna skiing. Luck—bad luck—would have it that it was on the very same slopes where Angelis had been vacationing. It is much too small a world."

"Did anyone see her here?" I asked.

"Not that I've heard," said Geoff.

Talon agreed with Geoff.

"What's her last name?" I asked.

Talon smiled. "Actors don't tell last names," he said.

"Not real ones anyway," said Geoff, gazing in my direction and winking. "So you really haven't heard any police gossip. I hear that you're in tight with the local constabulary."

Talon looked over my shoulder and said, "Here comes trouble."

I didn't have time to reassure Geoff that I didn't know more about the murder than I already told him. I looked back and saw Becky Hilton headed our way.

Geoff stood and held out his arms. "Hello, my dear," he said.

Becky frowned but still gave him a European peck on each cheek. She then leaned toward Talon, who had also stood and was only a foot away from the midfifties, sharp-featured financier. Both men stood in my way of standing, so I remained seated. Becky looked down at me. A hard life showed in her face. "You're Chris?" she said.

I started to edge Geoff out of the way and stand. She said for me to stay where I was, and she shook my hand. Apparently, assistant gofers don't receive the air-kiss treatment from people who finance films.

I was certain that God had given Becky the proper facial muscles to smile; it was just that I'd never seen her exercising them. Her scowl was directed at Talon. "How much longer are you going to drag out this damned disaster of a project?"

He looked down at the grass, glanced toward Geoff, and then returned her gaze. "I'm sorry, Becky, I don't know. The schedule—"

"Don't tell me about your freakin' schedule," she interrupted. "I don't care if you have to shoot around the clock; get it done or you'll never work in the industry again. Do I make myself clear?"

"Look, Becky," said Talon, "it's not my fault that the star you insisted on hiring had the audacity to get himself killed. What'd you want me to do? Prop his corpse up in a chair and continue to shoot? Do you think—"

She waved her hand in his face, turned, and briskly walked away. Geoff looked at the food truck like he hadn't heard anything. And I took a keen interest in my Crocs.

Talon started to follow Becky but stopped and returned to our table. "How does she think we can go faster?" asked Talon. He slammed his fist on the table.

I figured he was talking to Geoff, so I remained silent. Geoff looked over at me and then said, "I don't see how. We've been shooting extra hours. Do the best you can, Talon. It'll be fine."

I couldn't see how it would be fine. They were far behind schedule, and checks were bouncing. It didn't look like they were anywhere near wrapping up the shooting, but I also figured that was their problem. I wanted to come back to something Talon had said before Becky shared her charm and warmth.

"Talon," I said, "you mentioned the conflict between Donna and Angelis."

He took a deep breath, blinked twice, and unclenched his fist. "You bet there was," he said.

"Have you told the police?" I asked.

"In fact, I have," he said and nodded. "Yesterday I was visited by that detective you mentioned from Charleston."

"Callahan?" I asked.

"Think so. A young guy, sharp. He's been talking to everyone on the set."

"He talked to me too, old chap," said Geoff. "Asked numerous questions."

I was pleased to hear that Callahan was vigorously working the murder, considering how poorly his predecessor, Detective Burton, investigated a case last year. I was nearly killed because of his poor police work.

Despite the confidence I was beginning to have in Detective Callahan, I still had the feeling that too much emphasis was being placed on Donna and not enough time was being spent looking at others. Even today, Geoff seemed to be working hard to see what the police knew. What was he afraid of?

CHAPTER 23

CHARLES CALLED THE NEXT MORNING to say that he was pulling together a party at Melinda's. It seemed out of character for my friend, but I agreed that it was a good idea and volunteered to bring drinks. He even said that if I wanted to pick up chips and a couple of veggie trays from Harris Teeter, he would let me. Charles was generous like that. I also knew he had no way of getting to the store, and I would do anything for his aunt.

Charles greeted me at Melinda's door and instead of asking me in, he said, "Good to see you. Here, let me help you get the rest of the food out of the car."

There was nothing surprising about the offer other than the fact that all the food and drinks were beside me at the door and in my hand, and Charles knew it. I set the two plastic bags down and followed him to the front of the building.

He whispered, "I wanted to have this gathering because I don't think Aunt M.'s doing as well as she lets on. I thought having friends over would cheer her up."

I told him that I understood and that I thought it was a great idea. He thanked me and smiled.

"It's about time the beer got here," said Melinda. She was on the couch, in the same pose she was in the last time I was here. She wore a different color blouse though, which meant she had moved.

I was pleased to see Chester Carr sitting beside her. Chester was in his late eighties but had told Melinda he was a decade younger when they met shortly after her arrival on Folly. He stood, pushed his large, Coke-bottle-thick, black-framed glasses back up on his nose, and shook my hand. If Chester had been seventy years younger and Melinda had been fifty years younger, I would have said that they were an item. Melinda had said that they were only "good buds." Regardless, they were good for each other, and I was glad to see him.

Heather was in the kitchen. She hollered out a greeting and then asked me to bring the drinks to the refrigerator. Melinda said that they better not stay there long and to bring her a beer before she turned to dust.

A veggie tray, a party-size bag of chips, and a six-pack of Budweiser disappeared quickly, and I was beginning to think I'd need to make another trip to Harris Teeter. Melinda took to her role as the center of the party. She sat straighter, laughed louder, and kept patting Chester on his bald head. Charles and Heather shared an ottoman, and I pulled an old kitchen chair into the room.

Melinda leaned over and kissed Chester on the cheek and then turned to Charles and Heather. "So when are you lovebirds tying the knot?"

Chester wiped the slobber from Melinda's kiss off his cheek and turned his head toward the "lovebirds." He didn't turn as quickly as I did.

Heather turned to Charles. "Yes, Chucky, when?"

Charles didn't turn to anyone but did turn crimson, matching the color of his University of Denver long-sleeve T-shirt. "Umm, now, Melinda, one thing at a time; this party is all about you, not us."

Heather shook her head and hugged Charles. "Men! They can't think of more than one thing at a time."

Melinda laughed, looked at Charles and Heather, and then turned to me. "Boobs," she said.

"Huh?" said Charles.

He took the question right out of my mouth.

"Boobs," repeated Melinda. "Proof that men *can* think of more than one thing at a time."

I had learned over the decades that there are times that silence is golden. This was a 24-carat moment.

Heather was much younger and hadn't learned that valuable nugget of wisdom. "There you go, Chuckie. We can enjoy Melinda's party, and you can still answer her question." She squeezed his arm.

Charles turned to me with a bail-me-out gaze. It didn't work. I sat back, folded my arms in front of me, tilted my head, and waited for his next words.

Charles's bail out came from an unlikely source. "Now, M.," said Chester, "that's something that the kids might need to spend a little time working out. I'm sure they'll have some good news for us before long. Isn't that right, Charles?"

"Umm, sure," he said. He then reached over and put his hand on Heather's hand—the hand that held the death grip on Charles's arm.

"I'm not a doctor," said Melinda. "Not even a psychic like adorable Heather here, but I'm inside this frail body, and I have a feeling that you two better not dillydally too long with all that 'talking about it' stuff. If I'm going to walk down the aisle with you as *best aunt*, wedding bells better be ringing soon."

That didn't bring the party to a halt, but it slowed it considerably. After a moment of awkward silence, Chester hopped up—hopped as well as someone nudging ninety could hop—and said he was getting more drinks for everyone. I offered to help, and he said that he'd appreciate the assistance. Charles lovingly moved Heather's hand from his arm and moved over to plant a kiss on Melinda's head. I couldn't hear what he said, but she reached up and hugged his neck.

We spent the next fifteen minutes finishing off another round of drinks while Chester, a lifelong resident of Folly Beach, regaled us with stories about other actors who had ventured to our small piece of heaven while filming in the area. He then shared that he'd figured out that someone local had killed Wynn and that it had been done to send a message: Anyone who wanted to film there was not welcome. I told him that it was an interesting theory and I was certain that the police were looking at it.

Melinda said that she really liked Chester but that his theory was "hogwash." Heather said that she agreed with Melinda and that her psychic vibes told her that the killer was one of the actors. Charles, the collector of all things worthless, asked Melinda what hogwash was and if she knew the origin of the word. She said that she didn't know and for him to stop cluttering his overworked brain with hogwash.

And I sat back and realized that Charles's idea to have a party bordered on genius.

CHAPTER 24

CHARLES HAD CORNERED ME AS I was leaving Melinda's party last night and asked if I could meet him for breakfast at the Dog. It was cool, so we sat inside; it was also early, and most tables were empty. It was Amber's day off according to Brittany, who was quick to the table with coffee and a smile. Charles returned the smile, but he wasn't as chirpy as usual.

Charles stared into his mug. "She doesn't have much longer," he said.

I reluctantly had to agree. "How did she do after I left?"

"Put on a good front until Chester left." Charles paused and then frowned. "You know she's been sleeping on the couch."

I didn't know but remembered the last couple of times I'd seen her she was in the same position on the substitute bed.

Charles's gaze returned to the mug. "She says it's more comfortable than that 'danged old rent-a-bed,' but it's really because she doesn't have the energy to go back and forth. She doesn't want me to see her in bed all the time." He looked up from the mug. "What can I do?"

We'd been over this before, but Charles was used to doing something, even if it was the wrong something, when he was faced with a difficult situation or when he saw a friend in trouble.

Truth be known, he'd be compelled to help a copperhead if it was in danger.

"Think she's in pain?" I asked.

"Not really. She says she's comfortable but always comes back to saying she's a tad weak."

"Then all you can do is to be there for her."

"I know," he said and shook his head. "I know."

Brittany returned and asked if we were ready to order. Charles said that he wasn't hungry, but I convinced him to order bacon and eggs.

He waited for the waitress to leave and said, "We talked a lot about the murderer after you left."

"Who is it?" I asked.

"Melinda and Chester are pretty sure it's Geoff. They say he killed the first director, tried to kill Wynn with the fire, and then succeeded in bumping him off at the creek. I'm not that certain, but they make a good case."

"I thought Chester said it was a local," I said.

"He did. Then he didn't. And then he did again, then didn't remember what he thought and agreed it was whoever Melinda said it was."

I wasn't as convinced, considering the proclamation was made by Detectives Melinda, Chester, and Charles.

"Whatever," I said. "I understand the argument for Geoff killing Wynn, we've talked about that before, but why kill Cesar Ramon?"

"Our thinking's vague on that one. Chester says it's because Cesar must have demanded that Wynn play the lead and that by bumping him off, there was a chance that Talon would see the light and switch to Geoff as the star."

"That makes almost no sense," I said.

Charles shrugged. "True, but remember, Chester had been a detective only a couple of hours."

"Cesar's death was probably an accident," I said. "I don't want to, but I can see Geoff killing Wynn. He was talking to me at the fire and walked away. He went behind the wood pile and then returned shortly before it fell. He could have moved some of the lumber or done something else to cause the accident, but that would have been risky and not a foolproof plan for it to land on Wynn."

"Two bullets in the back were more foolproof," said Charles. "Geoff—"

"Geoff what?" said Cindy, who had stealthily appeared at the table.

"Whoa," said Charles. "Where'd you come from?"

She put two fingers on her temple. "Let's see, forty-nine years ago, I was born in Knoxville, Tennessee, and then when I was three my family moved to—"

Charles huffed. "I meant now."

Cindy smiled. "And I thought you were interested in my family tree."

Charles rolled his eyes and then offered her a seat. She surprised me by accepting. She asked how Melinda was, and Charles gave her a shorter version of what he had told me. She then asked us what we had been saying about Geoff when she arrived. Charles told her what Chester had said.

Cindy frowned. "Detective Callahan is still pursuing Donna Lancaster hot-and-heavy. He's convinced that she's good for the murder. He makes some valid points, and until she turns up, I have to agree. But." Cindy paused and looked around. "But—"

"But what?" interrupted Charles.

"Hold your donkeys," she said. "I'm getting there."

"Donkeys?" I said.

She looked at me and rolled her eyes. "Remember the first part of my life history—East Tennessee. Now hold on."

"We're all ears," said Charles. He then put a hand behind his left ear and pulled it forward.

"That's better," said Cindy. "Remember you kept saying that we needed to expand our suspect pool?"

I nodded but made sure not to say anything.

"I haven't liked Becky Hilton from the beginning. She treats me like dirt, not the best way to endear her to me. Anyway, I checked her out. Couldn't find much, but the rumor here is that she's connected with loan sharks in New York, New York, and a string of marriages that would make Madonna proud. She's in trouble with her money source and is under pressure to keep the production moving. Unlikely she would kill the lead actor and slow things down."

That was consistent with what Becky had said to Talon and Geoff at the food truck.

"Who else did you check on?" asked Charles.

"Chris asked me to check on your good bud Geoff."

"And?" I said.

Brittany arrived with our food and took Cindy's order.

Cindy leaned back in her chair. "Did you know Geoff isn't really Geoff? Seems he's Stanley—Stanley Kleinert."

"Yep," said Charles, smiling at Cindy. "We knew that."

She didn't return the smile. "Then did you know he's from somewhere a lot closer than jolly ole England?"

"Oklahoma," said Charles. He loved knowing things others didn't know.

"Okay," said Cindy. "Try this one. Did you know that twelve years ago he killed a man in a bar fight and did a nickel in the pokey?"

Charles's smile disappeared, and Cindy had my full attention.

She smiled at Charles. "From the look on your scraggly mug, I surmise that's news to you."

"What happened?" I asked.

"Seems that he and two other actors were taping one of those intellectually stimulating reality shows in Maine or somewhere up there. They got in a confrontation after work with four locals, and things went all to hell. Lots of beer guzzled, lots of words exchanged, lots of profanity thrown about, and then lots of bar furniture disassembled. Bottom line: one local dead; one actor named Stanley left holding the table leg and standing over said dead local."

"Five years in jail?" I said.

"Yeah," said Cindy. "Local court, out-of-state actors. Geoff was lucky to only get five. He pled to manslaughter although no one in the bar was certain what had happened. The point is that your friend, whatever his name is, has a temper and is not immune to violence."

"Does Detective Callahan know?" I asked.

"Does now," said Cindy. "I called him."

"What'd he say?" asked Charles.

"Said he'd look into it but still had his sights on Donna."

"What do you think?" I asked.

Cindy shook her head. "Don't know. About all I'm certain about after being on most of the sets and watching the actors interact is that truth is something that's alien to them."

"Remember," said Charles, "Geoff said that all actors are liars."

I would expand that to everyone involved with the movie.

CHAPTER 25

I T WAS MIDNIGHT, AND I had been asleep for an hour when Charles called. I wasn't completely awake, but I knew that something was wrong when he said, "Hey, Chris, did I catch you at a bad time?"

I was usually asleep by eleven, and Charles knew it. And he never started a telephone conversation with something as normal as "Hey, Chris."

"What's up?" I groggily asked.

"I'm at Melinda's." His voice was tense. "She'd like to tell you something. Could you come over?"

I swung my feet over the side of the bed and looked at the clock for a second time to make sure of the time. "Now?"

"Yes, please."

Charles saying please erased any doubt that something was wrong, seriously wrong. "I'll be there in fifteen minutes."

"Hurry," he whispered and hung up.

It was Saturday night—technically Sunday morning—and a cacophony of competing music from bars and restaurants along Center Street assaulted my ears. Rock music from outside bars at the Folly Beach Shrimp Company and across the street at Snapper Jack's entertained a steady stream of vacationers and locals who filled the sidewalks between the bars and the Folly Beach Crab Shack.

The sights and sounds barely registered. All I thought about was Charles's call and what I'd find at Melinda's. The porch light on Melinda's boardinghouse was on. I slid to a stop on the gravel parking area and rushed up the steps.

"Come in, it's open," said Charles as soon as I knocked.

Melinda was lying on her back on the couch. She was wearing the same clothes she had on at the party. A bright green, lightweight blanket covered her legs, and her head rested in Charles's lap. She slowly turned her head in my direction.

"Hope Charles didn't wake you," she said. Her voice was weak, and her words intermittent.

I said I wasn't asleep. I then noticed a shattered flower vase on the floor beside Charles's feet. I nodded at the shards of glass. "What happened?"

Charles looked down at Melinda. "I accidently knocked it off—"

She turned her head away from me and up at Charles. "Danged fibber," she said. She turned back in my direction. "Charles was going to call 911 and have them take me to the blasted hospital. Had to throw it at him to get him to hang up." She gave a weak smile. "It worked. I told him to call you instead."

Charles smiled, but I noticed tears streaming down his face. He wiped them away with his left hand while rubbing Melinda's head with his right hand.

I pulled the stool up to the couch, sat down, and reached for Melinda's left hand. It was skin and bones and cold.

"Charles said you wanted to tell me something," I whispered.

A tear ran down her cheek. "Chris," she said and blinked twice. "Don't expect I'll be seeing sunrise."

"Now, Melinda," I said. "Don't say—"

She squeezed my hand. "This is my story," she said and tried to smile. "Let me tell it."

I glanced up at Charles. His eyes were closed, and he made no effort to stop the tears. "Okay, sorry," I said.

"In case the book ends before I finish this story, let me tell you what I wanted. My nephew here," she said and slowly pointed her other hand toward Charles, "is the best relative I've ever had, and that includes my four husbands. The boy cares deeply about others, loves animals, hates injustice, and although he'll never tell you, he says you're the best friend he's ever had." She hesitated and had trouble catching her breath.

"Just relax, Aunt M.," said Charles. "No need to talk."

She sighed, caught her breath, and ignored her nephew. "Anyway, Chris, Charles cares so much that he has a tendency when he sees someone in trouble to step in manure to help them when everyone else will walk around it." She paused and licked her lips. "He's also the best thing that's happened to me. My only regret is that I didn't move here years ago so I could get to know him better."

"Aunt M.," interrupted Charles. "You do know that I'm here, don't you?"

"I do," she said. "But I'm talking to Chris."

"Yes, Aunt M."

"Chris," said Melinda, "will you please, please try to keep him out of mischief. He's too dear to me to let something happen to him." She closed her eyes, her breathing shallow. "I won't be here to look after him, but you will."

"That's a tall order, Melinda," I said. "I'll give it my best shot."

"That's all I can ask," she said. "A few other things. Would you please make sure he ties the knot with Heather. It's too late for rug-rat Charles's scampering around, but the old one here needs to be hitched."

I wondered how she was even able to speak, much less make so much sense. I smiled. "That's even a taller order, and Heather will probably have some say in it."

"Don't worry," said Melinda. "She's on board."

"Thanks, Aunt M.," mumbled Charles.

"Still not talking to you," she said and slowly turned her head back to me. I leaned closer to hear weakening voice. "Tell Dude that I'm sorry he won't have a chance to teach me to surf."

"I can definitely do that," I said and wiped back a tear.

She closed her eyes and didn't respond. I squeezed her hand and got a faltering squeeze.

She slowly opened her eyes and said, "Now, Charles, you have my written funeral arrangements, so you'd better follow them to the letter. Especially, don't forget the cremated part, but make sure that I'm really dead before they shove me in the oven. You can tickle the bottom of my feet. I'll giggle if I haven't croaked. I've always been ticklish there."

"Aunt M."

"Hang on," she said. "There's more. I'll be looking down—or up—at your wedding, Charles, so you'd better be good. Don't tell Heather I said this, but don't let the blushing bride sing at the ceremony."

"Melinda," I said as tears began streaming down my cheeks, "we'll take care of that. Please don't worry. Now just rest."

Charles bit his lower lip and looked to the ceiling. Tears continued to roll down his cheeks.

"Now, boys," she said barely above a whisper, "I'm really tired. If you don't mind, I'll have to check out of this party and drift off to sleep or—"

Melinda closed her eyes and exhaled. The only sound that I heard was a clock ticking in the corner of the room and Charles sniffling.

We sat in silence for fifteen minutes.

Charles caressed Melinda's head. He wiped the tears with his other hand and said, "God's got his hands full now."

"Both he and Melinda are better off for it," I said. I wiped the tears from my face and patted her hand one more time. "I don't know what's supposed to happen now. Think we should call Cindy?"

"Why don't you step outside and call," said Charles. "I'd like a few minutes. Might even tickle her foot." He smiled, but his heart wasn't in it.

I called Cindy from the front porch. Fortunately, she was at work and not asleep. She was at Melinda's door in five minutes. She nodded at me and then went over to Charles, who still had Melinda's head in his lap. Cindy put her arm on his shoulder and whispered something to him. She then looked down at Melinda and said that there was no need to get the coroner's office or more police involved. Melinda's death wasn't suspicious, and we should call a funeral home.

A month ago, while sipping beers and watching the sunset over the marsh behind his apartment building, Charles and I had somberly talked about what funeral home he wanted to handle her arrangements. I suggested that he call the one that handled the cremation of my ex-wife after she had been killed a year ago. Charles said that he would have suggested it but was afraid that I'd still have too many bad memories about Joan's tragic death. I appreciated his sensitivity but said that it would be the best funeral home to use since I'd already worked with them. I didn't tell him at the time that not a day goes by without me thinking about the day the killer slit her brakes and that her habit of not wearing a seat belt probably caused her death. I was with her in the car that tragic day but had my seat belt on. It saved my life.

I made the call for him, but it would be at least an hour before someone from the funeral home could get there, so I went to the tiny kitchen and brought bottles of water for both Cindy and Charles.

Charles delicately moved out from under Melinda and slipped a pillow under her head. He looked at Cindy and then at me. "Aunt M. would be mighty peeved if she caught us moping around like this. Cindy, say something funny."

"Gee, Charles," she said, "I let my stand-up comedian card lapse. Besides, the jokes I know can't be told in the presence of this sweet, dear lady."

Charles smiled. It wasn't his best, but a glimmer of humor peeked through his devastation. Thank you, Cindy.

Charles spent the better part of the time before the funeral director arrived telling us stories about his childhood and how Melinda had taught him to cuss, to drink, and how to religiously avoid work. He paused between each story and aimlessly walked around the small apartment. Melinda had been an excellent teacher. I had heard most of it before, but Cindy seemed to enjoy the stories, and Charles's mood elevated slightly. After about forty-five minutes, Cindy asked if we wanted her to stay until they came for Melinda. Charles knew that she had to get back on patrol and told her he was okay. He thanked her for coming, and I slowly closed the door after she left.

Charles walked around the small apartment but kept returning to the couch, so I suggested that we go into the kitchen until someone arrived. He started to protest but instead followed me into the kitchen.

"I don't think she suffered, do you?" said Charles.

"She didn't suffer," I said. "She was where she wanted to be and with the person she loved dearly."

The rest of the night—morning—was a blur. Fatigue, stress, sorrow, and missing the cheerful smile, voice, and attitude of Melinda took its toll on both Charles and me. We told the two men from the funeral home that we would come to their office later in the morning and make arrangements. I asked Charles if he wanted me to stay with him the rest of the night. He said that his apartment wasn't big enough for an obese cockroach, much less me. I could picture Melinda saying the same thing.

I asked if he wanted me to get Heather since her apartment was only a couple of doors away. He said that he would rather be alone. I didn't think it was wise but told him I'd pick him up at ten o'clock and go with him to make arrangements. He thanked me and then did something that was totally out of character. He hugged me.

***

I spent the next three days in a fog, or so it seemed. I barely remember taking Charles to the funeral home and helping him with the many forms and disclosures needed for her cremation. Charles barely spoke above a whisper, and his eyes were still red. He didn't leave his apartment the next two days. I tried to get him to go out for food, or for a walk, or to visit the movie set, but he responded with a halfhearted smile and a firm no. Heather visited him a couple of evenings and took him food, but she wasn't at his apartment long and shared that she'd never seen him so down.

I visited the movie sets each day. I figured it would distract me from worrying about Charles and from my own grief over losing a good friend, someone I had a great time being around, and someone who was an inspiration to all of us who wasted energy worrying about the small things in life.

The production appeared back on track. Talon, with increased help from Billy, began moving the project along at a much quicker pace. Scenes were being shot on schedule, and

Cal had been paid, so I assumed that all the others had been paid as well. The financiers still hovered over the shooting, and from their facial expressions and lack of temper tantrums, they appeared satisfied with the progress.

Dude and Cal told me that there hadn't been more accidents—something that everyone shared a sigh of relief over. Geoff appeared to be taking to his new role seamlessly. He was in more scenes than anyone since he had to make up for footage that included Wynn that had to be reshot. He was spending more time signing autographs for the increasing number of fans who were hanging around the set. He not only smiled at the fans, but clearly enjoyed his new starring role.

Karen managed to sneak away from her job catching murderers in Charleston and spent one afternoon and night with me. She had apparently forgiven me for supporting her dad for mayor. We walked around town and took in the bustle of vacationers who were arriving in larger quantities each day. We had supper at Woody's Pizza, dessert at Rita's, and burned off some of the calories with more dessert at the house. That part I did remember.

But then the thought of Melinda's death filled my thoughts as I tried to sleep. Not only was the loss of Charles's aunt tearing at me, but it dredged up memories of my final days with Joan and how our relationship that had remained dormant for so many years had begun to surface. How would my life have been different if we had not divorced a quarter of a century ago? How different would it be today if she had not sought me out to help her find the person who killed her husband, a search that led to her murder and me almost losing my life in the process? Sure, I tried to tell myself that I had moved on and that the past was not dragging me down. But I knew I was only trying to convince myself—and not very well.

CHAPTER 26

THE WEATHER THE DAY OF Melinda's funeral was supposed to be chamber-of-commerce perfect for late March with sunny skies, highs in the midseventies, and low humidity. Charles wanted the funeral at sunrise, and several of us gathered at the Atlantic end of the pier at six thirty, approximately a half hour ahead of time.

All I knew about the service was that Charles would sprinkle the ashes off the side of the pier, legal or not. He had told me just to show up, that he was taking care of everything.

The sky had lightened considerably even though the sun had not yet made an appearance over the horizon. Black storm clouds were off in the distance and moving away from the barrier island, and overhead, a few puffy, white clouds reflected the rising sun.

When I arrived, Charles, Heather, Chester, Cal, Brian, and Amber had already gathered at the far end of the structure. I felt bad that Karen couldn't get away from work and reminded myself to share her condolences with Charles.

Charles wore a black, long-sleeve T-shirt unadorned of any college identification and dark gray slacks that I hadn't seen before. He greeted me with a solemn handshake and thanked me for coming—both uncommon gestures for my friend. His eyes were red and puffy. Chester leaned on the wood railing at the end of the pier and stared out to sea. Cal was in his rhinestone-infused coat and wore his road-weary Stetson; he had replaced his usual hatband with a black ribbon. His guitar case sat at his feet like an obedient hound, and beside it was a large, 1980s boom box.

I acknowledged the others, and Charles whispered that he had wanted our friend William Hansel to sing but that he was in Cancun on a field trip with his students. William had a voice that the greatest singers in the Western world would give their vocal cords for. Charles said that Cal and his boom box were his second choice—a distant second, but second nevertheless. I didn't have the heart to ask if Heather was part of the musical offerings.

Charles walked to the side of the pier and waved to someone on the beach. I had walked over to Brian and Amber and couldn't see who it was.

"This is a sad day," said Brian. "Melinda brought a spark of life to our island. I wish she had journeyed over here years ago."

I agreed and told him that Charles had said the same thing. Amber hugged me and said that she would miss Melinda's fun-filled visits to the Dog, and then she looked around and asked where Karen was. I told her that she had an early meeting and wouldn't be able to make it.

Charles moved to the far end of the pier and stood beside Chester, who was facing the shore. Charles held a simple, pine cremation box under his left arm that reminded me of the urn that held the cremains of my ex-wife. I shook those thoughts away and focused on Charles. It wasn't that hard to do since he was almost yelling as he tried to pull the group together.

I got to the rail and could see who Charles had been waving to. I saw, but it was hard to believe.

Dude was on a surfboard and paddling alongside the pier, and a couple a feet behind him was Sean Aker, the adventurous skydiving, scuba-diving, surfing attorney. My biggest shock was seeing Dude's tattoo-covered, rude, snarky employees paddling behind Sean.

Charles moved closer to me, looked at the surfboard procession, and said, "Surfer funeral. It's a paddle-out circle or something like that. Dude's idea. Said that he was bummed out that he didn't get a chance to give Melinda lessons and wanted to pay his respects."

I said that I was surprised that Dude's two employees would be here.

"They liked Melinda," said Charles. "Only met her twice, but she asked them what each tattoo meant and said she'd like to get some herself. One of the guys even started designing one for her." He hesitated and looked out at the surfers and smiled. "They called her 'geezer gal.'"

Charles looked to the east where the sun had started to glance over the horizon. He moved his arm in a circular motion to Dude and then told Cal he could begin. The rest of us huddled together along the rail where we could see the surfers below and the sun to our left.

Charles looked out to sea and said, "Abraham Lincoln said, 'In the end, it's not the years in your life that count. It's the life in your years.' I don't know enough numbers to count the years of life Aunt M. lived. She's happy today, she really is."

Cal had taken his guitar from its case and had begun strumming the first notes of "Just a Closer Walk with Thee." The only other sounds were squawks from three seagulls who had flown closer to see what was going on.

"*I am weak, but Thou art strong,*" sang Cal.

I knew my vocal limitations and softly hummed along. Heather stood beside Charles, who had his head bowed, and thankfully sang in a voice barely louder than the seagulls. Amber moved closer to me, reached for my hand, gave it a squeeze, and didn't let go.

Dude, his two employees, and Sean sat on their boards and faced each other. The formation looked like a square with each board about eight feet from the next. With only four surfers, it would have been difficult to form a circle. Someone from the group had thrown a bouquet of spring flowers into the center of the square.

Cal continued.

"When my feeble life is o'er,

"Time for me will be no more,

"Guide me gently, safely o'er,

"To thy kingdom shore, to thy shore."

"Amen," said Chester.

"A moment of silence, please," said Charles.

Amber squeezed my hand harder, and Charles moved to my other side and put his left arm around my shoulder.

"Amen," said Charles. He then moved to the center of the group and kissed the urn. He opened the top, undid the plastic lining, and slowly poured the contents into the waters below. It must have been five minutes before Charles broke the silence.

"Now we will honor dear Aunt M.'s final wishes."

Cal slowly bent down and pushed a button on the boom box. Noise that reminded me of a seagull that had been hit by a surfboard screeched from the machine.

Cal quickly turned the volume dial. "Whoops, sorry," he said.

The next sound emitting from the box was Frank Sinatra.

And now the end is here,

And so I face the final curtain.

I looked at Charles. With his left hand, he wiped a tear from his cheek and then broke into a wide grin. Amber squeezed my hand tighter. Even Chester, who hadn't shown any expression since the unique ceremony began, looked over the railing to where Melinda's remains had been scattered and then looked toward the sky. He removed glasses, wiped both eyes, returned the glasses to his face, and laughed.

I couldn't help but smile and looked down at the surfer funeral playing out on the calm sea below. Dude had begun slowly paddling in a large circle, followed by the three other surfers. It wouldn't win a synchronized-surfing contest, but the group's movements were in time—almost in time—with the music.

Charles moved close and put his hand on my shoulder. "Aunt M. would be standing here laughing and applauding." He paused and watched the surfers paddling in a circle, which, to be honest, was shaped more like an inebriated oval. "She loved this kind of silliness."

The record shows I took my blows and did it my way.

Chester channeled Melinda and applauded. It wouldn't have seemed quite as silly if he hadn't been applauding an over-the-hill boom box. Three early-morning fisherman had gathered a few feet away from where we were standing. To no surprise, Charles knew them and invited them to join in the funeral. One of the three, named Louis, I believe, waved for his fishing buddies to join him, and they moved closer, quietly asked Charles who had died, nodded respectfully, and looked over the rail at the strange sight below. The surfers had stopped their whatever when Sinatra stopped singing and were waiting for the next part of the funeral. I noticed that Brian Ross, a friend who worked at the Tides, had also inched closer to our gathering. I waved him over and briefly explained what was going on. He said that he was taking an early morning walk before heading to work, saw us gathered, but didn't want to interrupt.

Charles thanked Ross and Louis and his friends for attending the funeral, a strange choice of words, I thought, and then asked Cal to continue with the musical selections.

The familiar opening guitar riff of the Beach Boys' "Surfin' USA" enveloped the pier.

If everybody had an ocean
Across the USA,
Then everybody'd be surfin'
Like Californ-I-A.

Yes, Melinda was definitely doing it her way. I looked down at the sea, and the four surfers had now moved farther out and had lined up parallel to the beach and patiently waited for the perfect wave to ride in on. The fishermen were tapping their feet to the music, and one of them was singing along with the Beach Boys. Chester was laughing, and Charles shook his head and smiled.

Amber let go of my hand and gave me a long hug. I thanked her for being here, and she said nothing could have kept her away.

I moved over to Charles. He was smiling, but a couple of tears continued to slowly roll down his cheek. "She planned it all," he said and waved toward the surfers and then at the boom box. "In the note that she wouldn't let me see until she was gone, she said that if I didn't do exactly what she wanted, she'd send a bolt of lightning down even if there wasn't a cloud in the sky. She said it'd strike me silly, more silly than I already was." He hesitated and looked at the perfectly blue sky. "She said she'd be talking to the chief lightning maker up there and make sure it happened." He turned to me. "You do think she's up there, don't you?"

"You can bet on it," I said, with confidence.

I looked over Charles's shoulder and saw Geoff walking toward us. I gave him a subdued wave. He nodded and moved close to Charles and gave him a dramatic stage hug. I didn't hear what he said, but Charles said that she sure was and thanked him for coming.

Geoff pulled me into the conversation and apologized for being late. He said that he had a "wee bit too much libation" last night and had overslept. He started to say something else, but Chester interrupted to share more sympathies with Charles and to tell him that since he was nearly "a million years old," he had been to "many-a-funeral." He said, "This was the strangest—I mean strangest good, not bad."

Charles said that he understood, and Chester slowly shuffled away. Amber and the chief were waiting behind Chester and also expressed their sympathies before leaving. Geoff saw Cal heading toward Charles.

"I've got a call in a half hour," said the actor. "Got to run." He looked at Cal, who was still a few feet away, and continued, "I'm going to check something out about the murder; I'll let you know what I find."

Geoff headed to the early-morning shoot at Bert's. Cal tipped his Stetson to Charles, thanked him for letting him be part of "such a moving funeral," and headed to his bar.

Heather wrapped her arms around Charles and said, "Let's go to my place. I'll fix you breakfast."

As I left the pier, I did exactly what I suspect Melinda would have done. I asked myself what Geoff had to check out. I also remembered that Melinda was convinced that he was the killer. I didn't have a good argument to refute it.

Was Melinda right?

CHAPTER 27

I WALKED AROUND TOWN INSTEAD OF going home. I passed the surf shop twice and wondered if I'd been wrong about Dude's two employees. Melinda didn't have near the difficulty making friends with them. I thought that I accepted others, regardless of how different they were, yet Melinda had been on Folly only six months and had connected. I needed to give that more thought, but not today.

I stopped at Cal's where a shoot was in full swing. A few vacationers had gathered in front of the building to get a glimpse of one of the stars even though there was a miniscule chance that they would recognize any of the actors if they met them at Harris Teeter. Stargazing was still a huge draw.

Billy B. was standing by the ProCatering truck and walked over to me when he noticed me standing with the other gawkers.

"Hear there was a nice funeral service for Charles's granny," he said.

"His aunt," I corrected. "Yes, it was nice."

"I wanted to be there," said Billy. "I'm wearing so many hats with this project that they're giving me a headache." He smiled.

"It's rough with a small budget, I suspect," I said, mainly to make conversation.

Geoff was going to get with Charles after work, and I asked if he was in the scene this afternoon.

"Not this one," said Billy. "He was at Bert's earlier, did three takes of two scenes, and then left in a hurry. He's been acting strange," added the harried assistant director.

"How?" I asked.

"Don't know. He keeps asking peculiar questions; doesn't seem to trust anyone. It's almost like he knows a really big-ass secret and doesn't know what to do with it."

Like he killed his competition so he could have the starring role, I thought. "What kind of questions?"

"Asking about Becky and Robert, like where did they get their money, or where was everyone when the boat capsized and did anyone notice where he was." Billy shook his head. "Funny stuff. You know how those Brits are; never know what they mean."

"Know where he went?" I asked.

"Nope," said Billy. "He should be on the beach around five for a shoot."

The side door at Cal's opened, and one of the grips looked around and yelled for Billy to get inside. I continued my walk, this time on the beach for a few blocks toward the Washout.

My phone rang as I stepped into the kitchen. I had just finished my extended walk and thought a nap would work well in my unbusy schedule.

"Hi, old chap—sorry, I mean Chris," said Geoff. "I've tried to get a hold of Charles, but no one answered. I figured you would do almost as well."

I acted like I wasn't insulted and asked what I could do for him. I wasn't ready for his response.

"I know who killed Wynn."

That's not a statement I hear every day, and the word caught in my throat, "Who?"

"Can't tell you over the blower," he said.

"Blower?" I said.

"Phone."

"Oh, go ahead."

"There's something I have to explain. Tell you what. Let me come to your house after we finish at the beach. I'll have to run by the house first, so let's say seven. Will that work?"

"Sure," I said. "I'll find Charles and see you then."

"Umm, okay." He hesitated. I heard voices in the background, and then he continued. "Stop by this afternoon's shoot. It should be a doozy."

He told me where they'd be, and I said that I'd try.

Charles may not have been home when Geoff called, but he answered on the second ring when I tried. I told him about the call, and he said a few choice words. He couldn't believe that I hadn't dragged the name of the killer out of the actor. I patiently listened until his tantrum had lost steam and then told him that since he and I had put Geoff on the top of our suspect list, I was going to call Brian and see if he could be at the house when Geoff arrived. He reluctantly agreed that it was a good idea and suggested that I keep Brian out of sight. He didn't want to scare Geoff off and speculated that if the actor pulled a gun, he'd probably have time to kill just one of us before Brian jumped out and captured the faux-Brit. I told him I thought that was a terrible idea and said Brian would be close enough to handle Geoff if we were threatened. Charles said that didn't sound like nearly as much fun but that he would go along with it and that he would join me at the afternoon filming on the beach.

I reached Brian on his cell, but after three dropped calls and a garbled response about where he was, I figured out that he was a hundred miles away in Myrtle Beach, attending a Homeland Security training session. He asked what I wanted, and I said that it was nothing important, that I just wanted to see if he had more information on the killer. He said no but that of all the people in the universe, I would be the first person he would call if he learned anything. I told him that I appreciated his sarcasm and wished him a good meeting.

I was more successful when I reached Cindy LaMond. I told her what little I knew, and she said that the plan was "as worthless as a kernel of unpopped popcorn in the bottom of a cold pan" but that she would go along with my harebrained scheme. I could tell that she liked it. She also said that she had been "sliced and diced" out of her security job with the film production because they were now using movie extras to provide crowd control.

We didn't know how long the filming would last, so she said she would join me on the set, and when it was finished, she would be at the house before Geoff arrived. We agreed that it was far from a perfect plan, but it was the best we could come up with.

I wasn't naïve enough to believe that there was a perfect plan, but I was betting my life on it being good enough. I tried to not give it much thought before walking to the beach for Geoff's big scene. I failed miserably.

CHAPTER 28

CHARLES WAS AT THE SET when I arrived. He wasn't gofering—budget cuts and all—but since Geoff had said that this was going to be such a critical scene, he didn't want to miss it. He then explained that Geoff's character was going to confront the cousin played by Haney Lawrence. Geoff discovered that Haney had been lying to him about not bringing cocaine and marijuana to Oceanside. He and Haney would get in a shouting match, and then Haney would pull a pistol from under his loose-fitting shirt and fire at Geoff but miss. Geoff would take a small handgun out of his coat pocket and shoot Haney in the leg. That explained why Geoff was dressed in a suit and tie even though it looked foolish since he would be standing where the surf lapped onto the beach.

Charles, who had apparently studied the script in great detail, said that Haney would "moan loudly while facing the camera," go down on his left knee, mumble a profanity, and "with trembling hands" raise his weapon and fire two shots at Geoff. Both shots would hit Geoff, and he would topple backward in the sand.

Cindy arrived and moved close to Charles. She asked him what was going on, and he proceeded to tell her exactly what he had told me. Since I was hearing a rerun, and the scene hadn't yet been committed to digital, I watched three movie extras moving into place on surfboards eighty or so yards offshore. Three couples standing outside camera range were laughing and getting prepared to walk through the scene. I didn't know what they were supposed to do when the gunfire erupted. I wasn't about to ask Charles.

Charles regained my attention when he reached the point in his story where Geoff was getting shot. He patted me on the back and said, "Welcome back." He then pulled Cindy closer and waved for me to move to his side.

"They're almost ready," he said. "We don't want to screw up the scene."

He lowered his voice to a whisper, and Cindy and I leaned closer to him. "After Geoff is shot," continued Charles, "he'll wobble up on one knee and fire three shots at Haney." He shook his head. "This time, he won't hit Haney in the leg."

Cindy looked at Talon, who was huddled with Geoff. Billy was giving Haney last-minute directions. She then looked at the three extras lying on their surfboards. "And what are they supposed to be doing?"

"Surfin', duh," said Charles.

Cindy rolled her eyes. "Hmm. That explains the surfboards."

I gave in and asked, "What about the three couples?"

"They'll be walking hand in hand along the beach. When Haney shoots at Geoff, they'll act startled," said Charles. "Talon said it would be more realistic if the girls screamed and ran away when the shooting started. The guys will initially follow the gals, but when Haney bites the dust, or sand, they'll rush over and try to revive him."

Before Charles could tell us every excruciating detail of the rest of the scene, Billy's assistant slammed down the clapper and yelled, "Marker!" Cindy, Charles, and I turned toward the empty spot on the beach where Geoff and Haney were going to meet. The assistant yelled "Action background!" and the three surfers started paddling out in hopes of catching a wave while the cameras rolled. Billy's assistant clearly enjoyed giving commands. He smiled and then yelled, "Roll sound," followed by "Action!"

Haney entered the scene from the right, stopped in what was to be the center of the frame, and slowly lit a cigarette. He took a long draw and turned toward the surfers. Geoff then entered and walked briskly toward Haney. He had a scowl on his face. One of the background couples entered the scene from the right.

"Cut!" screamed Talon, who jumped from his director's chair and frantically waved at the couple. All action stopped, and Talon pointed at the extras and screamed for them to get out of the frame. They were too early, and he let them know it—loudly, profanely, and leaving no doubt that they'd screwed up. They meekly moved back to their starting spot, and one of the crew moved in behind them and wiped their footprints out of the sand with a large rake. Both Haney and Geoff moved back to their starting spots and watched as the crew member wiped out any evidence that they had been on the set.

Billy's assistant did his thing again, and Haney and Geoff walked through the shoot exactly like they had the first time.

Geoff stopped inches from Haney. "You moronic half-wit," he growled and knocked the cigarette out of Haney's hand. "You come to my town and start spreading drugs to the—"

Haney slapped Geoff's hand away and took three steps back. He reached under his shirt and yanked out a revolver. Geoff looked down at the gun and backpedaled four or five steps.

The young couple that had started too soon during the previous take moved into the scene. Haney ignored them, raised the gun, and fired one shot at Geoff. He missed. Geoff started to turn away but instead reached into his suit's coat pocket and pulled out his weapon. He quickly raised his gun and fired at Haney.

A blood squib on Haney's right thigh fired. A metal plate had been attached to his leg, with a small explosive charge detonated by one of the crew. Movie blood spewed from his thigh and would have convinced anyone that it was real. Haney looked down at his leg, moaned, mumbled, "Shit," and then fell to his knees.

Geoff took a step toward Haney when the wounded cousin raised his gun again and quickly fired two shots at the mayor.

Blood spewed from Geoff's chest, and he toppled backward. The three couples were now in the scene. The surfers had finally caught a decent wave.

"Cut!" screamed Talon.

From everything that Charles had said would take place, it went off flawlessly.

I was wrong, dead wrong.

Geoff had been scripted to push himself up on one knee and shoot Haney. Instead he was splayed out in the sand. The couples moved. The surfers moved. Everyone moved except Geoff.

Haney looked at the gun in his hand, dropped it, and rushed to the fallen star. He was quickly followed by Talon, Billy, and the cinematographer who had been shooting close-ups with a handheld camera.

Someone yelled for help. Someone else yelled for an ambulance. Cindy charged over to where at least a dozen people had gathered and pushed two of them out of the way so she could get to the motionless actor. She grabbed her handheld radio from her belt and called for an ambulance. Charles had followed Cindy and frantically motioned with his cane for others to move back.

I stared at the scene and couldn't believe my eyes. I bent over and put my hands on my thighs and struggled to take a deep breath. Haney's gun was still in the sand where he had dropped it. I slowly stood, gained confidence that I could walk, and moved close to the weapon. Geoff had been shot by the gun at my feet, and I wanted the police to be the next to handle it. Everyone had seen who pulled the trigger, and there may not be any helpful fingerprints on its surface, but there could be some on the bullet casings.

Charles, with help from Billy and a grip, firmly moved everyone back from Geoff. Cindy was on her radio again, and I could hear the sirens of two Folly Beach police cars rapidly approaching. Cindy then grabbed the old megaphone that was in the sand near where Talon had been barking directions and yelled that no one was to leave. I remained over the gun and looked at Charles. He saw me and shook his head. Geoff had finished his final scene.

Two police cars arrived almost simultaneously, and I heard the distinct wail from the ambulance in the distance. It would be a wasted trip. The first officer to rush from the car was new, and I didn't know him. He went directly to the body and listened as Cindy described what had happened. Allen Spencer, an officer I had known since I moved to Folly, was quickly out of the second car. He looked at Cindy, his colleague, the prone body of Geoff, and then looked in my direction. I was still standing over the pistol, and Allen used all of his experience to figure out that it might have some significance.

I acknowledged Spencer, and he asked what had happened. I gave him a brief explanation, and he went back to his car to get an evidence bag. By now, the ambulance had arrived, and one of the paramedics needlessly rushed to Geoff. I was surprised to see Detective Callahan walking behind the paramedics. Instead of his usual navy sport coat and gray slacks, he had on light-green shorts and a white polo shirt. He gave me a quick wave and went over to where Cindy and the other officer were standing by the body.

Spencer returned and lifted the gun with his pen through the trigger guard and dropped it in the evidence bag. The wind was getting stronger, and clouds of sand were flowing through the air. The sun was descending behind the island; darkness would soon follow.

***

It was nearly midnight before the police had interviewed everyone who had been on the set and a handful of locals who had watched the ill-fated shoot from the side of the road. The video had been confiscated, and the gun that was supposed to shoot blanks had been sent to Charleston for analysis.

The witnesses had been given rides by the police from the set to the station, and we were spread out in every available vacant space in the building. Other officers were called in to ensure that we couldn't compare notes with others being questioned. Charles was one of the first to be interrogated, supposedly because he was officially a member of the crew. He saw me waiting outside the station and said that he'd meet me at Cal's when I was finished.

I told Detective Callahan what Geoff had said about knowing who killed Wynn. He interrupted and asked if I knew whose name Geoff was going to reveal. I said I didn't. I also told him about our half-baked idea of Charles and me meeting Geoff at my house. I included the part about having Cindy hide because we were suspicious that he was actually the killer and that he had learned that we were suspicious and that he might try to kill us. He didn't laugh, but I could tell there was a smile hiding behind his straight face. "Appears that you were wrong about him being the killer," he said.

Way wrong, I thought.

CHAPTER 29

FROM CAL'S ANTIQUE WURLITZER JUKEBOX, Garth Brooks worried about "If Tomorrow Never Comes." Loud, slurred voices from a dozen inebriated members of the cast and crew drowned out most of Brooks's words. The familiar smell of greasy fries and beer filled the air. And Charles, Cindy, and I sat in the quietest corner of the dark barroom. Cal's regulars had wandered home hours earlier. It was two in the morning, and if Charles hadn't wanted to talk, I would have been asleep, probably having nightmares about Geoff's final scene.

Charles drifted between teary remembrances of Melinda to laughter about some of the humorous things she had said during her all-too-brief stay on Folly. Cindy wisely listened to Charles and nodded at all the right times. I added a few comments since I had known Melinda better than Cindy had, but I tried not to control Charles's mood swings.

After a few moments of rare silence, Charles turned to Cindy. "Why'd they question us so long? There can't be any doubt what happened. Geez, two cameras recorded the whole thing."

Cindy had been around Charles enough to not be surprised by his awkward transition. She reached over and pinched his cheek. He had been nursing his second beer for the last hour, but Cindy was on her fourth Budweiser and was looking around for the waitress to "round up another one." "Twern't lookin' for what the cameras caught, my cute friend," she said. "What they didn't shoot's the important stuff."

"What'll happen to Haney?" I asked.

"Probably nothing," said Cindy. "Unless we find a motive. I don't see one, do you?"

"No," I said.

"Zero," said Charles.

"He had no way to know that someone had switched bullets for blanks," said Cindy.

"Unless he did it himself," said Charles. "He would've figured that no one would think he was that stupid to kill Geoff in front of God, country, and two movie cameras."

Word had spread quickly that the movie was shut down until further notice. Most of those involved felt that "further notice" would never come. A couple more actors joined the loud group on the other side of the room, and a few had begun drifting out of the bar.

"I Think I'll Just Stay Here and Drink" sang Merle Haggard. Several members of the cast and crew had beaten the country legend to it.

Cindy finished her beer and looked around again for the waitress. She stood, slowly weaved her way over to the bar, and then returned with another beer in hand. "Chriso," she said. "You sure Geoff didn't tell you who the killer was?"

Beer had a hold on Cindy, so I didn't waste time by saying that if he told me I would have mentioned it. I said, "He didn't say."

Charles stood and said, "Have a seat, Billy B."

I hadn't noticed, but Billy had walked over from the boisterous group and was standing behind me. He looked like Cindy would feel in the morning.

He pulled a chair from the next table and plopped down in it. He leaned his elbows on the table and looked down. "It's my fault. I killed him," he said.

"Whoa. You killed him?" said Charles.

"Yeah," said Billy. He put his head down on the table. His shoulders shook. "I killed him."

"How?" I asked.

He slowly raised his head and looked at Cindy, who set her bottle on the table with so much force that beer splashed out the top. She stared at him. He then turned to me. "The gun was my responsibility," he said. "It's my fault."

"Where was it?" I asked.

"I've already told the police—told the police," he said.

"I know," I said. "I was curious."

"You've seen that large, red, wood crate with wheels, haven't you? It's got all those old movie stickers on it."

"About the size of a Leonberger house?" said Charles.

Cindy, Billy, and I turned to Charles. "What the camel snot's that?" asked Cindy.

My thought but not my words.

Charles rolled his eyes. "Really, really big dog, duh."

Cindy and I followed Charles's lead and rolled our eyes. Billy said, "Yeah, I guess. We keep the small props in there—wigs, fake dope, cell phones, stuff like that."

"Guns," added Charles.

Billy finally looked up and tried to smile. "Prop master is another hat I wear. Sounds important, and on big-budget projects, it is. It's a big job. On this cheap-ass film, it means I have to keep up with all the things they'll be using."

Cindy stared at Billy through her bloodshot eyes. "Who else has access to the box?"

"Plum near everyone," he said and shook his head. "Can't keep it locked. People need to get in it all hours, day and night."

"What about the gun?" I asked.

"What about it?" asked Billy.

"Who loaded it and when? Is this the first time it's been used in the film?" I said.

He put his forefinger on his chin and then looked at the ceiling. "It was in some scenes early on. Haney 'borrowed' it a few times." Billy shook his head. "He flashed it around in here to impress the ladies." He looked around the room. "It wasn't loaded."

Cindy sat up straighter, getting into the story now. "You loaded it, right?" she asked.

"Yeah," he said. "Two days ago. I had a break and knew it would be used in today's—I mean yesterday's—shoot. I'd be busy and thought I'd better do it when I had time. Loaded it myself from the box of blanks in the prop box." He closed his eyes and shook his head. "On those big-budget films, they have one person whose only job is to handle the weapons, keep them secure and working good. The armorer—that's what he's called—checks everything out before scenes with his stuff in them. Makes sure they're safe."

"And on films with hardly any budget, that's you," said Charles.

"That's me. I killed him."

"You can't blame yourself," said Charles. "Who could've switched bullets?"

"Could've been anybody," said Billy.

"Then who had access to the script? Who would've known that Haney was supposed to shoot Geoff?" I asked.

"Bunches of folks," said Billy. "Changes in the script were made as late as two days ago. Haney and Geoff were only supposed to get in a fistfight, but the money lady, Becky, said that the film needed more punch and made Talon add the shooting."

"So not everybody with the production would have known about the changes?" I said.

Billy thought for a second. "Guess not everybody. Talon, Haney, Becky, Robert." He paused and then looked at the ceiling. "Rodney, Donna, Geoff, of course, the crew that was going to be working the shoot." He turned back down at us. "Umm, hells-bells, don't know who wouldn't have known. Sorry." He shook his head. "I don't know why anyone would have done it."

Billy may not have known why, but the rest of us around the table were certain we did. Geoff was going to identify the killer who then somehow found out that he knew and chose a creative and macabre way of stopping him. Clearly, the killer would not stop with killing Geoff if he suspected that anyone else was suspicious about him—or her.

That was frightening.

Fatigue, sorrow over Melinda's passing, the shock of witnessing a murder, and alcohol blurred the rest of the conversation. The boisterous group of movie people went their separate ways about a half hour before Cal visited our table and politely told us that he was locking up. He said that if we wanted to stay, sweep the floor, wash the dishes, and mop behind the bar, he'd give us a key. We just as politely declined.

CHAPTER 30

THE NEXT MORNING, I WOKE with a headache and the vague memory that Billy had said something at Cal's that struck me as strange, but with everything else that was going on, it didn't stick. I called Charles to see if he remembered anything unusual. He didn't answer, so it didn't matter if he remembered or not. My next call was to Cindy, who was probably working but, unlike Charles, had a cell phone.

From the sound of her voice and a well-timed yawn, it was clear that she either wasn't at work, or if she was, our tax dollars were being wasted. She said that unless I was calling to tell her that I had discovered a pill that would make her lose twenty pounds in three days without having to exercise, I was in a heap of "Leonberger poop."

I told her that I was impressed that she had remembered the name of the dog breed and that I hadn't discovered a pill. I added that she was gorgeous the way she was and didn't need to lose an ounce. She said that lie had probably saved my life.

With the "pleasantries" out of the way, she asked why I was harassing her on her day off. I told her about my vague recollection that Billy had said something important but that I couldn't remember what it was. She said that after she had "over-enjoyed Cal's fine libations," she wouldn't have remembered if

Billy had been wearing a gorilla suit and riding a unicycle, much less anything he had said. I thanked her for being so helpful, and she said she was going back to sleep and if she dreamed anything that Billy had said that she'd wait until three in the morning and call me.

I was batting 0-for-2 and decided to go directly to the source, if only I knew where to find the young assistant director now that the production was shut down. My first stop was the production trailer. A sound tech was in front of the trailer reading a handwritten note taped to the door. The tech, whom I had seen several times, mumbled something to himself, stormed down the trailer's steps, and then walked toward the beach. I asked him if he knew where I could find Billy. He helpfully said that he didn't give a rat's ass where he was. I thanked him anyway. The note taped to the door explained his surliness. It read *Production on hiatus. Don't bother to knock* and listed a phone number with a 323 area code but added *If it's about your pay, don't call.* I assumed that the number was in Los Angeles.

I walked to the Dog for an early lunch instead of wandering around the island looking for Billy and possibly running into more disgruntled members of the film's entourage. My luck changed when I entered the restaurant and saw the object of my search at a table against the far wall, sitting across from his assistant and a young, attractive extra I had noticed when they were shooting two scenes at Bert's. The three of them appeared as if they were at a funeral home visitation. In a way, they were.

I approached the table, and Billy nodded recognition, but the other two looked at me expressionless. I told Billy that I would like to talk with him after he had finished and asked where we could meet. The other two said that they were on their way out and I could have him now.

"How are you feeling?" I asked as the others walked toward the door.

"If I've felt worse, I don't remember it," said Billy.

I didn't know if he felt bad because of how much he had to drink at Cal's, the very public murder of Geoff, if he felt responsible, or if he was out of a job. I told him I was sorry and paused.

"It's my fault, you know," he said.

I didn't remind him that he had said that roughly a dozen times last night. "It's not your fault, Billy. It could have been anyone with access to the prop box."

"I should have kept a better eye on the props, especially the gun."

"You said that several people needed to get in the box, so you couldn't be there all the time."

He looked down in his empty coffee cup. "Yeah, there were several."

Then I remembered what he had said last night that jiggled something in my brain. "Last night you were talking about people who knew about the script change from a fistfight to the shootout."

"Yeah, so?" he said. He held his empty mug in the air and looked for someone to refill it.

"You mentioned Donna. I assumed you meant Donna Lancaster."

Amber arrived at the table, refilled Billy's coffee mug, and asked if I wanted anything. I said coffee would be great. She gave me her 500-watt smile and went to get my drink.

Billy watched her go and then said, "Umm. I did?"

"Yes," I said.

"Okay, it's like this," he said. "Day before yesterday, I was at craft services. Talon had left a stack of the script revisions on the picnic table. Actors grab them when they're eating. I was heading back to the production trailer and caught a glimpse of the back of a woman with the revised script in her hand. I was in a hurry and didn't think much of it and didn't really get a good look, but I think it was Donna."

"Did you say anything to the police about it yesterday?" I asked. "They've been looking for her."

Amber returned with my mug, and Billy stuffed a piece of gum in his mouth.

"I wasn't thinking too clear after the shooting," said Billy as he watched Amber move to the next table. "I was lucky to remember my name."

"You didn't say anything to the cops," I said.

"They just asked about what happened on the set. To be honest, I forgot about seeing the woman, and I'm not positive it was her." His head bobbed toward the table. "It's my fault."

I'd never aspired to have a second career as a life coach, so I told him once again that it wasn't his fault and changed the subject.

"What'll happen with the production?" I asked.

"That a really good question," he mumbled. "I wish I knew."

"Any rumors?"

Charles would have been proud of me for asking.

He looked up from his stupor and appeared to give the question serious thought. "I hear the money people, especially Becky, are bouncing off the walls. They say they've sunk so much into the project that it must continue. Some of the crew have already headed out. They're not saying the movie is snake bit; now they're calling it cobra bit."

I wouldn't argue with that. "How could it continue after Geoff's death even if everyone wanted it to?"

"Movie magic, my friend, movie magic. I've heard that Talon has already contacted his actor friend that he wanted to star from the beginning. It'll be tough reshooting Geoff's scenes, but it would be a way to save the project."

"What about the crew who've left?"

Billy snapped his finger. "They can be replaced like that. The industry is feeling tough times like everyone else. There're way more skilled crew members out there than jobs, and actors are three cents a dozen."

"What're you going to do?" I asked.

Billy smiled—only the second time I'd seen him smile in the last two days. "First I'm going to finish my breakfast. Then I'm going to call my mother and tell her that I'm okay in case she heard about Geoff's murder. After that, I'm going to grieve a day for Geoff. And then I'm going to suck up to Talon, tell him how great he is, how I know he can pull off finishing the project and receive rave reviews, and then beg him to keep me on." He leaned back and continued chewing on his gum.

I smiled back but wondered how many more people would have to die before the project was finished and received rave reviews.

I called Detective Callahan on the way home. I suspected that he'd already heard that Donna Lancaster might be back, but I didn't want to take a chance that he didn't know. It seemed unlikely that she would have come back to kill Geoff, especially if she'd suspected that the police were looking for her. If she knew that Geoff'd known that she killed Wynn, why wouldn't she have simply shot him earlier? Billy hadn't thought to tell the police, so others who may have seen her may have also failed to share the information. Donna was the prime suspect in Wynn's murder, and now Billy had said that she would have known about the deadly script change.

I was afraid my call to Detective Callahan was about to go to voice mail when he answered. I said who I was, and he chuckled. "Figures."

"What's that mean?" I asked.

"You're getting quite a reputation around the sheriff's office," he said and chuckled again.

"Good?"

"Mostly," he said.

"Mostly?"

"Yeah," he said. "Story is that you've stolen the heart of one of our best detectives. That's irritated a couple of our officers who've had eyes on the lovely lass."

"That's the good part, right?"

"For you, not for them. You're even starting to convert the COF."

Because of circumstances far beyond my control, I'd learned a lot of cop lingo since moving to Folly, but that was a new one.

"COF?" I said.

"Umm," he said and then hesitated. "Detective Burton— Cranky Old Fart. You didn't hear that from me."

I laughed and knew exactly what he meant. Detective Burton had been my nemesis for several years. If he had his way, I would have been run out of South Carolina for butting into his work, or more accurately, lack of work.

I assured him that the source would remain anonymous.

"Anyway," he said, "I don't suspect you called to shoot the breeze about the COF, but I'm certain it has something to do with you butting into the movie murders."

"Guilty," I confessed. I then proceeded to tell him what Billy had said about possibly seeing Donna Lancaster at the catering truck and that I'd heard that she was a person of interest in Wynn's murder. I explained about the revised script and that Donna could have known about the change. She knew where the props were and could've switched bullets. He asked if Billy had said that anyone else had seen her. I said no. He said that he would be surprised if she had actually been back on Folly since the sheriff's deputies and the Folly Beach police had been looking for her.

I told him that Billy wasn't certain that it was her and that with everything going on with the production, he could have been mistaken. I was pleasantly surprised when he said he would get with Billy. And the most surprising part, he thanked me for letting him know.

If I'd waited three hours, I wouldn't have had to call Callahan.

CHAPTER 31

I HAD WALKED IN BERT'S AND was greeted by Eric with, "Need my special hangover cure?"

Thank goodness I didn't, but I asked why he'd asked.

He clapped. "If you don't, you're the only person with a connection to the movie who hasn't needed the cure today."

I didn't ask why he thought I was connected to the project but agreed that I wasn't surprised after the events of the last twenty-four hours. He started to tell me a funny story about one of the cinematographers when his story took a backseat to the person who walked in the door.

Donna Lancaster took two steps into the store and looked around. It wasn't hard to recognize her in hot-pink short shorts and a skintight, black T-shirt. Eric and I were the only people around. She turned and started out, stopped, pivoted, and walked toward us.

"You're, umm, you're—"

"Chris," I said to end her awkward moment. "I've seen you on the set a few times."

"Okay, right," she said. "You saved Wynn from that terrible fire. Sorry, I'm a little out of it."

Eric stepped back and said he needed to get some food prepared in the small room beside the deli counter.

I watched him go and turned back to Donna. *What do I do? She's wanted by the police. She could have killed both Wynn and Geoff and is now standing in front of me waiting for me to say something.*

"I'm sorry about Wynn," I said in as sympathetic a voice I could muster while possibly standing two feet from a killer.

She lowered her head. "Thank you." She then jerked her head back up. "What happened to the movie? I just saw the note at the trailer, and nobody's around."

"After Geoff was killed, they—"

She covered her mouth with her right hand and stared at me. Finally, she said, "Whoa!" Her green eyes widened. "Geoff killed? You serious?"

I nodded.

"When?" she asked. "How?"

Something didn't compute. "Oh," I said, "I'm sorry. I thought you were here before he was shot."

"When?" she asked.

I explained that it was yesterday around sunset. I described the scene, what had happened, and the aftermath.

"I was here the day before yesterday and yesterday morning," she said and looked blankly at the coffee urn beside me. "I thought I could come back to honor Wynn. Figured someone would be having a memorial service. He was liked by all, you know." Her voice cracked. "I was wrong and left again. I stayed in a two-bit hotel just off the interstate—no damned self-respecting bed bug would have stayed there."

Six construction workers entered and were talking like the others were near deaf. They headed toward the beer cooler. They were followed by three surfers who made a beeline toward the junk-food section. The quiet, peaceful grocery was now full of hungry, thirsty, and loud customers.

"Feel like a walk?" I said.

She looked at the gathering crowd and said, "Okay."

It must have been in the low nineties when we left Bert's, and Donna asked if there was somewhere we could sit and get a drink. My house was the closest spot, so I pointed to my yard and asked if that would be okay. She nodded, and even though she wouldn't have any reason to not trust me, I started wondering what I was doing by inviting a suspected murderer home with me. I figured that if I didn't say anything to make her suspicious I'd be okay.

It was a relief to step into the air-conditioned living room. Donna entered behind me and looked around.

"Nice," she said. "Live by yourself?"

I should have told her that I did but that there were two police officers with their guns pulled standing behind the door in case she tried anything, but instead, I said, "Yes."

She walked around the room and peeked into the kitchen. "Have anything to drink?"

I recited the drink menu: water, Diet Pepsi, cheap Chardonnay, and beer. She chose the beer, and I grabbed a soft drink and joined her in the living room. She was already in my favorite chair, so I took the stool.

She looked at the beer bottle and said, "Benjamin Franklin said that, 'Beer is proof that God loves us and wants us to be happy.'"

Considering Donna's situation, I wasn't quite as certain as old Ben but agreed with her anyway.

She took a long draw.

"So you didn't know anything about Geoff getting killed?" I asked.

She pointed toward Bert's. "Not until you told me."

"Did you know that the police have been looking for you?" I asked and then held my breath.

She grabbed the chair's armrest with her left hand. "They asked me to hang around, but I didn't see any reason to. What do they want?"

"To ask you if you know anyone who might have wanted Wynn dead," I said, knowing fully well that the police would have already asked her that, but it was better than saying that they thought she killed him.

"I told them I didn't," she whispered. "I was hurt when I thought he left to go into rehab without telling me. To be honest, I thought he was clean. The bottom fell out of my world when they found his body."

"You left without saying anything to anybody?" I said, already knowing the answer.

"I didn't know what to do," she said. A tear rolled down her left cheek. "All I could see was black, an abyss. I was scared. What if the killer came after me? I couldn't go to California and face my kids; I couldn't stay here. What could I do?"

I nodded sympathetically. "That had to be terrible," I said. "Where'd you go?"

She wiped the tears from her face. "I packed up and drove inland. Didn't have any idea where. Got to Columbia and followed the signs to Charlotte. I'm a West Coast gal and had never been there, but the name sounded nice. I stopped at a Cracker Barrel outside Charlotte and heard the family sitting next to me talking about their vacation in Blowing Rock; they were on their way home. I asked them where Blowing Rock was, and they said about a hundred miles farther. I said why not."

"When did you get back?"

"Day before yesterday. I almost didn't leave Blowing Rock. It's a cute, little burg on the edge of the mountains; everyone there was so friendly. I found a quaint bed-and-breakfast right in the center of town, and I figured I could get my head on straight and then head back to California. After a few days, I knew I had to come back here. It wasn't fair to the memory of Wynn to skip out on the people who knew and loved him."

Most people there knew him, but I doubted the part about loving him. Several didn't like him, and one had put a gun to his back and pulled the trigger, twice. Nothing about that shouted "love."

"You don't know who could have killed him?"

There was a long period of silence before she said, "I thought a lot about that when I was walking around Blowing Rock. I went in circles trying to figure it out."

"Who would have benefited from his death?" I asked.

"Geoff, no doubt. He got Wynn's starring role, didn't he?" I nodded.

"Then there's Billy B.," she said.

"Billy Robinson?" I said.

"Yeah," she said. Her face was still red, but the tears had stopped flowing. "He was always sucking up to everyone, but I knew he resented Wynn."

"Why?"

She looked at the floor. "He hit on me a couple of times. Wynn found out and told him if he tried anything, he would break both his legs and then make sure he never again worked in the industry."

"I can see where that would have turned Billy against him," I said and smiled.

I was pleased when Donna returned the smile. "Billy stayed away from me after that."

For the next twenty minutes, she shared stories about Billy, Wynn, even her two children in California. It seemed like she wanted to relive some of the better moments from the last couple of years rather than the reality of losing her boyfriend, learning about Geoff's death, and the gut-wrenching loss.

I needed to bring her back to the present and reality. "Anyone else have reason to kill Wynn?"

"Talon might have harbored some resentment. He wanted his actor friend from California to get the starring role, but the two footing the bills vetoed it."

"That doesn't seem like enough reason to kill him, does it?"

"Not really, but hey, they're in the movie business," she said as if that explained everything. "Oh yeah, speaking of the financiers, I wouldn't be surprised if they, or more specifically, the bitch Becky Hilton had something to do with it."

"What motive would she have?"

"Publicity's everything to the industry. Old-time actress Bette Davis said, 'I wouldn't consider dying during a newspaper strike.'" She rubbed her eyes with her left hand and then lowered her head. "Wynn always said that nothing sold more tickets than some disaster while a movie was being filmed. His … murder fit that bill." She started to cry.

I walked to the kitchen to get her another beer even though hers was still half-full. She needed a few minutes with her memories, and I needed time to figure out what to do. I returned ten minutes later and handed her the beer. She thanked me and asked what I thought she should do.

"You should tell your story to the police. They have some questions, and you might be able to help."

She looked up from the floor and tilted her head. "I'm scared."

"Want me to call, and you can stay here until someone comes to talk to you?"

"Would you?" she whispered.

I nodded and then grabbed my cell phone and moved to the kitchen and punched Detective Callahan's number. He answered on the second ring.

"Is that you, Chris?" he asked.

I hate caller ID. "Yes."

"Are you okay?"

I thought that was a strange question but said that I was fine.

"Is Donna Lancaster there?" he asked.

Okay, now I was freaked. I said yes, and he asked where she was. I told him that she was in the living room.

The phone went dead, and seconds later the front door flew open.

Then the gates of hell imploded.

CHAPTER 32

T HE DOOR FRAME WAS BARELY wide enough for six cops to squeeze through, but they managed. They wore bulletproof vests and scowls, and each of them carried a handgun. I knew that because each firearm was pointed at the lady in the hot-pink shorts and black T-shirt.

"Hands in the air!" yelled Brian Newman, the first cop through the door.

I was in the doorway between the kitchen and the living room when Donna flung both arms toward the ceiling. The beer she had in her left hand dropped to the floor, and she started to say something.

Then a forceful voice from behind me yelled, "Get out of the way!"

If I had anything in my hand, it would have followed Donna's drink to the floor.

Officer Spencer and two members of the Charleston County Sheriff's Office pushed their way through the kitchen and blocked the rear escape route. Two of the officers who had entered the front door had already twisted Donna's arms behind her back and were restraining her wrists.

Detective Callahan was behind Chief Newman but stepped around him and faced Donna.

"Ms. Lancaster," said Callahan, "you're under arrest for the murder of Wynn James."

He was halfway through reciting her Miranda rights before I realized that my legs were shaking so much that I was about to collapse. One of the kitchen chairs was within arm's reach, and I took advantage of the perch.

Callahan, along with what seemed like fifty or more police officers but was probably only a handful, had already begun escorting Donna out of the house. Brian Newman and Cindy LaMond watched the parade out the front door and then came into the kitchen. They were followed by Officer Spencer, who came back into the kitchen and said he'd close the back door on his way out. He also suggested that I get a more secure lock; it took him all of fifteen seconds to jimmy it.

I said, "Thanks, I guess."

"Are you okay?" asked Brian.

Cindy didn't say anything but came over and put her hand on my shoulder.

"I was," I said, "until every police officer in South Carolina stormed into my peaceful abode. How'd you know she was here?"

Cindy smiled and turned toward Brian. "Smart-ass Chris is fine."

I looked at each of them and toward the living room. "I know you're quick, but I hadn't hung up on Callahan when the population of my house increased dramatically. What's going on?"

Cindy looked at her boss. Brian smiled and then nodded. "You tell him," he said.

Cindy pulled one of the chairs from the table, turned it around, and straddled the seat. "Dispatch got a call from Woofer—"

"Woofer?" I interrupted.

"Yeah," said Cindy. "Don't know his real name. He cuts lawns and weeds out here for money and surfs for peace and happiness. He's been finding his fame lately as an extra in the movie. Been in two of the surfer scenes. I've known him—"

Brian aimed his palm at Cindy. "The story."

Cindy rolled her eyes at Brian and then turned back to me. "Anyway, Woofer was in Bert's with a couple of his surfer friends earlier and saw you and Eric and a chick talking. Actually, he said that he saw Eric, an old geezer, and a chick talking. Knew you'd want me to be accurate." She paused and winked at me.

Thanks, I thought and nodded.

"Woofer said that his attention was drawn to the 'hot-pink shorts that barely stretched around the chick's ass.' After taking in the view, Woofer's gaze stopped at the black T-shirt that was, 'way too small for the anatomy it was covering,' and then finally he noticed that the person wearing the captivating attire was Donna Lancaster. He recognized her from the set. He knew that the police were looking for her, said everyone on the island knew it, so he did his civic duty and called us. Probably the only time in his life that Woofer exercised his civic duty, but anyway—"

Detective Callahan walked in the room and stood behind Cindy. He said that about the same time the civic-minded surfer called the Folly Beach police, the sheriff's office received an anonymous call telling them that Donna Lancaster's old Mazda was parked in front of the liquor store behind Bert's. He called the chief, garnered the troops, and checked out her car. Brian then took the handoff and said that when he got to her car, he saw a clear, plastic sandwich bag that appeared to contain marijuana on the front passenger seat. That was enough to enter the vehicle. The door was unlocked, so they didn't have to break in. They also saw a handgun sticking out from under the passenger's seat, a handgun the same caliber as the bullet that killed Wynn.

Brian hesitated long enough for Cindy to chime in. "I went in Bert's looking for Donna. Woofer was standing in the corner patiently waiting for someone to talk to him. I asked what he'd seen, and other than tapping the concrete floor with his foot like Mr. Ed counting to five, he didn't offer anything we didn't already know. Eric came over and said that he had seen the 'lady in the fetching attire' leave with you. He said that Donna wasn't holding a gun to your head or a Samurai sword to your throat, so he figured you weren't in danger. Cops are worrywarts. When Detective Callahan showed up, we figured we needed to be cautious. Your house was the first place we checked. The chief peeked into your kitchen window, and you looked safe. And then Detective Callahan got your call. You know the rest."

I sat back and tried to let the story sink in. I grasped what had happened, but I couldn't quite put it together with the calm, convincing conversation I had just been having with the frightened and confused girlfriend of the late Wynn James. Callahan and Brian had taken the other two seats at my table. I couldn't remember the last time all four chairs had been used at the same time. It was a strange sight in a strange day.

I shared as much of my conversation with Donna as I could remember. I acknowledged that she could be Wynn's killer and could have set the stage for Geoff to be killed if he had learned that she was guilty of killing Wynn. I also shared how sincere she had seemed and how surprised she was when I told her about Geoff. I asked why she would have stuck around after killing him. "What would she gain by staying? Wouldn't she have been better off to distance herself as far as possible from Folly Beach? And doesn't it seem mighty far-fetched that she would have left the evidence in clear sight in her car? Looks like a frame to me."

Cindy nodded. "Our job is to catch. God created juries to do the rest."

CHAPTER 33

PEACE HAD BEEN RESTORED. REPRESENTATIVES from two police departments and one alleged killer were off to wherever they were going, and I was standing on the front porch watching the last police car as it pulled into the flow of traffic.

"Yo, Christer, what be happening?" asked Dude, who was leaning against the hood of my SUV and dressed in his usual tie-dyed, florescent T-shirt and ratty cargo shorts.

I walked over to him. "What makes you think something *be happening?*"

He held both arms out like he was trying to hug my yard. "Could be flock of flashin' red and blue beams stuck on rides with word po-leece on side." He pointed at my entry. "Could be fuzz flashin' bullet-throwers at your minding-its-own-business front door."

I leaned on the fender beside Dude. "Did you see all that?" I asked.

"Be buying bundle of bananas at Bert's. See commotion. Figure movie shootin' at *su casa*." He then tapped his temple with his forefinger. "Then figure, no moviemakin' machines in yard. Something be askance."

It was hot standing against the vehicle, but I wasn't ready to go back in the house. "Up for a walk?" I asked.

"If not far—Connecticut be too far," he said with a straight face.

"We'll cut it short," I said with an equally straight face. It reminded me of the conversations Charles and I would have, this one with fewer words, of course. I'd need to check on him later. My life would be in greater danger than it was with Donna if Charles didn't learn from me what had just happened, and learn quickly.

We walked a block behind Bert's and then away from town. I gave Dude my version of how I'd spent my day, and he said something that I think meant that my day was more exciting than his.

He took a couple of steps into a front yard of one of the rustic, pre-Hugo houses and then stopped in the shade. "Bag-o-weed be sittin' in view in Barbie's car?" he said.

"That's what the chief said," I said as we turned and headed back toward Center Street.

"Me not weed partaker," he said and winked. "If I be, its resting spot wouldn't be in view of Sun God and fuzz. That'd be asking for trip to pokey."

I remembered what Brian said about Donna's car being unlocked. "You think someone planted it?"

"Me be 97.3 percent sure," said Dude.

I didn't question his math, but I totally agreed.

"Killer not be Donna," said Dude, radiating confidence. "She be picture framed."

His confidence came to an abrupt halt when I asked him if not Donna, then who? He said that was what the *po-leece* were paid to figure out.

***

Dude said that he needed to check on his two clerks to make sure they hadn't insulted too many customers, so our walk ended at the surf shop. I said that must be a difficult task, and he told me that I didn't know the two-thirds of it.

I left Dude to save the surf-stuff buying public from his employees and walked five more blocks to Charles's apartment. It took several knocks before he opened the door. He looked like he had aged a decade since the funeral. His eyes were buried deep in their sockets, and his hair, never groomed well enough for a salon ad, had taken on the appearance of a rats' nest after a wine-and-cheese party. His clothes sagged on his already trim frame.

He stepped aside for me to enter but didn't say anything. Floor space in his apartment was always at a premium, but today it was so cluttered with empty beer bottles and pizza boxes that I had to kick a couple of them aside to get to a rickety chair. The smell of stale air and aging pizza permeated the air. Charles slowly closed the door and moved to the chair opposite me.

I asked one of the most stupid questions that had left my mouth in months. "How're you doing?"

He blinked a couple of times, scooted an empty box out of his way with his foot, and then looked in my direction. He missed my face with his gaze. "Better than Aunt M."

"The last thing she'd want would be you moping around," I said. It sounded harsher than I had intended.

He finally looked me in the eyes. "I know. I know, but ..." he hesitated. "It hurts."

"I know," I said in a softer voice.

"Chris, I'm trying to hang on. Thomas Jefferson said, 'When you reach the end of your rope, tie a knot in it and hang on.' I'm at the bottom of that rope and am having trouble getting the knot tied."

I looked around the room. "When was the last time you were out?"

He looked toward the door. "Don't know," he said. "Few days ago."

"Get your shoes on and let's take a walk," I said. "Got a story to tell you."

He hesitated, but the promise of a story motivated him to get up, slip on his tennis shoes, wipe pizza crumbs off his shirt, tuck his long hair under the brim of his Tilley, and head toward the door. I asked if he wanted to take his camera, something that almost always got a positive response. He said no, so I knew that he had a long way to go to reach normal—Charles normal.

I slowed down more than once during the first couple of blocks since he was moving at the speed of an iceberg, pre-global warming. I shared what had happened with Donna, and Charles started to move faster. He asked questions, and glimmers—however slight—of the old Charles began to reappear. He agreed with Dude and me about someone planting the drugs and the gun in Donna's car. He said that he was certain that Geoff had been killed to keep him quiet. It couldn't have been Donna or she wouldn't have returned to Folly after she switched the ammunition.

His pace quickened more as he told me that he had heard before the shooting that moneybags Becky Hilton was broke and that her source of funds was ready to cut her off with a hint of doing something worse if she didn't get the production finished.

I told him that I had a bad feeling about Billy Robinson. He seemed to want to pass the suspicion on to Donna, and he had been sucking up to everyone. He seemed too sweet. He wanted something, I said.

"Too much syrup turns to fat," said Charles.

"Did some president say that?"

"Not that I'm aware of," he said. "Why?"

"Never mind. Need anything while we're out—food, drink," I sniffed the air and facetiously said, "deodorant?"

He smiled.

"Let's swing by the post office," he said. "I haven't gotten the mail for a few days. Never know when I might get a check for a million bucks."

I knew the answer but turned and walked with him to the post office. Since the overstaffed and underfunded United States Postal Service didn't provide home delivery on Folly Beach, a daily excursion to the post office was a tradition if not a necessity for many residents.

Charles was off retailers' radar since he didn't have credit cards, never bought anything online, and to my knowledge, wasn't even a registered voter. His trips to the post office were more for exercise and the chance to talk to people than the expectation of anything being there for him. The barrage of irritating junk mail that most of us were accustomed to had passed him by.

He acted surprised to receive an oversized, brown envelope with his name and address handwritten in pencil on the front. There was no return address, and the envelope was postmarked Folly Beach. He looked at me and shrugged. I suggested that we walk across the street to the River Park where we could sit in the shade. Other than a middle-aged couple seated in the small pavilion across the small park from us, the area was deserted. We sat on a bench shaded by the palmettos and live oaks that dotted the perimeter of the park.

Inside the envelope, there were two sheets of copy paper folded in half. The ink was faint, and on the bottom of the first sheet was what appeared to be a drink stain. The pages looked to be several years old.

The copy was formatted like the script pages that I had seen on the sets, so I assumed it was a film script. There was a yellow Post-it note stuck to the top page. *In case I miss you, here's a preview. Wait until you see the rest!* was written on the note in the same handwriting as the envelope and was signed with a large "G."

"Geoff?" I said.

"That's my guess," said Charles. He looked at the front of the envelope again—still no return address. "But why'd he send it to me? He talked to you the day he was killed."

"True," I said, "but he wanted to talk to you. The only reason he called me was because you weren't home."

"So you think he dropped this in the mail before he called?"

"Looks like it," I said and pulled the Post-it note off the top sheet and held the copy paper out so Charles and I could read it at the same time.

Halfway down the first sheet, it read:

> *EXT. HUBBARD LAKE—NIGHT* at the left margin followed by:
> *Overturned canoe drifts away from Chet and Harvey. Harvey moves up behind Chet, grabs him around neck, and pushes him under water. Chet struggles but cannot get leverage.*

The second sheet apparently was not the actual next page in the manuscript since it said that Harvey was in a bright red rescue boat surrounded by three people. It was still night, and centered on the page, it read:

> *HARVEY*
> *I tried to reach him, but he floated away.*

RESCUER 1
Could he have reached shore?
Harvey wipes a tear from his eyes. The
rescue boat bobs in the water.
HARVEY
No, he's gone. I couldn't save him. God, I'm sorry.

Charles silently read the two sheets a second time and then pushed them closer to me. "Any idea what this is about?" he asked.

There weren't instant answers on the two sheets, but I said, "Looks like pages from a script. It's not from *Final Cut* since the scene's on Hubbard Lake, wherever that is, instead of the ocean."

"Could have been an early draft," said Charles as he looked back at the first page.

"It could," I conceded, "but it seems unlikely. Most everything in *Final Cut* is centered on the ocean—surfers, beach bars, sand, and surf."

"True," said Charles. He hesitated and looked at the couple in the pavilion and then back at me. "One hell of a big coincidence in here." He took the first sheet from my hand and waved it in front of my face.

"Cesar Ramon having the same fate as Chet?" I said.

Charles pointed in the direction of the beach. "Looks like Cesar's drowning out there in that big, blue Atlantic Ocean was scripted on this paper."

"One big difference though," I said. "No one could have known that the fishing boat would capsize in the storm."

"No," said Charles, "but once it did, someone on that boat already had a plan to kill one of the passengers—a plan that he, or she, had written." He waved the paper in my face again like I would have already forgotten what he was talking about.

"That's what it looks like," I said.

Charles looked at me and then back down at the script. "If this was what Geoff wanted to talk to us about, and somehow it proved who killed Cesar, Wynn, and I guess Geoff, why didn't he say who it was?" he asked.

"He was an actor," I said. "Drama, suspense, mystery—he probably sent this to tease you; he said it was a preview. He wanted to star in the big scene and tell you in person who the killer was."

"Too bad he'll never get to shoot that scene," said Charles.

The puzzling script gave Charles something to get his mind off Melinda. He read the pages several more times and then said that he was hungry. I suggested we go to the Grill and Island Bar, located a block from where we were.

It was hot but not unbearable, so we sat on the patio, where Charles had always preferred because it was close enough for him to talk to people passing on the sidewalk along Center Street. He wasn't in a talking mood today, but I thought I would tempt him with the chance to yell at people he knew and talk to their dogs as they walked by. The manager escorted us to a table closest to the sidewalk and said that he was sorry that the movie had been shut down. He knew that Charles had been part of the production. I was also certain that losing the revenue from the visitors from California was hard on all the local restaurants and bars.

"Help me remember who was on the boat," said Charles. "Cesar, of course, the captain, Wynn and Donna, Talon, Billy, Geoff, and who else?"

"Becky and Robert."

Charles looked up from the menu. "Think that's it?"

"I don't recall anyone else."

The waitress stopped at the table, and Charles ordered a vegetable enchilada and a beer. I settled for a hamburger and chardonnay. Charles's increased appetite was a good sign.

The young waitress moved to the next table, and Charles continued, "My astute power of detecting tells me that Geoff didn't kill himself. Cesar didn't kill anyone, but if the script means anything, one of the others managed to drown Cesar."

I told him that I couldn't argue with his logic and asked if he wanted to call Detective Callahan and tell him about the script. Charles thought for a second and took a sip of water from the glass that the waitress had wordlessly set on the table.

"WWMD," he said and then took another sip.

"Huh?" I articulately asked.

"What would Melinda do?"

I smiled. "She did have a way of letting us know what was on her mind."

Charles looked at the empty chair beside me where I had placed my Tilley. "If she was there, she'd say, 'Now, Charles, the smart thing would be to call the police and turn those papers over to them and butt out.' Then she'd wiggle her finger at me and say, 'Heck, that wouldn't be a spit of fun. You and Chris need to figure out who killed your friend Geoff. You'd better figure it out quick before you get yourself hurt. Stop dallying.'"

I laughed. "You're absolutely right. But, we still need to get these pages to the police. If Geoff had more pages that were more incriminating, and if they haven't already, they need to search his house."

Charles looked back at the empty seat. "Tomorrow would be a good day to give them the script."

I didn't see why we couldn't do it now, but I knew Charles wanted time in case a miracle happened and we figured it out before then. He wanted to solve it for Melinda.

Our food arrived, and so did a stream of questions from Charles.

"How did Geoff get the pages? Who would know that Geoff had figured out who killed Wynn? Why was Wynn killed? If Donna didn't kill Wynn, who did? Who on the boat would have benefited by Cesar's death?" He took a deep breath, exhaled, and then continued, "Who would have benefited by the ceiling beam and lights falling at Cal's? Was the bonfire supposed to fall on Wynn? If it was rigged, who would have benefited? Where … never mind, that's enough questions."

For a second, I felt like Charles and I were at a speed-dating lunch and he wanted to get in as many questions as possible before the timer went off and we had to move on. That thought quickly left my mind, and I tried to focus on remembering the questions. Failing at that, I took a bite of hamburger.

"Well?" he asked. "What do you think?"

Something about the script had bothered me since Charles opened the envelope, but I couldn't put my finger on what it was, so I tried to address his questions—the ones I could remember. Age seems to be removing as many of my brain cells as it has my hair.

"That's probably the reason Geoff was killed," I said and looked down at the envelope sitting beside Charles's water glass. "Wynn's killer found out that Geoff had these pages and others that could incriminate him and had to stop him from telling anyone."

"Makes sense," said Charles. "But other than Donna, who would have wanted Wynn dead?"

"I keep coming back to the publicity the deaths would draw for the film. It could be a box-office smash, regardless how good the film turned out to be. If the light bar had been sabotaged, it wouldn't have landed on the stars, just increased publicity. Extra publicity would have benefited everyone, so that doesn't narrow it down. Or from what I've seen, jealousy, resentment, and hate among actors could be powerful forces, all possible motives."

Charles nodded. "Billy told me that some famous director had said that, 'In Hollywood, it's considered bad manners to stab someone in the chest.'"

"Again, that doesn't narrow the field. What were some of your other questions?"

A horn beeped on Center Street, and I turned and saw Dude's classic El Camino slowly drive by and turn into the parking lot beside the restaurant. The aging hipster hopped out and headed toward us. He waved at the manager and then walked directly to our table.

Charles motioned to the seat beside him. Dude saluted and then sat. Charles asked where he was going.

"No eight-track tape player store on Folly," said Dude as he waved his right hand over his head. "Believe that?"

Not an eight-track tape store left anywhere in the world, I thought.

"Is there one in Charleston?" asked Charles.

"Don't know," said Dude. "Headin' to W-world. If not there, it don't exist."

The last time I'd seen an eight-track tape was in the early 1980s, and I was fairly certain that even Walmart to most, W-world to Dude, didn't sell the machines.

Dude looked at my hamburger and then toward the door into the restaurant. "Chowin' down better idea." He then reached over and took one of my fries.

He got the waitress's attention and pointed to my plate and said something that was interpreted as him wanting a hamburger. He then turned to Charles and said, "Hear Gidget-Donna now behind bars. Bumpin' off Wynn, and Geoff be frowned on by fuzz."

"Think she did it?" asked Charles.

"Two rude employees say no way. They be right for a change."

"Why do they say that?" I asked.

"She be hot," said Dude. "Too cute to kill."

That's an argument you don't often hear in court.

"Is that their only reason?" I asked.

"Yep," said Dude.

"Who do you think did it?" asked Charles.

"Me know cost of surfboards. Me know how to work credit card machine. Me know name of eighty-eight constellations." He pointed to the sky. "Me know *nada*, zip, *suihou* about who be killer. Except it not be Donna."

I continued to have this feeling that somewhere in my subconscious I knew more than Dude, but for the life of me I still couldn't remember what.

I hoped that it wasn't literally for the life of me.

CHAPTER 34

DUDE PATTED CHARLES ON THE head before leaving the restaurant and again said that he was sorry about Melinda. Dude then pointed off-island and said, "W-world or bust."

Charles watched the El Camino pull out of the lot and head for the bridge. "That boy sure has a way with unwords," he said.

There were still a couple of hours of sunlight left, and I suggested that instead of heading to Charles's apartment, we walk to the end of the pier. We'd spent many hours there, and we both enjoyed the peacefulness of being three football-field lengths past where the tide met the beach.

"Tell me again why you don't think Donna killed anyone," said Charles as we reached the far end of the pier. "She has the best motive and no alibi."

"You hit it earlier," I said. "Why would she return?" I shook my head. "I also saw her face when I told her that Geoff had been shot. She was shocked; she wasn't faking."

Charles took off his Tilley and sat it on top of mine on the wooden bench. I gave him a dirty look.

"Didn't want to put it in bird poop," he said and then smiled.

"That makes it okay?" I said.

"You bet," he said.

"Do you think she's guilty?" I asked.

"Not for a sec. But the fact is that she's in the hoosegow, so somebody thinks she did." He stared at two dolphins frolicking in the surf near a buoy in front of the Tides. "If I were a betting person, I'd put *your* money on Becky Hilton."

"Why?"

"Ever since the first accident at Cal's, there've been rumors about her money. Folks who should know say she borrowed most of it from seriously bad guys with lots of leg-breaking ball bats and guns. They say the bad guys' patience is running as thin as Saran wrap."

"That doesn't make sense," I said. "Each delay in filming costs big bucks. Wouldn't she want it finished as quickly as possible?"

"Exactly what I asked Billy B.," said Charles. He then stood and slowly moved to the rail and looked down into the surf.

I walked over to him and started to say something but noticed the sun glistening off a tear in the corner of his eye. I rested my arm on his shoulder and followed his lead and stared at the water.

A seagull squawked at one of its traveling buddies, and Charles shook his head and walked to the other side of the pier. I followed.

Charles looked toward the beach, took a deep breath, and then said, "Billy said that he hadn't been around nearly as many films as most of the Hollywood crowd, but from what he could tell, *Final Cut* was going to bomb. That's even if it makes it to the big screen. He said he doubted it would ever appear 'where customers buy popcorn.' Publicity, tons of publicity, was the only thing that could save the film."

Billy's comment struck a chord. Not because it was accurate—since I had no idea if it was—but because he had been spending an awful lot of time recently badmouthing people. He'd hinted that Becky could be the killer. He had talked about Geoff acting funny; said he didn't trust anyone and had been asking a bunch of questions. He had confided that Donna had the most reasons. He also had made no bones about wanting to make a name for himself. He'd sucked up to everyone who could help him. Now with the extra publicity, he would have nearly as much to gain as Becky. He'd been on the boat. He had access to the ammunition. And as assistant director, he had the ear of most everyone in the production and could observe everything that was going on. He was young, and none of the old-timers took him too seriously. Billy fit in everywhere and flew under the radar.

I shared all that with Charles, and he listened, but his mind was somewhere else. It was a mistake to bring him out here. This was where we had "buried" Melinda. Too soon, way too soon.

I offered to buy him a beer at the outdoor bar at the Tides. He said yes and started next door to the luxury hotel before I had time to pick up our hats from the bench. I was right about it being too soon for him to be here.

"What could those pages have to do with Billy?" asked Charles as he took his beer to the stool-height seats at the fifty-foot-long wooden bar.

"What do they have to do with anyone?" I answered his question with a question and sat beside him. We faced the ocean.

"You do know what Aunt M. would tell us to do, don't you?" said Charles.

"Tell me," I said.

"She'd wave the pages in the air and say something like, 'Crapola, these don't mean diddly-squat by themselves. Get your expanding butts out of those chairs and go ask Billy what they mean to him.'" He stopped and laughed, the first time I'd seen that in days. "Then she'd say, 'Heck-fire, the worst the young whippersnapper could do is kill you.'"

I laughed. It was so like her. The sun had disappeared behind the nine-story hotel, and darkness was rapidly approaching from the east. Charles leaned back in his chair and sighed. A smile followed—he was relaxing. It was a welcomed sight.

"Think Melida'd be too upset if we waited until tomorrow to track down Billy?" I asked.

"Nope," said Charles. He pointed at his beer. "She'd want us to finish these and have a couple more for her. She'd be sitting here with us if she wasn't busy getting God straightened out."

A young, bearded musician sat on a stool in the corner by the bar and played a medley of soft-rock hits from the eighties. Three college-age women sat at the table closest to the musician and sang along with him. A half dozen conventioneers, conspicuous by their stick-on *Hello I'm* ___ nametags, had gathered along the rail separating the hotel property from the beach. Each held a beer, and from their laughter, it wasn't their first. And Charles and I honored Melinda's heaven-sent request for us to enjoy a couple more adult beverages before we called it a night. I offered to walk him home, but he said that he was quite capable of finding it on his own and besides he needed time alone. I wished him well on his journey, and he did the same to me.

I hit the bed as soon as I got home, but sleep was slow to come. I had never imagined that I could have been so attached to Charles's aunt in the small time that I'd known her. It was even harder to imagine how much her being gone would affect Charles. He had survived several decades without any contact with family. During those years, he had met many people and had casual friendships with several. Melinda had told me that I was his best friend, and I was humbled but also felt sad that there weren't others close in his life. Now Melinda had come and, all too quickly, had gone.

Charles and Heather were close, but I had a hard time picturing it when Melinda talked about them getting married. Melinda had confided that Heather wanted to get married, but Charles and I had never had a serious conversation about the topic. I hoped that Melinda's wish for holy matrimony wouldn't be the only reason Charles would take the leap.

Once again, my overnight thoughts also went back to my ex-wife, Joan, who, like Melinda, had reappeared in my life after years of being only a bad memory. Then after nearly getting me killed and rekindling memories and feelings that had been long gone, I had lost her, again. These disconcerting nighttime images and memories were coming more frequently.

Sleep kindly prevailed despite my mind's tumultuous efforts to keep me awake. A horn blast from what sounded like a large truck on the street jarred me awake a little after eight—late for me. Somewhere in the middle of the night between thoughts of Charles, Melinda, Heather, and Joan, I remembered that I had to pay some bills I'd left at the gallery.

It had rained overnight, but the sky had cleared, and it appeared that a beautiful spring day was to be. I stopped at Bert's for coffee and then headed toward the gallery, but before I had walked a block, a City of Folly Beach patrol car pulled up beside me and lowered the passenger-side window. My heart skipped a beat like most people's would if a police car stopped next to them. Then I saw Cindy driving. She asked if I had a minute to talk and if I could walk around the corner where she could pull off the road without drawing too much attention. She pulled the patrol car off the road onto the sandy berm, and I leaned in the open window.

"Figured you'd want to know this," she began. "You know Sam Allia?"

"Don't think so," I said.

"Guy who owns Folly Fries & More," said Cindy, who then looked in her rearview mirror.

"That Sam, yeah. What about him?"

Cindy smiled. "Thought you'd never ask. The other night he was in Loggerheads and was three beers past soused." She giggled. "Right before he fell off the barstool, he told two guys who were standing around watching him make a fool of himself that he had 'showed that interloping food-truck guy that it don't pay to hog in here.'"

"Which meant?" I asked.

"Which meant that he'd slipped tainted food on ProCatering's buffet line. Which meant that when Dude and Wynn ate it, they got food poisoning. Which meant that the early rumors were true about one of the local restaurants sabotaging the food truck. That enough *which meants* for you?"

"How'd the police find out?" I asked.

"One of the guys standing around listening to Sam was an off-duty Charleston cop. He's not a detective, but was sharp enough to know that he had detected a crime and told his supervisor, who called our chief. Now Sam's got himself into a scrambled-eggs pile of trouble."

"What'll happen to him?"

"He probably won't serve time, but he can kiss his business license *adios*." Cindy snapped her fingers and pointed one at me. "Want to buy a hamburger stand cheap?"

"Why not," I said. "It couldn't be more unsuccessful than the gallery."

Cindy smiled and then looked back in the rearview mirror. Her face turned serious. "Got a question," she said.

I nodded.

"The chief keeps talking to me about offering me his job if he gets elected mayor. He thinks I could do a good job."

She paused. "I don't know, Chris. I'm happy doing what I'm doing. And you know God didn't give me an overabundance of patience. I'm not sure I could put up with the politics and crap that goes with it. It'd also be hard for me to have to look at one of my fellow cops in the eye and fire him ... or her. It'd be about three time zones outside my comfort zone. I don't know; I just don't know."

I waited for a couple to peddle past us on bikes and turned back to Cindy.

"Let me put it this way," I said. "If you decide to go for it, I'll be your biggest supporter. If you decide to stay where you are, I'll support you 100 percent."

She tilted her head. "Thanks, but that sure as hell doesn't help any."

"Then let's try it another way," I said. "You'd be an excellent chief. You'd be different from Brian, way different, but because you're different doesn't mean you'll be worse. In fact, you'd bring a breath of fresh air to the job. You are firm but have a way of putting people at ease. You have a certain charm that can be effective in working with the many kinds of people you'll have to deal with. And you've been on the job long enough to know about each quirk and cranny of the island and everyone who hangs out here."

"Thanks again," she said. "I don't know if I agree, but even if you're right, will it be the best move for me?"

"Officer LaMond," I said, "only you can decide that. My vote's yes."

Before she responded, a white Mustang convertible squealed its tires and sped by on the cross street in front of us.

"Geez," muttered Cindy. "Guess I'd better go use some of that charm you were talking about. What an idiot."

I stepped back, and Cindy spun her wheels in the sand, hit her siren, and headed after the Mustang.

I postponed my trip to the gallery and walked to the Lost Dog Café. All the early-morning thinking about Cindy's decision made me hungry.

I started toward the door when I noticed Billy B. at a table by himself in the back of the patio to the right of the building. He saw me and waved. This would be a good time to talk to him about what Charles and I had talked about last night. We were the only two customers on the deck, so it was a couple of minutes before Billy's waitress came out to check on him and noticed me. I ordered French toast.

"Has anything been decided about filming?" I asked.

"Beth and Robert have made it scary-clear that production must continue," he said and chewed on his gum.

"How's that possible?" I asked.

He chuckled. "With lots of smoke and mirrors and major script revisions." He then looked past me to the street. "Speak of the devil," he said and bowed his head.

I turned and saw Becky Hilton and Robert Gaddy walking toward the patio. They were in deep conversation and didn't notice us as they grabbed a table near the front. A second waitress must have seen them and was at their table before they were situated. Becky had her back to us, and Robert sat to her side rather than opposite her.

Billy seemed relieved that they didn't see him and whispered to me that they both had been in horrible moods and biting the heads off anyone who came near. I wasn't surprised considering what they had at stake and with the production collapsing around them.

I leaned closer to Billy. "Have you ever written a screenplay?" I asked, remembering the two mysterious pages Charles had received.

Billy looked down at his coffee, glanced at the financiers on the other side of the patio, and then glared at me. "Why'd you ask that?"

I should have kept my mouth shut, I thought. "It seems that everyone in your business wants to write one. Just thought you might have." I smiled and hoped that I hadn't raised suspicion.

"I started one," he said and giggled. "Maybe someday I'll finish it. You know, I'd love to, but right now all I'm trying to do is get better known, trying to get recognized as someone who can get the job done and land bigger jobs on bigger productions. I need to get back to Hollywood where the money and opportunities are—no offense, Folly Beach." He waved toward town.

"I'm sure the island isn't offended," I said, moderately sarcastic. "What's your screenplay about?"

Billy looked at his watch. "Have to run, got to meet Talon. Nice talking to you." He left three ones on the table to cover his bill and walked around the edge of the patio, as far away from Robert and Becky as he could. When he reached the street, he nearly collided with Charles, who had arrived on his classic Schwinn bike.

Charles glanced my way and then said something to Billy, and they both laughed. I was pleased to see Charles laugh. Billy then walked toward town, and Charles made a beeline to my table, tapping his cane on the wood deck along the way. He tipped his Tilly to the financiers. They ignored him.

"You're in good spirits," I said.

"Thought I'd give it a try. I'm tired of being depressed."

"How's it working?" I asked. I smiled but was dead serious.

"Gonna take more work."

Breakfast arrived. Charles looked at my plate and told the waitress that he'd have the same. "Know who the killer is?" he asked. "Did you ask Billy B. about the script? Figured you did since he came from back here."

"Don't know who the killer is. He said he'd started a script but left before telling me about it. I do know who the food poisoner was though."

"Huh?"

I told him what Cindy had said. Charles seemed disappointed that the food poisoning wasn't an effort to kill Wynn but just a struggling restaurateur's gross stupidity. I then returned to Billy and how he'd reacted suspiciously when I asked if he had written a screenplay.

Charles started to say something, but then he did one of the things he excels in. He leaned in the direction of Robert and Becky and began eavesdropping. I couldn't catch everything they were saying, but it had something to do with revising the script and bringing in another actor to take the lead.

Charles almost fell over in his chair from leaning toward the other table when the financiers jumped up and headed to their car.

Charles rearranged his chair and then began filling me in on their conversation. He hadn't gleaned much more than I had overheard, but we were convinced that every effort was being made to continue the film. Charles kept interrupting his summary by saying that he didn't trust them, especially Becky. I wasn't as certain about her as he was but couldn't disagree.

Charles picked up his cane and pointed it in the direction of the Robert and Becky's car.

"President Madison said, 'All men with power ought to be mistrusted.'"

CHAPTER 35

I SHOT UP IN BED. If I were a cartoon character, a light bulb would be flashing over my head. It finally clicked. The first time I'd met Talon at the food truck, he'd mentioned having written two movie scripts. He'd said that he and Cesar Ramon had discussed the ones they'd written. He hinted that they were talking about them because Cesar had bemoaned how much better their works were than the crap that he had to direct.

Could Talon be the killer? He was on the fishing boat and definitely would have had motive for drowning Cesar. He would eliminate his roadblock to directing the movie and also knew that the production needed all the help it could get to be a box-office success. What better way than to have it known as a snake-bit production. He was in Cal's when the lights fell. He was on the set when the bonfire mysteriously collapsed. He had access to the props and the gun that proved to be Geoff's downfall. And hadn't there been talk about him wanting a friend to have the lead role rather than Wynn? Wynn's death would have opened that door, but it was quickly closed when the two financing the production insisted on Geoff taking lead. If one of his scripts had a drowning scene and somehow Geoff got ahold of it, and Talon found out, it could have signed his death warrant.

On the other hand, the similar script could simply be a coincidence. I knew that everything tying Talon to the accidents and to the deaths was circumstantial, and it would be a waste of time to go to the police. So how could I prove it?

The good thing about calling Charles at five a.m. was that he was home; the bad thing was that he was home—and cranky. He slurred something about sleep and did I know what time it was. I said that I did know what time it was and that's why I didn't call earlier. He said something that sounded like "ha, ha," or maybe it was garbled profanity. Either way, it finally dawned on him that I wouldn't be calling that early unless it was important. He said it would be best if I came to his apartment because he was afraid that our phones were bugged, but I knew he really meant that he needed time to wake up.

Forty-five minutes later, I was in Charles's living room, surrounded by about a million books and staring at an awake version of the Charles I'd shaken out of a sound sleep. I had finished sharing my realization and how I believed Talon was connected to the tragic events. Charles had listened attentively, and a few times he nodded agreement. Twice his nod had more the appearance of him falling back asleep, and I talked louder until he rejoined the conversation.

"How do we know that the two pages were from Talon's script?" he asked.

"We don't," I said.

"How do we find out?" he asked.

"Don't know," I said.

"Think he would confess if we asked him politely?"

"Probably not," I said.

"Aunt M. would say that we're bright enough to trick the information out of him," said Charles, who then looked at the front door as if Melinda was joining us.

"Then let's try," I said.

Charles jerked his head in my direction. "Really?"

"Sure. There's nothing to lose as long as we don't make him suspicious. Know where he is?"

"He's probably asleep like all sane people," said Charles, who then wrinkled his nose and yawned. He then surprised me when he said, "After he wakes up, he's going to be at the production trailer until noon. They're having a meeting to figure out how to rewrite the script and switch the actors around so they can finish the film."

"We need to talk to him then," I said.

"If we're there when they break, we could innocently say something like, 'Hey, Talon, can we buy you lunch? Got some questions about how we can stay involved—maybe even work free.' Free help will get his attention."

I said that I'd meet Charles at Bert's a little before noon so we could casually walk across the street to the trailer when we saw the meeting breaking up.

***

Charles and I were in front of Bert's at noon. Charles spoke to everyone who was headed to the store and knelt to pet, speak to, and kiss each pooch that accompanied its owner. I kept an eye on the production trailer.

I was beginning to believe we had missed the end of the meeting when Billy rushed down the steps and jogged in the direction of Center Street. I pulled Charles away from dog smooching, and we casually scurried to the trailer. Becky Hilton was next to leave and didn't look happy. She was closely followed by Robert Gaddy who was talking to Talon. They stopped about twenty feet from the trailer, shook hands, and Robert followed Becky to their car.

Talon looked around and saw us approaching and waved. Luck was on our side.

"Hi, Talon," said Charles, playing his part to the hilt. "What's going on?"

"Meeting about what to do next," said Talon.

Charles looked down at his watch-less wrist and then back at Talon. "Chris and I were on our way to Locklear's for lunch. Want to join us? Even the best producer on Folly Beach needs to eat." Charles smiled when he said it.

Talon looked back at the trailer and then to Charles. "Well, I … okay, sure."

Charles would have given Billy B. a run for his money in sucking up. From Charles's comments, you would have thought Talon was a cross between Steven Spielberg and Francis Ford Coppola. And that was before our fish sandwiches had arrived. You would have also thought that Talon's stomach was on fire, and Charles needed to extinguish it with beer. The director was on his third Budweiser before his plate was empty. His left arm was draped over the back of his chair, and he was humming "Do-Re-Mi" from *The Sound of Music*. He wasn't exactly where Charles wanted him, but was within millimeters.

"Didn't you tell me that you had written some movie scripts?" asked Charles with his most innocent voice.

"Umm, guess so," said Talon. "I mean, I have written some and guess that I told you."

"Bet they're better than any of the crap coming from writers today," said Mr. Suck-Up.

Talon focused on Charles. No simple task after so many beers. "Don't know about that. Think they're pretty good."

I looked at Charles. He gave a slight nod. "Tell us about them," I said and leaned closer to the table.

Talon finished his drink and held the bottle in the air. The waitress took the hint and brought another beer to the director.

"Okee dokee," said Talon. "One's science fiction and takes place on the planet Estremo. There are five Estremoeans who are the only creatures left after an asteroid wiped out the others. What happens is …"

Talon spent twenty minutes sharing, in excruciating detail, everything that happened on Estremo and with its five surviving residents. It took less than half that time to figure out that the two pages of script couldn't have come from the Estremo saga.

"That's fascinating, Talon," said Charles.

I prayed for another asteroid to wipe out the remaining five creatures.

Charles continued with much more enthusiasm. "What about the other scripts?"

Talon stopped and mentally returned to earth from Estremo. "It's no big deal," he said. His eyes narrowed. He took another sip of beer, set the bottle on the table, and then stared at it. "It's a love story with a murder. It takes place in current time and is set on a lake in Michigan."

Bingo! "Tell us about it," I said and glanced over at Charles who had leaned his elbows on the table and smiled at Talon.

Talon smiled back—attention cures many ills. "It's a twist on the often-told love triangle. Sexy wife, doctor husband, and the couple's handsome accountant. Now the twist, the husband and the male accountant are having an affair and, well, you can guess the rest." He stopped as if he was waiting for us to tell him how brilliant it was.

"Sounds interesting," I said. "Who gets killed?"

His head jerked in my direction. "You are an amateur detective, aren't you?" He smiled when he said it, but his eyes didn't show humor. They were probably dark brown but looked as black as the inside of a coal mine.

I laughed. "Not really."

"How'd someone get killed?" asked Charles.

Talon wiped his face with the napkin from his lap. "Whoops," he said. "Time's getting away. Sorry, guys, I got to run. Let me get the check."

Charles looked over at me and then back at Talon. "No way, we've got it."

With that, Talon was on his feet and headed to the exit.

"Think we struck a nerve," I said and grabbed the check.

I hoped we didn't strike anything more dangerous than a nerve, I thought.

Had I only known.

CHAPTER 36

W<small>E LEFT</small> L<small>OCKLEAR'S AND WALKED</small> to the far end of the pier. Charles appeared more comfortable than he had on our last visit to the landmark. There were so many seagulls cackling and people fishing, laughing, and yelling that I almost didn't hear my phone ring.

I covered my right ear, blocked some of the distracting sounds, and said, "Hello."

"This is answer-man Mel," came the powerful voice of Mel Evans. Charles and I had met the former marine a few years earlier. He ran marsh tours, mainly for college students who couldn't care less about the flora and fauna of the marsh but simply wanted a way to go out in the water and drink, and drink, and drink. His boat was named *Mad Mel's Magical March Machine*. That said it all.

"What've you got?" I said.

Charles leaned close to listen, but the sounds of the beach made it impossible.

"Guess who rented the fishing boat that capsized?" said Mel.

I glanced up at the circling seagulls and then said, "Talon Hall."

"Not only did he rent it, but he asked for the captain by name," said Mel.

"I'm not surprised," I said.

"There's more," said Mel. "The storm had been predicted before he rented the boat, so he could have known about it the day before he made the reservation. That's all I got."

"That's enough, Mel," I said. "Thanks."

"You owe me," he said and then hung up.

"What?" asked Charles. "What?"

I shared what Mel had said, and then Charles asked if I'd asked Mel to look into it.

I smiled. "Yep. Figured since he runs charters he'd be able to find out about the capsized one without raising a stink."

"Good thinking," said Charles. "So it wasn't rented because of the reduced rate but so that a drunk would be at the helm."

"That would be accurate," I said.

"He couldn't have known it was going to capsize," said Charles.

"No," I said. "But it would have increased the chances, especially after he had asked the captain the capacity of the small boat. He then surprised the boat's owner when he arrived with two more passengers than the boat should accommodate." I thought for a second and then continued, "With that many people on board, even if it didn't capsize, the passengers would have been distracted by the storm, and he could have conked Cesar on the head and pushed him overboard without anyone noticing until it was too late. If nothing happened, and he couldn't get rid of Cesar on the boat, nothing would have been lost. He'd just wait for another chance."

Charles looked at me and then out to sea. He then waved his hands over the edge of the pier. "I believe Aunt M. helped us catch another killer."

I nodded and said, "He's guilty, but we still need more. The similar script could still be a coincidence."

"Maybe," said Charles, "but we have enough to hand it to the cops on a silver platter. We've got to give them something to do. If Callahan's half as good as everyone says, he'll find proof."

Then I remembered something else Geoff had said when he asked us to meet him after what proved to be his fatal last scene. He'd said that he would need to go to the house before meeting us at my cottage. I didn't think about it at the time, but why would he have needed to go there first?

I grabbed the phone and called Cindy.

"What now?" she said.

Caller ID: the downfall of civil communication.

"Did you find any papers on Geoff's body?" I asked.

"Only his wallet," she said. "Why?"

"Just curious," I said.

"Hmm," said Cindy. "Suppose you'll tell me when you're ready."

"I will. Talk to you later," I said and tapped *End call*.

Charles pointed his cane at me. "What was that about?"

Before I could tell him, a South Carolina summer shower dumped buckets of rain on the pier. Charles and I were not spared. We ran to the covered, two-story pavilion on the Atlantic end of the structure as the sky, already losing its light to sunset, became even darker as ominous, black clouds rolled overhead. Like most Lowcountry afternoon showers, it was over as quickly as it had begun, but the rumble of nearby thunder portended more storms to come.

"The call to Cindy," said Charles. "What's up?"

"We're going to take a ride and break into a house," I said.

By the time we reached my cottage, our clothes were more dry than wet, and Charles had asked me three different ways, whose house and why.

I ran into the house and got a flashlight while Charles waited outside. We got in the SUV, and I said, "Remember I told you that Geoff said he had to go home before meeting us here?"

"Not really," he said. "His murder sort of erased all that stuff from my head."

I pulled out of the drive and headed away from town. "His note said that he had more to share with us, but Cindy just said that there was nothing but his wallet on him when he was killed. So where was whatever he wanted to share?"

"Ah," said Charles. "So we're headed to his house."

I nodded.

"Wouldn't the police have already searched it?" asked Charles.

"Probably," I said, "but they didn't know about the script and its connection to Talon."

The small, older home where the production company had moved Geoff after he took over as star was five blocks from the house and ominously dark.

"So now what?" asked Charles as I pulled in the drive.

"Suppose we'll have to go around back and hope the door has a glass window near the lock," I said, like breaking into houses was one of my regular activities.

A porch light from a house two doors down provided enough illumination for me to see three small windowpanes in the back door, and Charles handed me a softball-sized rock that he found beside the drive. The houses on either side were rentals and equally dark, so I figured the shattering window wouldn't draw attention.

I raised the rock to smash the small window when I heard footsteps crunching on the gravel drive. Charles stepped back off the porch, and I nearly fell down the step behind him when I turned to see who was coming. The distant porch light was enough for me to see the business end of a matt-black Glock pointed at my face.

"You don't give up, do you?" came the steel, cold voice of Talon Hall. "Go back to your car. No quick moves, no noises; don't even think about running. I know how to use this, and believe me, I won't hesitate to."

He had already killed two people that I was aware of, and most likely a third. Nothing would be gained by not following his directions. Charles and I returned to the SUV's front seats, and Talon moved to the backseat; the Glock never wavered.

"Slowly drive off the island," growled Talon.

"Why—" said Charles as he turned toward the voice. He was rewarded with a blow to the side of his head from the barrel of the semiautomatic weapon.

"You don't listen good, do you?" said Talon. "Look out the front window."

Charles obeyed, and I continued the short distance to Center Street and then turned right toward the bridge connecting Folly Beach from the rest of South Carolina.

I kept my head facing the road and said, "Where are we going?"

Talon made a noise between a grunt and a cackle. "Don't worry. I'll tell you all you need to know."

We crossed the bridge off-island, and I goosed the accelerator and sped up to ten and then to fifteen miles-per-hour over the limit. I doubted that Talon would know about the reduced speed limit in this stretch of road, and I prayed to be pulled over for speeding.

It worked. I looked in the rearview mirror and saw the flashing blue lights of a Folly Beach patrol car closing on me. Talon looked back, uttered a profanity, and then turned back to me. "Pull over. You even twitch when the cop gets here, and you and your shaggy friend will have bullets in your heads before you can say help."

I pulled to the right berm and took a deep breath. The patrol car, with siren blaring and lights flashing, didn't even slow as it sped past.

"You lucked out," said Talon and cackled. "For now."

I eased back onto the street and continued toward who-knows-where.

"Why us?" said Charles, who started to turn toward the backseat. "What'd we do?"

Talon jammed the barrel into Charles's ear. "I said look straight ahead."

I glanced at Talon in the rearview mirror and repeated Charles's question. "Why us?"

Talon leaned forward. His elbow rested on the console between the front seats. I could see the faint glimmer of the navigation system reflected in his eyes. "You did what everybody said you'd do. You butted in where it was none of your business. You think I didn't see you whispering and cuddling up to Geoff? You think I didn't see you talking to Billy while glaring at me. Then today at lunch, your questions about screenplays."

"We were only—" interrupted Charles.

"Shut up!" said Talon. "I blew it when I told you about the one I'd written with the drowning. I saw the look in your eyes. I knew that you knew." He hesitated and then mumbled something that I couldn't understand. His breath smelled like onions. He then continued, "I knew that you must have seen the pages or that Geoff told you about them. I waited until dark to come over here and see if they were still in his room. I was three houses over when I saw your damned car pulling in the drive."

He then tapped the side of my head with the gun. "You're loose ends—loose ends to be tied up before you go blabbing to the cops."

I saw where the police car had been going in such a hurry. Traffic was stopped in front of us. It had started to rain again, and there was a minivan stopped in the middle of the lane just past Oak Island Drive. Two cars were off to the side of the road, and it looked like one of them had been broadsided by one of the other vehicles. A Folly Beach fire engine had the left lane blocked, and one of the police officers was igniting flairs and sticking them in the sandy berm.

"You drowned Cesar, didn't you?" asked Charles. A few taps on the side of his head weren't going to stop him from talking.

He didn't answer, so I took his silence as yes. "Like in the screenplay you had written?" I said.

"Ah," he said. "Life imitates art. A perfect plan," he said. "Perfect until that damned Brit broke into my motor home and stole pages from the screenplay. He only took a few pages, thought I'd never notice them missing. I wouldn't have if I hadn't seen him slithering away like a snake." He laughed, a sinister laugh. "And we all know what to do to snakes. Chop off their heads."

"Why kill him?" I asked.

I didn't think he was going to answer, but he finally said, "Do you know how much more a director makes than a damned assistant director?"

Charles turned toward the backseat and said, "I guess that it's—"

"Shut up and turn around," said Talon. "It's a hell of a lot more money, and I'm ten times a better director than that hack. The money and the job should have been mine from the beginning."

I looked in the rearview mirror and saw another police car in the oncoming lane passing the cars stopped behind us. I saw Cindy driving as it passed. We were no more than a distraction from her goal of getting to the wreck. Would we have a chance if I bolted out the door? Would we have a better chance if we sat tight and hoped for a better plan to come to me?

"How'd you plan for the boat to capsize?" asked Charles.

"I didn't," said Talon. "That was luck, good luck. I knew that a big storm was supposed to hit, and I'd heard about the captain and his fondness for brewski. I helped it along by graciously inviting more people than the drunken captain said the boat should hold. It was one of the few times that wishful thinking actually came to fruition. Was a fine directing job on my part."

"There's no way you could have known that the boat was going to be swamped," I said.

He laughed. "You've got me on that one. My plan was to be out on the boat and make sure everyone, especially the captain, got soused. I was going to get Cesar alone and clobber him with a wrench or something heavy that I knew had to be on the boat. Then I'd slip him overboard along with whatever I'd hit him with. The best special effects person in Hollywood couldn't have created a better storm. It did most of the work for me. It almost got all of us killed." He hesitated. "That wasn't in the script."

"So the boat capsized, you managed to get Cesar where no one else could see you, and you held him under," said Charles.

"Couldn't have said it better," said Talon. "Pretty easy actually; he was too cocky to wear a life jacket. Good for me, deadly for him."

Between swishes of the windshield wipers, I saw the yellow, flashing lights on a wrecker moving into position in front of the minivan. If Charles could keep Talon talking, perhaps he would be distracted enough that I could wrestle the gun out of his hand. Maybe.

"Did you fix the light bar to fall?" asked Charles.

"You sure are a nosy one," said Talon.

If only he knew the half of it, I thought. In addition to Charles's extra chromosome for nosiness, I knew he was trying to keep Talon talking. It might not help, but nothing good would come from dead silence.

"Curious," said Charles.

"Yeah," said Talon as he leaned back in the seat. "I did it. I got what I wanted when Cesar, with a little help from me, kicked the bucket. I was now the director, but I also knew that I was directing a dog. *Final Cut* would never be a hit without a lot of publicity. We already had a dead director, and if I could rustle up more ink and airtime, there was a chance that the gullible movie-going public would buy lots of tickets."

"Who were you trying to kill?" I asked. "The light bar landed on a small-time actor and our friend Dude?"

"Wasn't trying to kill anyone," said Talon. "That'd get too much attention. Didn't want cops snooping around." He leaned up and moved closer to Charles's face. "Didn't want a couple of local yokels snooping either."

The wrecker's wench sounded like two angry cats on steroids. This was the distraction I needed. I moved my left hand to the door pull handle. Charles saw what I was doing and leaned toward Talon and said, "You think you're smart enough to get away with it?"

Talon touched his ear with the Glock. "I know I am," he said.

Charles slapped his left hand on the leather console. "Don't bet on it."

Talon leaned even closer to Charles.

I yanked the handle and pushed the door open. The interior lights came on.

"Open it another inch and your friend's brain will be splattered all over your car."

Talon was quicker than I thought he'd be. Charles's eyes were shut, and the killer's gun barrel was lodged in Charles's left ear. I couldn't risk it, so I stared straight ahead and slowly pulled the door closed.

"Smart," said Talon.

The wrecker had begun towing the demolished minivan, and the brake lights in front of us glowed bright. Engines of the stopped vehicles roared to life. We were about to move.

Charles had opened his eyes and gave me a slight nod. "Did you set up the bonfire accident?" he said.

I continued to stare ahead but could see that Talon had moved the gun barrel from Charles's head and was waving it in the air between the two seats.

"One of my finer moments," said Talon. "I even called Channel 4 so they'd be there for the fun-filled event. Years ago, an old stuntman showed me how to build something to fall that looked stable. He would have been proud of me. I didn't figure it would kill Wynn, but if it did, all the better. Either way, it would have been more press for the beleaguered movie. And if Wynn had died, it would have been icing on the cake."

The cars in front of us began to inch forward. My window of opportunity was quickly shutting, but I couldn't risk Charles's life by making a stupid move.

"Then why kill Wynn?" I asked.

Talon seemed surprised that I had asked. He kept the gun pointed at Charles but turned toward me. He was almost between us as he leaned over the console. I wondered if Charles could have grabbed the gun if I distracted Talon, but remembered how quickly he had reacted when I opened the door.

"He was getting suspicious," said Talon. "He casually mentioned that he had seen me rearranging the logs on the backside of the bonfire. He didn't say it, but he had given me

FINAL CUT

a look that would have bored through a steel wall. Besides, if he was out of the picture—ha, ha—I could have brought in the actor I wanted in the first place, a real actor, not a hack like Wynn."

"So you faked the e-mail about him going into rehab," I said.

"Easy to do," said Talon. "I had his phone after he met his untimely demise. I sent the e-mail to the gullible Ms. Lancaster. The stage was set: lights, action, and Wynn was in rehab. No one questioned it considering his history with drugs."

The rain was getting harder, and the wipers slapped in time with the rhythmic pounding of my heart. The cars in front of us were accelerating, and I followed closely behind them.

We passed Bowens Island Road on the left and then the iconic Folly Boat that had welcomed *Final Cut* at the start of the production. I wondered if I'd live to see the popular landmark again.

Talon rammed the gun barrel into my shoulder. "Turn left at the light."

I didn't see any choice, and before I reached Harris Teeter, I turned at Sol Legare Road. I hadn't traveled the road often but knew that it dead-ended in about three miles at the Battery Island Landing boat ramp. The road was sparsely populated and, with this weather, exceptionally dark.

The rain was so intense that I barely saw the security lights on the side of a seafood company on the left. Lights may have been on in the few houses scattered off to the right, but I couldn't tell. Small smatterings of oak trees appeared along the road.

Charles said something about why Talon had killed Geoff.

"The damned Brit figured it out," said Talon. "Yesterday morning, he asked me where I was—where I was exactly— when Cesar drowned. And then thinking that I was an idiot, he asked where I was when Wynn was shot. The damned Brit

| 269 |

sounded like he was still playing the police chief. I'd gone too far for him to start accusing me of murder, stirring up the police, getting them looking under every rock until they caught me." He sighed. "I was too late; he had already told you."

I didn't say how little Geoff had actually told us.

Talon then chuckled. "Who else could have directed a murder with such precision," he said. "Billy almost caught me switching bullets, but he wants to get ahead so much that he'd have overlooked anything I was doing. The plan was perfect, it was simply perfect." Talon glanced out the window into the dark and then laughed again. "The shocked looks on everyone's faces when Geoff didn't get up. I wanted to jump up and applaud my directing." He hesitated and then tapped Charles on the head. "Too bad I won't get the directing credit for such a perfect scene."

Charles was doing what he could to distract Talon. It was up to me to figure something out. I suspected that Talon was having me drive to the end of the desolate road where he would kill us. He could then run the car into the water, and with luck it would sink. Even if we were found, no one would have known when it happened, and Talon would sit back smiling at another outstanding directorial feat.

Then the memory of my ex-wife flashed back in my mind, and a plan began to emerge—a possibly fatal plan. It was all we had.

CHAPTER 37

I GLANCED AT CHARLES AND tugged on my shoulder harness. "Joan lives somewhere out here, doesn't she, Charles?" I said.

Charles got a quizzical look on his face at the mention of my ex-wife. He glanced at my shoulder harness and said, "Yeah, she—"

"Shut up!" shouted Talon.

Charles then cocked his head to the side, gave a barely noticeable nod, and touched his shoulder harness with his right hand. At that point, Talon returned to basking in the glow of his perfect and fatal directing job. He was still leaning on the center console.

We were a mile from the end of the road—in more ways than one. Houses along the street were farther and farther apart and set back from the street. I had to act quickly.

I slowly pushed down on the accelerator. Charles nodded again and then turned to Talon.

"You'll never get away with this," he said. "You're not nearly as smart as you think."

Talon leaned close to Charles. "One thing's for certain," said the killer. "Nobody will hear what you think."

I noticed out the corner of my eye that he braced himself with his left elbow on the console and had rammed the barrel of the pistol in Charles's left temple. My friend winced, and a trickle of blood ran down his cheek. I was afraid Talon was going to pull the trigger.

Instead, he moved the gun to within a couple of inches of Charles's head. "You think you know everything," said Talon. "We'll see—we'll see."

I continued to accelerate, and Charles continued to distract Talon. "Chief Newman and Detective Callahan will hunt you down. You don't stand a chance. The next thing you'll be directing is *Jailhouse Rock*."

I finally saw what I'd been looking for, a small grove of live oaks on the left shoulder. I said a silent prayer, pushed firmer on the accelerator, and steered the SUV toward the group of trees.

Talon tensed; he knew that something wasn't right. He turned from Charles and saw the trees in front of us. The speedometer inched past fifty.

"What—" he yelled.

The SUV collided with the largest tree. The airbag slammed into me like a ton of rocks. It felt like the seat belt had cut me in half. The screeching sound of the mangled steel pounded my ears. It happened in an instant, and then everything went black.

The continuous sound of a blaring horn dragged me back to reality. I thought I heard moaning to my right but wasn't certain. The deflated air bag was pressed against my lap, and then an eerie red glow illuminated the interior of the vehicle. A branch the size of a baseball bat was sticking through the windshield to my left. I turned my head to the right. Pain radiated down my neck. Talon's face was inches from mine. His eyes were open, and blood from a three-inch gash above his right eye slowly trickled into his unflinching eyes. The shattered windshield pressed against the top of his head. He startled me until I realized that his body was facing the other direction and his neck was twisted in a way that no living human could endure. He had directed his last killing.

The horn abruptly stopped its irritating wail, and popping sounds began to come from under the dash. The red glow had become brighter. The shock of seeing the mangled face of the late Talon Hall was replaced by the realization that the car was on fire.

I elbowed Talon's lifeless body away from the seat belt buckle and pushed the red release button.

Nothing happened.

"Get off me," Charles mumbled. "Who are you?"

Charles's eyes were closed, and he was shoving Talon back toward the console.

"Are you okay?" I asked and continued to pound the red seat belt release.

"Melinda," he said. "Is that you? What happened?"

The smell of overheated radiator fluid was replaced by the toxic smell of burning rubber and plastic. Smoke began to fill the SUV. Charles was alive but out of it, and I was trapped by the same seat belt that had saved my life seconds earlier. The latch was stuck, and I couldn't budge it with my fleeing strength. The glow from the burning engine compartment grew brighter. Heat from the fire rolled into the cabin from under the dash, and Charles was in never-never land. The SUV was about to burst into flames, and Charles and I would breathe our last breath.

A Swiss Army knife was in the storage bin in the center console, but Talon's body held it down. I tried to shove him out of the way, but he was wedged between the front seats. There was nowhere for him to go. Where was the gun?

Luck finally changed. The weapon was stuck between Talon's right side and Charles. I dislodged the firearm and considered firing it at the latch but quickly discarded that idea. I put the barrel against the red button and pounded my hand against the butt of the weapon. Still nothing. I slammed it harder, nothing. On the third swing, the button moved and the latch released. I dropped the gun and threw the restraint out of the way.

My luck improved even more when the door pull worked. The front of the vehicle was mangled, but the door opened with only minor resistance. I pulled myself out of the car using the door as a crutch. Pain shot through my left wrist and forearm, and the pain in my neck was intense, but all my body parts seemed to work. Flames lapped out from under the front of the SUV. Thick, black smoke rolled out from the engine compartment.

I ran to the other side of the vehicle and grabbed Charles's door handle. It didn't open as easily as my mine, but I was able to get it about halfway and reached across to Charles's seat belt latch. It unhooked. Charles had begun to return to reality.

He looked at me and said, "I think it's time to get out."

I breathed a sigh of relief and asked if he thought he could get out on his own. He said he wouldn't know until he tried. I pulled the door open as far as I could, and he shoved it from inside. He fell out of the SUV, and I caught him before he hit the rain-soaked grass. Flames illuminated the trees in the grove and reflected off the passenger-side window.

"Can you walk?" I asked as I looked at the SUV.

"Won't know until I try," he said for the second time.

"It's time to try," I said as I grabbed his elbow.

He pulled his cane from between the seat and the door and stumbled three steps but regained his balance and moved with me about fifty feet from the vehicle. He fell to one knee, and I bent down beside him. He lay back on his elbows and then stretched out in the bristly, warm weeds along the side of the road. I did the same. The rain had eased but still pelted my face. It had never felt better.

The Infiniti didn't exactly explode. It was more of a loud whoosh with flames bellowing out the open front doors. Talon's lifeless silhouette was visible in the center of the vehicle.

The flames continued to burn, and one of the front tires exploded. Charles took a deep breath and then leaned up on his elbows and looked at the burning SUV and then over at me and back at the vehicle.

"Cut," he said.

EPILOGUE

IT WAS PEAK VACATION SEASON, and we were standing at the long, outdoor bar at the Tides watching the hotel's crew on the beach setting up the sixteen-foot-high, twelve-foot-wide inflatable movie screen. The bar was packed with vacationers and locals who considered the bar their regular hangout.

"I can't believe that it's been four months since you torched Talon and ruined a perfectly good oak tree," said Charles.

Not to mention totaling my vehicle and nearly getting ourselves killed, I thought. "Four months, five days to be exact," I said and rubbed my wrist that had finally healed after its collision with the air bag.

The inflatable screen was being prepared for, as Charles called it, the universe-wide premiere of *Final Cut*. On a more modest scale, yet still a hyperbole, the special showing had been touted by the financiers as the North American premiere.

After Talon's untimely death, the real money behind the project firmly informed Becky and Robert that stopping filming was not an option. Billy B. Robinson was given the unenviable task of creating ninety minutes of cinematic magic with little to work with and a condensed postproduction schedule. The first two directors were dead, the first two lead actors had been killed, and two weeks of around-the-clock rewriting had created a hodgepodge of convoluted plot lines, with the lead actor emerging from a weak supporting cast. Charles and I had suggested that the lead should go to our favorite city council member Marc Salmon. We said that he was ham enough for the part, could outtalk the best actors available, and being a politician, was familiar with fiction. Marc told us that he knew he was movie-star handsome but would stick with city government. He said he already had enough two-faced people to work with there and didn't need more raving lunatics in his life.

It was still an hour before the premiere, and three hotel employees were setting up white folding chairs facing the screen. What the film may have lacked in quality, it more than made up for in free publicity. The premiere and the hoopla surrounding it was being covered by Charleston's television stations, the local newspapers, and even one of the national fish-wrapper magazines had sent a reporter and a photographer to the event. Talon, looking up from the gates of hell, would have been pleased.

"Yo, Chuckster and Chrisster," came the familiar voice of Dude. He had walked up behind us and carried an amber-colored drink.

"Join us," said Charles as he moved a couple of feet to the left to open space for Dude.

"Watching me be famous?" asked Dude.

"You bet," I said.

Dude had more small appearances than in the original script since he played a bartender at Cal's and cost cutting had necessitated a greater number of scenes in that venue. Billy had told us that Dude had only one tiny speaking scene where he was to say, "What's your pleasure, pal?" Billy had then shared that it had taken Dude "only" eleven takes to get it right. I could have saved the writers a bunch of time if they'd asked me about giving Dude words to massacre.

I watched as Officer LaMond—excuse me, Chief Cindy LaMond—walked across the beach to talk to two of her officers who were stationed beside the giant screen. Brian Newman had won the special election by a landslide and, good to his word, had promoted Cindy to chief. A couple of the cantankerous old-timers had threatened to move off the island if "that gal" was appointed chief, but that not only didn't discourage the new mayor but probably sped up the process. Of course, instead of the old-timers moving, they stayed so they could exercise their Constitutional right to complain about everything.

A hundred tickets had been distributed to the various VIPs, but that only meant that they would be able to sit in the seats in front of the screen. Anyone else who wanted to watch the premiere could stand within viewing distance on the beach or on the hotel's deck.

Fifteen minutes before the film was to start, Brian Ross, who had coordinated the screen and chairs from the Tides, grabbed the cordless mike off a portable lectern sitting beside the screen. He introduced Billy and turned the mike over to him. Billy asked the VIPs to take their seats and said the prepremiere festivities were to begin in five minutes. I suspected that fewer than half the VIP tickets would be used and noticed that the crew who was supposed to be taking the tickets were more interested in three coeds standing behind the inflatable screen.

A couple of minutes later, Billy tapped on the mike and asked everyone to pay attention. He looked like a high school kid playing the part of a movie director in a class play. He wore a white linen shirt with the top two buttons open, pressed jeans, sandals, and had a tiny lens around his neck attached to a lanyard as if he would be previewing a scene to be shot. His dyed blond hair was slicked back, and he continued to chew gum.

There was a shortage of true VIPs, so Charles, Heather, Karen, and I were in the third row. Dude and Cal were in the second row because of their roles in the production. I was pleased to see Donna Lancaster at the other end of our row. She had been cleared of all charges and had said she wanted to be at the premiere in memory of Wynn. Thirty or so locals who had been extras throughout the production filled in seats behind us.

Billy thanked everyone for coming and then introduced the "stars" to polite applause from the VIPs and a couple of cheers from clusters of slightly inebriated college students who had taken time from their night of partying to see what was going on.

Charles leaned over to Karen and me. "Don't run off after it's over," he said. "I have—"

Opening credits began to run, and the Rolling Stone's "(I Can't Get No) Satisfaction" boomed from the large speakers near the screen before Charles could finish his sentence.

Ninety-three minutes, which seemed like two eternities, later the credits began to roll, and the audience began to disperse. There was a smattering of applause. I suspected it was because the film was over rather than praise for the production.

Charles rolled his eyes and said, "If you entered that in a beauty contest, a manatee would've beaten it."

I looked around at the people walking away. "It's a tad shy of *Gone with the Wind*," I conceded.

Karen elbowed me in the ribs.

Charles nodded. "Was a mighty fine performance by Dude though," he said.

Dude cornered Charles, Karen, and me and asked us to follow him to the water's edge, about a hundred feet from the screen. Cal and Heather joined our small group as we gathered in the pitch dark except for the lights on the pier. Clouds covered most of the sky, and the people who had been there for the premiere had gone their separate ways.

I thought of Joan as I walked to the water and how her death had given me the idea for how to save Charles and me. I also thought of Melinda and the killer-catching party she had thrown for Charles and me only nine months earlier.

Heather took white candles out of her oversized purse and handed each of us one as we gathered at the water. Cal, who didn't smoke but always carried a Bic lighter, lit each candle. I didn't know what Heather and Dude had in mind, but quickly found out that they had planned something.

The aging hippie removed his sandals, took five steps into the surf, and then turned to the rest of us who had lined up on shore facing him. Water lapped over his ankles, and he held his candle at face level and said, "Nod thy noggins."

We bowed, and Dude began:

"Sun God sending us Melinda's smiles,

"Moonbeams be M. watching over our sleep,

"Wind be M. telling us to laugh,

"M. be here—be here always."

A seam appeared in the clouds, and moonbeams glistened on a patch of surf behind Dude. I looked over and saw the faint reflection of the candle in a tear on Charles's cheek. I wiped tears from my face and then put my arm around him and looked up at the moon.

Charles also wiped away his, nervously shuffled his right foot in the loose sand, and then said, "Y'all step closer."

I looked at Karen, and she shrugged as we moved closer to Charles.

"Heather Lee," said Charles as he faced her, dropped his cane, and followed it down as he planted his right knee in the sand, "want to get hitched?"

Heather squealed.

And I knew that Melinda had gotten her final wish.

Printed in the United States
By Bookmasters